NEVER MORE HUMAN

NEVER MORE HUMAN

JOANNE McLAUGHLIN

For Michael, who is my immortality.
And for Josie, who is his.

Three times the thanks to Rhonda Dickey,
Kevin M. Smith, Lynn M. Ross, Amy Junod Placentra
and Dawné Dominque.

So Many Lifetimes Ago

BOHEMIA, MAY 1864

The blacksmith watches the gentlewoman who has been watching him these last days. A small woman in mourning garb; young, he guesses by her bearing, her stride as she advances and retreats. She does not come close enough for him to see her features beneath the veiling, or to intuit the nuances of her form beneath yards of black fabric. One day, a carriage set her down on the cobbles across from his forge at the edge of the village, close enough to the road to bring him the custom of travelers yet also near enough to the townspeople to draw their trade. She has returned to this spot each day for a week now, to what ends he cannot even speculate. She is a stranger to these parts.

He is at work pumping the bellows, his shirt soaked through with perspiration though it is only mid-spring, when he feels her presence at his side, smells the faint fragrance she wears—lavender, he thinks, though he knows little of such things.

"Smith," she whispers, "I would like to engage your services."

He looks up and sees she has raised her veil to better transact her business, whatever it may be. Her eyes fix him with a gaze of brilliant green. Her hair, he supposes from the hue of her brows, is a rich reddish-brown. The smith straightens to his full height, wipes his sooty hands on a cloth, and inclines his head.

"Milady, how may I be of service?"

She lowers her eyes then lowers her veil. "I am told that you are a gifted artist, a goldsmith capable of crafting memorable works of jewelry. It is as such I desire to retain you."

A gifted artist? He cannot recall anyone ever describing him so. His jewelry, while admired by his kin, has brought him little renown, still less coin. Yet a man must feed his family, so a blacksmith, not a goldsmith, he remains, and an ironmonger, as well, selling what others make if their work will also bring in a kreuzer or two for him.

"Surely, milady, there are goldsmiths, jewelers of great skill, artists as you put it, in the city who might accomplish your commission." Not that he wishes to turn down her patronage, since it appears that she has purposefully sought him out, of all people.

"I require discretion, smith. Are you capable of such? I will pay handsomely for it." From her cloak, she retrieves a pouch and offers it. "Will this suffice?"

He hefts the pouch, opens it. "A generous sum, milady, but for what? How am I to know whether this is sufficient when I know nothing of what it is you seek?"

Into the folds of her cloak she reaches again, this time proffering a scroll, a sketch of a pendant, its chain a thin course of gold links from which hangs a bright red stone.

"A necklace for yourself, milady?" he asks, understanding more.

"Two of them actually," she replies. "One for a woman roughly my size, one for a man approximately yours."

The blacksmith studies the drawing. "The man's chain must be thicker than depicted here, to support a slightly larger, slightly heavier gem. Or do I presume too much?"

She nods that he presumes quite correctly.

"I must see the gems before I can begin, measure them and evaluate their weight to determine how best to forge the chains."

Again, she nods, then turns toward the street. "I will fetch them here to you tomorrow. Of course, you will understand that

I cannot entrust them to you until you are ready to set them. The rubies I have in mind are both rare and expensive, because of their cut, and hence not easily replaced."

Of course, she will protect her investment. And that will be a boon to him, he thinks. He will require several more visits from her, certainly, before the commission can be completed.

"Of course, milady. How quickly will you want the pendants readied?" He senses her smile beneath the veiling, senses its beauty.

"Before the solstice, you have six weeks. Here is my calling card. I will return tomorrow afternoon." She lays the card on a crude shelf and departs.

"Mistress Eugenie Verlaine," it reads.

* * * *

The next day, he hurries through his quotidian duties, the horseshoes, the axles, the tools and hinges and other metalwork that facilitate the labor of man and horse and farm and shop. She arrives mid-afternoon, removes the rubies from a velvet pouch, and arrays them side by side. The blacksmith lifts each stone, weighs them in his hands, runs a finger along the bevels, feeling for any roughness, peers carefully as if looking for an inner liquid core. Each stone is, in fact, oddly moist to the touch, slickened with something pleasant he cannot identify. She observes as he measures, writes down his calculations.

"How long?" she asks.

"Long, milady?"

"How long should the chain be?" She places her right hand in the center of his chest and spreads her fingers wide. "Down to here, I think, for the man's pendant. For the woman's, you will have to judge."

She places the blacksmith's hand at the base of her throat, runs it slowly down the plane of her bodice until it rests at the center of her own chest. "Find roughly the same point between my breasts," she whispers, and he flexes his hand until his outermost fingers brush against them.

"Yes," she murmurs, "that will do, I think."

His hand feels as if it has been burned. His cock stiffens.

"How thick?" she asks, her voice husky.

"Thick enough," he replies stupidly, his wits failing him.

"As you say," she agrees and laughs.

* * * *

Each workday, the smith feels more drawn to his patroness. She comes in the afternoon, about three o'clock, and regards him for about an hour. She distracts him so that he works later each day to keep to his schedule, well after foot traffic in the square near his forge diminishes, well after activity at the few nearby shops drops off for the day, then ceases altogether.

She says little, does little but hand him the gems and allow him to analyze whatever he must to achieve the design she has given him, then slips them back into their pouch when he finishes. He offers her tea; she declines, but insists he take his refreshment. As he drinks, he analyzes Mistress Verlaine, who no longer wears her veil in his presence. Most often, she watches activity on the street outside, watches her horse and driver as they wait for her.

By the end of the first week, he finishes the initial links of the more delicate handiwork he has come to think of as her chain, working long into the evening, past the hour by which he should be home taking supper with his wife. By that week's end, the smith is halfway to being in love with the widow Eugenie Verlaine.

By the time his assignment is complete, four days before the solstice, the chains fashioned and the clasps functioning and the rubies fit into their settings, he is smitten beyond all reason. He has slept at the forge these last nights, his wife complaining of his neglect and reminding him other men would not be so inattentive.

To carry the finished pendants away with her, Mistress Verlaine brings two hinged velvet boxes to the forge. That midsummer day, she examines his work and, without comment, lays the necklaces into their boxes. She hands the smith a pouch far larger and heavier than the one she first presented him and offers her thanks.

"It was my pleasure to execute such a beautiful design, mistress."

She smiles at him, and he feels he ought to be paying her for that glimpse of such loveliness. She extends her hand. He reaches for it, in hopes of kissing it, but snags a finger on the button fastening her glove closed.

"You are bleeding." She lifts his finger to her mouth and licks it slowly.

The gesture startles him, and the smith cannot wrest his eyes from her tongue. Pleasure rushes through him, straight to his groin, a pleasure like that he experiences with his wife in bed, but perhaps better.

No, surely better.

"These pendants are for myself and the man I intend to marry, though he does not yet know it. His is a gift, a surprise for his birthday, a key to open his heart to my love." She braces herself against the smith's hard chest, her small right hand over his hammering heart, and kisses his cheek.

"Thank you, smith. This is fine work, indeed."

He tosses in his sleep that night, aroused by a dream of making love to the widow, who hopes to woo the recipient of his creation instead. The smith awakens his wife and, for the first time in weeks, sheaths himself in her body, sating his lust if not his longing. He takes her repeatedly, until exhaustion claims him, pulling him away from visions of the auburn-haired beauty who has claimed his soul.

* * * *

The next time the smith sees Mistress Verlaine is the day— one year later—that she visits his forge at the edge of the village on the arm of her betrothed.

Stefan. His brother.

"Will you wish us happiness, Gregor?" Stefan asks, fingering the ruby pendant hanging from his neck.

"Of course," the smith replies, extending his hand without wiping the soot of the metalwork from it, intentionally staining the soft gray glove of the renowned musician Stefan Herz, returned triumphant from the Hapsburg court with his lovely bride-to-be.

Stefan smiles knowingly. "I had described for Eugenie your skills with gold and gems, brother. Imagine my pride when she presented me this gift on which you and she collaborated."

"Yes, I can imagine," the smith says.

What he imagines quite vividly, and not for the first time, is how it would feel to kill his brother with the hands he used to fashion that pendant. How good it would feel to murder his own twin.

Chapter One

OUTSIDE PRAGUE, MAY 2012

All across Europe and the Americas, in Czech and German, French and Italian, Spanish and English, the call went forth, summoning those loyal to the Court of Cruelty:

> *Attention! Achtung! Pozor!*
> *Hearken ye to the heralds' trumpets, heed the*
>   *drummers' tattoo!*
> *Torture is the bond that unites the vassals!*
> *Assemble at noon Sunday, 13 May 2012, for a final*
>   *tour of our monarchs' Eastern European palace.*
>   *See their home, listen to their music, purchase*
>   *a piece of their lives, and pay tribute to their*
>   *enduring legacy.*
> *Ticket proceeds benefit local charities and the*
>   *Sebastian and Emilie de la Coeur Foundation for*
>   *Blood and Bone Marrow Cancer Research. See*
>   *details at the Cruel website.*

The invitation was issued two weeks ago in the hope it would draw every fan with the money and means to travel, lured by the chance to pay homage one last time to the departed king and queen. An irresistible voyeurs' paradise, right?

I can only hope. Right now, all is quiet here, and dark. All I see is the wan moonlight slipping through the wavy glass in the 300-year-old windows. All I hear is Jackson's breathing, a steady, reassuring cadence of intake and outflow. All I smell, aside from his special, spicy blend of beautiful male, are the sharp odors of the ammonia and vinegar and polish the cleaning crews have employed in their quest to displace dust and grime and mildew.

All I feel at this late hour is the skittering of my anxiety and apprehension, the beating of my heart inside my chest, the pounding of my vampire brain against my better still-human sense that I should rest from time to time.

All I can think of is ridding myself of this house, as though by relinquishing it I finally will be able throw off those vile final memories of Sebastian de la Coeur—or, rather, of Teppan Nilsson, the man my father was in the year before his death. Put out of my life once and for all this grand collection of rooms he acquired as a young husband, a large property close enough to his mean Bohemian birthplace that it mocked the family that loved him, and maybe I can forget the predator he became.

Of course, I know that's not true. I could rip down every beam, topple every stone that comprises this edifice, and the graves where my father's former lovers were found would still be cemented into my consciousness. Four women, four stillborn infants, eight reminders of my father's obsession with procreating, of again producing offspring as he and Emilie once somehow produced me, the unlikely child of two vampires.

Destroy this house, and the memories would still be with me, like scars that fade only slowly—like the scars Teppan inflicted on Jackson. But it's a pretty illusion, and so is not easily shaken: Wake up one day soon and it will all be in the past, and only the good memories of Sebastian will remain with his still-hopelessly-devoted only daughter. It's humiliating to admit how much I miss him—not the murderous bastard he was at the end, but my Daddy Bastian, whom I adored then fled for so long. It's humbling to acknowledge how little power my adult feelings have to overcome everything the child in me remembers.

Mere weeks now until we close on the sale of this impressive dwelling, and here I am again, lying in this bed my father bought as Stefan Herz, this bed he used as Sebastian de la Coeur, possibly even conceived me in. It's just a bed, for the love of God, some sticks and nails joined together, not the muscle and sinew he was made from, though sometimes it feels that way.

It's as if he is imbued in the wood's every knot, as he is in my every cell.

"Just close your eyes and be still, Chloe, you'll soon be done with it," I command. It seems like I've been telling myself that forever.

Maybe I've said it out loud this time. Jackson grumbles sleepily, gathers me against the warmth of his chest, kisses my head, rests his wide palm on my stomach. The baby kicks against us.

"Now you've gone and roused her, too," he says. "You may not need to sleep, love, but Avalon and I do. Please settle down, just for a little while. If we're going to make this place look presentable for the vassals' convocation you've planned—we have all the outbuildings to go through still—tomorrow will be another very long day, and so will the next, and the one after that. Unless you simply want to finish shuffling furniture around and leave the rest for the buyer to sort through."

"No, I need to pick through it all, you know that. There has to be something that can tell us why Christoph Zwilling wants this house so badly. That's why I've called the vassals in—he'll have to show up to keep up the pretense that he is who he says he is."

Jackson moves his hand higher, onto my pregnancy-swollen breast, and squeezes gently. "I know what you need, C.J. Hart, and it's to concentrate on the fact that you're eight months along instead of working your tail off to achieve some sort of emotional exorcism. Zwilling says he's a Court of Cruelty fan, a vassal through and through, so of course he'll turn out for your gathering. He appreciated Sebastian and Emilie's music, and now he wants to own this old mansion of your parents' and replicate the architectural details. Why does there have to be any more to it than that?"

Because I *know* there has to be. Barcelona showed me that much.

"You mean it's enough that Zwilling is a vampire, the only other vampire I've ever seen besides my parents? And that my mother, who's usually pretty proper despite her stage persona, seduced and had sex with the man in a public place, in front of me and you and her lover and who knows how many more people less than three hours after meeting him? Or that none of us, apparently not even Zwilling if we can believe him, has heard from Katarina since that night last month when the inscrutable Mrs. Nilsson scrambled off his cock at Casa Cruella? Really, for a journalist, Jackson Fahey, sometimes you're remarkably non-curious."

He tugs me closer, nibbles my shoulder. "Oh, I'm curious about lots of things, like just what it is you think still might be discovered here in this old pile of mold and mortar, and just what you think your mother isn't making herself available to explain."

All hope of sleep evidently abandoned, Jackson swings his body over mine, traps me against the mattress with his much-longer arms and legs, stares at me with those dark-brown Irish eyes of his, strokes my cheeks lovingly. "You've said yourself that your mother will do what she will do. She doesn't want this house or anything in it, she's told you that; surely that means there's nothing here that will hurt you down the road. Let it be, and let Kat be. She won't miss the show. Matins and Vespers will do all the classic Cruel covers, and afterward you'll take Christoph Zwilling's money and we'll go home to have our baby."

Home? Which home? My barely habitable flat in London?

His barely habitable flat in Brussels? Or maybe back to upstate New York and Castle de la Coeur, which still looks like the equivalent of a war zone?

I need the money from the sale of this estate near Prague to cover the repairs to the Castle necessitated by my father's horrific death, as opposed to the phony double suicide Sebastian and Emilie concocted more than a year ago. This property is my only truly liquid asset right now, the only thing still not tied up in estate and contract issues. Inevitably, I must turn this place over to Zwilling and his band of architectural mimics to plunder. But for a few more days, we'll search the remaining structures and serve up the appropriately feudal decorating style needed to pull off the May 13 show, then we'll pack up whatever's worth taking and leave. Not until then; not before.

A kiss brushes my collarbone; lips work their way up my throat, suck at my earlobe. "I have to be sure I haven't overlooked anything, Jackson. Something that might come back to bite me. Something always does."

He blows into my ear, his breath sweet and soft and so distracting, just as he intends it to be. "Hush, love, no more worry for tonight, please." He raises himself onto his knees, inches back and presses his mouth against the swell of my stomach, inches back still more, moves his tongue along each thigh and everywhere in between until, finally, I sigh in surrender.

"You win," I murmur.

"If only for now," Jackson concedes.

He knows me too well. Leisurely, he kisses his way northward, caresses my every angle and curve, until at last his face hovers over mine. He leans in, rubs his neck against my mouth.

"Bite me," he invites, opening my legs with his knee, teasing me to attention with his hot, ready cock, entering me as I open his vein and sip.

"Persistent man," I say, gasping as he thrusts. He builds the pace, accelerates me to another climax.

"That I am." He surges deeply but gently, peering seductively over my baby bump. "The one who loves you best of all, my sweet Juliette. For as long as I am, I am yours."

As he comes, I bite down harder and imbibe the champagne that flows out of him, my delicious, delicious man.

* * * *

Avalon gives me a vicious kick, as though she wants out of me as badly as I want out of this house. "Patience, baby," I whisper. "Trust Mommy, it's nicer in there." She's lost a sister and a grandfather in the last few months; maybe she, too, has memories she'd just as soon shed. Hell, I've been lugging my emotional baggage through Europe with me since I graduated high school and left the name Clothilde de la Coeur behind for good, so I should know: Some things never change, they just get harder to carry.

After a while, Ava gets the message and quits the in utero gymnastics. But, of course, I'm all charged up again, like I'm on a triple-espresso buzz. I wriggle out of Jackson's arms without waking him, poor exhausted love. He's just back from three days of economic reporting in Croatia, for a series of radio and TV segments on the state of the non-eurozone nations. Heady stuff, as he would say, but he persuaded his BBC superiors that it would serve their purposes and his need to carve out time with me here until I close on my parents' erstwhile Eastern Europe pied-a-terre with Gregor Zwilling GmbH, Christoph Zwilling's architectural-fittings company. When Jackson wakes, he'll have to go out to find us breakfast. Except for enough chargers and flagons, platters and chalices to serve up a faux medieval banquet, the cupboards are pretty bare, the appliances sold off. Best to let him sleep as long as he can.

The sun is at mid-morning strength when I leave the house armed with a ring of unlabeled keys and an industrial-grade flashlight, my head tucked into the hood of the sweatshirt I've thrown over my shoulders to protect me from solar assault. The barn I'm heading for has few windows; I'll be all right to rummage there until noon arrives and vampire safety outdoors with it, assuming I can ever get inside. It's not apparent which key will open the padlock on the barn door. No matter how many I've eliminated, there are always more mystery keys. Maybe that was a low-tech defense against Soviet-era intrusions: Dazzle lazy party functionaries with a very large haystack and they'll decide your needle isn't important after all.

My fingers, gloved this brilliant, warm spring day, are tingling long before the eleventh key proves to be the right one. I slide the padlock off, slide the barn door open, slip inside, slip the magic key off the ring and into the pocket of my sweatshirt, fire up the world's heaviest flashlight, and get my bearings. Stacked nearly to the ceiling along the four walls are shipping crates, steamer trunks, cardboard boxes, even a few plastic bins like the ones I used to move my gear from dormitory, to rented room in a host family's home, to tiny graduate-student quarters over the course of ten years. Crowded into the center of this space are six black file cabinets, some dented, all scratched 1960s Communist-bloc military surplus, by the looks of them. I pull on the nearest drawer. It's locked, naturally, which, I hope, explains the half-dozen little keys on the ring.

I awkwardly climb the ladder to the loft, my center of gravity thrown off by my advanced pregnancy, but I don't have to go all the way up to see more of the same. More stuff, packed away in more seemingly random containers, much of it possibly worthless, but who can say for sure, so I'll have to open every last one of them—none of the outbuildings came with inventories of their contents. I back my way down the steps, regain the lower level, grab for the nearest carton, and slash through its packing tape with one of the many keys. Old magazines tucked into individual plastic sleeves: *Paris Match, French Vogue, Cahiers du Cinema*. My mother's downtime diversions from the musical whirl, I suppose, mostly from the late seventies and eighties. Makes sense: That's when Court of Cruelty was at the peak of its popularity, and thus at the peak intensity of its performance schedule. Probably some interesting articles here. I should pick through these before I consign them to the flea market or recycling bucket, but there's no time, on to the next carton.

Costume sketches, all done on acid-free paper, about three dozen binders full of them, dated and labeled by Cruel concert tour, with a corresponding number of transparent folders filled with the sewing patterns needed to create them. Gowns, chemises, corsets, stomachers, stockings for her; tunics, leggings, doublets, breeches, vests, cloaks for the guys in the band. At the bottom of each sketch: my mother's initials, *EdlC*, for the woman she became after she was Eugenie Juliette Roget Verlaine Herz.

Emilie's ephemera, more than I can sift through in two months, let alone the three weeks left to me before we close on the sale and/or I go into labor. Ava sticks a foot into my side. *"That's it, baby, put your feet up, relax. Mommy will do this all by herself."*

I spend about two hours eyeballing bits and pieces, then decide to move on.

Several of the shipping crates are bigger than I am; they must contain something more substantial than Emilie's wardrobe flights of fancy and old reading material. No keys needed here, but I don't have a crowbar either. What the hell, I kick through the plywood side of the crate closest to the door. Dressmaker's dummies, about a dozen of them, three about my height, the others more than six feet tall.

"Emilie just packed this stuff out of sight, out of mind, and now it falls to me to dispose of it," I complain aloud. "I can see the poster now: 'Designing Cruel: A new exhibition of de la Coeur whatnot at Aspect Ratio.' "

A throat clears behind me. "Surely, many will be interested in purchasing some of these memorabilia at your art gallery, Miss Hart. Your parents have amazing popularity more than a year after their deaths. A potentially lucrative afterlife, like Elvis Presley, yes? But in London instead of Tennessee, *und, naturlich*, here for a few more weeks."

That voice, like chalk dragged across a blackboard; cold, like the chill that washes over me as I recognize it. I wish I could say it doesn't unnerve me, even with the books closed on Interpol's investigation of my father's murdered paramours, even though I no longer have anything to fear from Julian Gippel.

"What an unexpected pleasure, Detective Gippel," I lie. "What brings you to my corner of exurban Prague today? It's certainly not to consult on the rock-and-roll collectibles market."

A smile curves his thin lips; my disdain always seems to amuse him.

"I have just finished with the Czech authorities identifying the bodies found in the mass grave nearby, just over your parents' property line. You will be glad to know that the victims were Dubcek supporters known to have incurred the enmity of the Soviets during the Prague Spring. They left their homes in 1968 and did not return. Shot to death every one, all sixteen."

I would be gladder if I knew where my parents had been in spring 1968, and whose side, if any, they had taken. Sebastian and Emilie left a secret under every rock around, why not with a few long-decomposed Cold War dissidents? Maybe it's the rush of unfocused anxiety Gippel's presence has created, added to my already quite-focused anxiety relating to this estate, but I feel faint suddenly, feel my legs go out from under me. Faster than he looks for a middle-aged man who smokes, Gippel catches me under the arms, eases me down onto one of the shorter crates.

"You are very pale, Miss Hart. Should I summon help?"

Then again, maybe it's just that I'm so very pregnant— sitting helps. I breathe deeply for a few minutes. He hands me a water bottle retrieved from a pocket somewhere in his impeccably tailored trench coat, he's like a film noir detective who keeps a valet on retainer.

"I just need a minute." I sip the water slowly. "Too little sleep, too much dust, too much to do in too little time before the sale of this estate is finalized to the Gregor Zwilling company."

Too strong a sense of déjà vu, as well, but he realizes that. Gippel and I have danced this pas de deux before; he nods in acknowledgment of our shared history. "Ah, yes," he says. "Herr Zwilling seems quite entranced with this property, if the media are to be believed. He is an aficionado of all things Cruel, yes?"

"A vassal? Yes, so he claims. I have yet to meet the man."

Gippel arches an eyebrow, an expression that all but calls me out as a liar though I'm telling the truth. "You did not meet Christoph Zwilling in Barcelona last month? Video of the Matins and Vespers concert shows you performed at the anniversary tribute to your late parents."

Gippel seldom asks questions he doesn't already know the answers to. He's here to fish for information.

"There were about five hundred people crammed into Casa Cruella that night. I could hardly have met them all, though I did meet quite a few before the riot. And I know you'll understand my reluctance to stick around once the flutes and the fists started flying," I say, resting my hand protectively on my extremely round stomach.

"Your good friend, Katarina Nilsson, provoked the disturbance, according to the news accounts, taking, shall we say, great pains to lavish attention on Herr Zwilling. Her friend, Eric Bohlander, took exception to Zwilling's overtures to Mrs. Nilsson, yes?"

He keeps up on his D-list celebrity gossip, I'll give him that. "That seemed to be the case, yes. As I said, I was eager to get out of harm's way."

"So you say," he nods. "You have seen Mrs. Nilsson since that night?"

As a matter of fact, I haven't. "We share a common interest in my parents' music, some mutual friends, and, of course, the fact of her husband's suicide at Castle de la Coeur in December, but not much more, Detective. We are, if anything, business colleagues rather than friends. Kat does not keep me apprised of her whereabouts, though I expect to see her shortly, at my charity event here. I understand from Christoph Zwilling's staff that he has been trying to reach her, too. I can give you the number I gave his secretary, if you like."

He shakes his head, backs up toward the door. "That will not be necessary, *danke*. Should you hear from Katarina Nilsson in the interim, please pass along my regards."

Sure will. "Why do you want to talk to Kat Nilsson, Detective? It's been almost six months since her husband confessed to the murders you were investigating and then killed himself. What interest can you possibly have in Teppan Nilsson's widow now?"

Gippel knows I'm fishing too. He nods his farewell and makes haste to exit the barn. Is it my imagination, or was there a warning there somewhere? And where the hell is my mother anyway? I pull out my mobile, tap out yet another text to her that will probably go unanswered: K, please call. C.

A few minutes later, as I try to identify which small key will unlock the first of several file cabinets, the phone rings. The caller ID shows my mother's number.

"Kat?"

"She left this phone behind three weeks ago. I was hoping she might be with you," Eric says, worry evident in his voice. "She must be with that bastard Zwilling. Why would she do that, knowing what he is? He can't give her what she needs."

Whatever that might be at this point in her very long life. "She isn't with Zwilling, or at least she wasn't as of yesterday. If you hear from her, have her contact me, Eric, and I promise I'll do the same. Please tell her it's urgent."

I need to speak to her, to be sure she actually turns up for the show planned during this open house, an appearance also intended to amp up sales of *In Service to the Court of Cruelty*, the album featuring Matins and Vespers' performances at a London nightclub last fall and the entire "Christmas at the Castle" benefit concert in December. We've already distributed CDs across the US via a certain humongous coffee company, and through the EU via some strategic partnerships with similar coffeehouse operations. The Castle repair bills are exorbitant enough, but I'm also still scrambling to pay for Jackson's medical expenses, the orthopedic and cosmetic surgeons, the burn specialist, the psychiatrist who treated his post-traumatic stress after my father took him hostage.

So much damage done all around. How will I ever make it right?

"Was that Gippel driving away just now? What did he want?" Jackson, awake earlier than I expected, sets a large decaf for me and a bag of croissants down atop one of the file cabinets, then takes a long drink from his own fully caffeinated, four-sugar brew. If not for the faint scar on his cheek and the stiffness in his limbs at the end of the day, the reminder of those gunshot wounds, you'd never know.

I kiss him gratefully, stroke along the scar with my fingertips. "Gippel, yes, it was. He says he was in the neighborhood to wrap up the final loose ends on the Soviet-era mass grave. All the bodies have been identified as belonging to 1960s dissidents. All shot, not a slashed throat in the bunch, vampire-free. *Dasvidaniya*, Detective."

Avalon lands a Beckham-worthy kick into my midsection. I grab a croissant, take a big bite in hopes of appeasing the baby diva within me. "Interesting thing, though," I say between chews, "Gippel was asking about Kat, whether I'd heard from her. So I called her number after he left, to give her a heads-up. Eric answered and said she'd left her phone behind three weeks ago. He thought she'd gone to Zwilling."

"But Zwilling's people are looking for her too." Jackson fishes a container of yogurt out of his jacket pocket, hands it to me with a plastic spoon and an unspoken order to eat. "Maybe she's at the Castle? You could call your godmother."

Ah, but would Gloria Dennehy, my parents' longtime confidante, tell me if my mother had returned there, information she's withheld in the past? I shrug and drink my coffee. Jackson's brought his laptop. Time to start cataloging what I have been able to find today.

* * * *

Jackson decrees that I mustn't climb, the reality of my vampire invulnerability unable to dissuade him from his expectant-father fretting, so he's opening the boxes up in the loft while I go through the file cabinets down below. As if Sebastian and Emilie assumed a similar gender divide, it seems the stuff upstairs is my father's exclusively, the stuff downstairs my mother's. It's slow going for my darling, who is fascinated by photography in general and Sebastian's in particular, and thus is captivated by the box-loads of it he's discovering.

"We're never going to get through all this, C.J.," he calls down. "We're going to have to pack it up and ship it to London. There's at least two exhibitions' worth here, and that's just the cartons I've opened, all Sebastian's signature themes, stamped with his name: nighttime city scenes; families dining, as seen from the street on the other side of a window. Fabulous images, all of them. There must be contact sheets and negatives here too, somewhere."

As the owner of an art gallery whose stock in trade has become the non-musical creations of the Family de la Coeur, I am most grateful. As the daughter with fewer than three weeks to see this property emptied, I am weary. "There must be. Seems like Sebastian and Emilie never threw anything away. Keep opening—I'll get the movers in here tomorrow to re-close the boxes and ready them for transport."

We work silently for perhaps another half-hour, cutting through tape, burrowing through straw and rags, old newspapers and their modern-day equivalent, bubble wrap, when Jackson shouts, "Holy Mary and the saints!" and scrambles halfway down the ladder. "I need you to come up and see this."

He jumps down to the main barn floor, reaches out, and hands me up the rungs, scrambles down again to retrieve the enormous flashlight. "I can't believe it."

"What?" I wait at the top for him, though I can see perfectly well through the afternoon shadows.

He shines the light onto some daguerreotypes he's positioned on an unopened crate, arrayed like three small soldiers. "Look at these. They're just like the daguerreotype Sebastian kept in that locked barrister bookcase outside his darkroom at the Castle, the one with the old cameras. Do you know the image I mean?"

I'm thinking, trying to remember. Those cameras, that bookcase, anything made of glass was laid waste by my father's cries of despair the night before he took his life; for months now, there's been nothing to remind me of what they used to be. But the daguerreotype would have been imprinted on metal, so it must have survived. I must have seen it at some point during the cleanup. I close my eyes, to bring up the scene Jackson describes from my now near-eidetic memory. "Was it a young man, dressed in a dark suit, maybe mid-nineteenth century? He looked like Sebastian. Probably was Sebastian."

"Yes, that's the one." Jackson takes my face in his hands and kisses me fiercely. "Now, Chloe mine, examine each of these closely and tell me what you see."

The first image is of two boys, teenagers the same height, all arms and legs and elbows, standing very straight in front of a curtain; one has dark hair, one has hair a lighter shade. The second image: the same two young men, maybe ten years later, in virtually the same pose. The third depicts a family: a man, the lighter-haired one, but a bit older, with a woman seated before him and his hand on the shoulder of a boy about five or six years old, all dressed in their Sunday best.

"Wouldn't it have been very expensive to have these made?" I ask the resident photography expert.

"Yes, so in all likelihood these represent special occasions, even if it was just a special market-fair day when the daguerreotypist visited. It's hard to say exactly, but my guess from their clothing is that these people were members of the merchant class, and thus able to save some money to sit for a photographer. Either that or perhaps the daguerreotypist was a friend or family himself and offered his services gratis. But look, Chloe, especially at this middle image, down at the corner, can you see what's there?"

Carved into the copper plate are four letters: SuGH.

"Stefan und Gregor Herz," I whisper in German, surprised and yet not. My father and his twin brother, a man whose face looks remarkably familiar. I run a finger over the inscription, a bit jagged still, despite the passage of more than a century.

Jackson lifts the third image, turns it over, feels for a spot, grabs my right hand and runs it over more lettering. He trains the flashlight on the copper: G-B-C.

"Did Gregor Herz marry?" he asks. "Could these be his wife and son?"

"I don't know, Sebastian didn't talk about his family. There might be something in the Bible he left me, but that's locked away in London in the safe at Aspect Ratio. It would take days to get it here."

"Not if you ask someone to look through the Bible for you and text you a photo of anything that seems to apply—you know, entries of marriages or births."

Benjamin Kwesi, my art gallery partner, doesn't know about the de la Coeur secret, but his wife, Meredith Grainger-Todd, my oldest and dearest friend, does. Is she even in London, given all I've asked her to do to help set up the vassals confab here? She might have flown back to Ithaca to work with the printers and web designers.

Jackson spins his laptop around on the crate behind me so

he can type. After a few minutes, he motions me closer.

"According to a company history posted on the Gregor Zwilling GmbH website, Gregor's wife was named Marie Beatrisa. Could the G-B-C on this daguerreotype stand for Gregor-Beatrisa-Christoph?"

The resemblance is undeniable. Jackson sees it too.

Is Christoph Zwilling my cousin?

Chapter Two

OUTSIDE PRAGUE, MAY 2012

Painters, carpenters and a set designer from London were banging around the grand home that had once been little more than a way station for Sebastian and Emilie de la Coeur, a place to do the laundry and check messages while tramping around Eastern Europe. To hear what was being fed Jackson Fahey's media comrades, the de la Coeurs adored this moldering old pile quite a few kilometers off the main highway out of the Czech capital and cherished its place in the republic's history and their own. As the tale was spun, Emilie and Sebastian conceived their daughter here, and who knew, perhaps they had. So the cosmetic blitzkrieg had begun, in an attempt to make the place seem actively lived in and loved.

Good luck with that, Fahey wished them as he set out to get some work done far away from the banging and hammering and the inevitable debate over which settee looked best where.

He'd spent the last three days either moving furniture or sorting through the piles of stuff Sebastian and Emilie had left behind, to the point where his old knee burned, his new knee ached, and the muscles in his back and arms felt relentlessly stretched. Overdid it probably, but honestly, it had felt good to test himself, to be certain that his strength had returned, that he'd done sufficient conditioning in his physical-therapy sessions to feel whole again. Still, enough already.

Thus had Fahey gone to the nearest village and settled into the corner of a café, empty at mid-afternoon except for him and the barista, and sent the tracks he'd recorded last night for his "economies beyond the eurozone" features. Croatia and Lithuania down, Denmark and Poland yet to be reported, he hoped to knock out at least one before the open house. He hated to leave Chloe for even a day, but she'd been able to manage her blood needs since they reconciled that night in Barcelona three weeks ago. Which is to say that since then, when Fahey had been in Brussels or on assignment, she hadn't turned to a certain willing supplier who'd been her lover during previous absences. If he never heard of Will Baumann again, if Chloe never saw Baumann again, Fahey would be very happy.

He was seated with his back to the door, earbuds in, listening to a BBC World Service report on new revelations of corruption in Nigeria, so Fahey did not notice the man who entered and ordered an espresso. The man took the table next to Fahey's, sitting in the chair that faced him, so Fahey could not help but see who it was as soon as he raised his eyes.

"We meet again," he said, losing the earbuds.

Behind them, the barista cranked up the music, a song that sounded like Court of Cruelty, yet not anything Fahey had heard before. Curious that, but weren't the Cruel constantly playing somewhere in the background of his life these days?

Unsmiling, body language less friendly than it had been in Barcelona, Christoph Zwilling nodded. "Charming little place you've taken over here, Fahey, more *konditorei* than Starbucks, and playing selections from your fiancée's latest enterprise, as well." He waved a copy of *In Service to the Court of Cruelty*, slashed open the CD's cellophane wrapper with a lethal-looking fingernail, and scanned the song titles.

"That tune playing now, what is that? Ah, here. It's listed as a bonus track: 'Weapons of Class Destruction.' Clever. Nice to see Miss Hart is keeping the family business going, though she seems to have less regard for the family real estate."

"Did you come to check in on your acquisition? It's in disarray now. I fled while the men with the rollers and brushes and tools were having at it," Fahey replied, gratified by the wince his comment evoked. "It will, of course, look lovely in the end. Chloe has her best people on it, including one of her gallery associates."

Daphne, Aspect Ratio's former intern and newest staffer (did he even know her last name, Fahey wondered), had gone to art school with the set designer, who was willing to work cheap, if indeed Chloe was paying her anything at all beyond expenses in exchange for the chance to head up a very high-profile project.

Zwilling shrugged, sipped from his demitasse. "So, the house is being styled with whatever furnishings your Ms. Hart has not yet sold off. Perhaps, then, I'll wait for the open house to see the finished product, maybe buy a few pieces myself. I've given some thought to keeping an apartment in Prague; perhaps I'll just keep a few rooms at the house instead. Wouldn't want all that tidying up to go to waste. As it happens, some of my ancestors are from this region."

Do tell. Fahey was sure he'd love to hear all about those Zwilling forebears. Or was the name Herz? He watched Zwilling stretch his long legs into the aisle between their tables; he was tall like Sebastian and his twin brother, if that daguerreotype image were true. The hair color was different, but the eyes were the same, and the jaw line and the cheekbones, the face handsome like Sebastian's. But this man carried himself with less grace, without that comfort in his own skin that his, what—uncle?—had. Christoph Zwilling seemed coiled, like a snake ready to strike. Why not poke him a bit to see whether he'd hiss?

"Do you have a wife, Chris? Children?"

Zwilling pulled his legs in, sat up in his chair. "Children, no. A wife, yes, only recently," he responded, in something quite close to the hiss Fahey sought. "I had hoped to meet her here, but she seems to be unable to get away. Unnecessary complications, she allows these to get in the way."

Which seemed less the complaint of a frustrated new husband than that of a man unused to being thwarted. Make that a vampire used to having his own way, Fahey mustn't forget, recalling Barcelona and Chloe's mother. He looked at Zwilling's left hand. On it there was, indeed, a gold band, as well as a pinky ring with two rubies, neither of which Fahey noticed when they first met in Spain.

"What word of the musicians?" Zwilling asked, as if he had read Fahey's mind.

Still nothing from Katarina, as far as Fahey knew. "You mean, will all members of Matins and Vespers be available for the performance this week? That I can't say, but the show will go on. Chloe is prepared to step in, if necessary." (She was, though he knew she dreaded the prospect.)

Zwilling raked a hand through his hair, as if ready to pull it out. "The show is of little concern to me. I wish to see Katarina. We have much to discuss."

Much Katarina evidently preferred not to discuss with the recently married Christoph Zwilling, since she'd gone incommunicado. What more had transpired in Barcelona that night, after Fahey and Chloe fled a club full of riotous concertgoers while Zwilling and Kat were so publicly bonding? How deeply, Fahey wondered, did vampires bond: body and blood and *soul*? Did trouble with Kat trump Christoph's trouble with his wife?

"Any message, should we hear from Katarina?" Fahey asked.

Zwilling's eyes darkened from deep brown to black, and he stood, looming over Fahey's table. "Tell her I meant every word I said: We are not finished, she and I." He swept the CD and its wrappings to the floor as he stormed out of the cafe.

Fahey thought himself lucky not to be standing in Kat Nilsson's thigh-high boots.

* * * *

At a stopping point, really, in his online research about the current state of the Danish and Polish economies, there was nothing to keep Fahey in the village. Nothing for it but to return to the house and the work crews and Daphne and her friend fussing, and also to Chloe ankle-deep in the excavation of the barn's treasures and her attempts to unearth the common secrets, if any, of the de la Coeur and Zwilling clans. He packed up his laptop, notebooks and phone, bought another coffee for the road, and headed back on foot; walking would help build stamina in the leg with the new knee, as well as in the other leg, the one Teppan Nilsson had left with merely a flesh wound in the thigh.

The afternoon had turned cool, the sun had ducked behind a cloud, and Fahey had stopped to zip his jacket when he heard the squeal of brakes and jumped back as a town car screeched to a stop next to him.

A tinted window lowered, and a blonde head emerged.

"Sorry about that. Driver doesn't speak English, and I certainly don't speak Czech. I finally screamed, "Halt!" and that he got. Get in, and we'll give you a lift home."

Meredith opened the door then slid along the bench seat, pushing a large old book across the leather ahead of her. Fahey folded himself in, closed the door, and the car peeled away. He turned and wrapped his arms around her, squeezing tightly. She slipped her arms around his neck and kissed him enthusiastically on the lips.

"Jackson, you look so healthy and strong again. Jesus, I've missed you! I've even missed those endless days at the hospital beating you at chess while you recovered from your shot-up arm and shot-up legs."

"I beg your pardon. I took you twenty-two games out of twenty-four. Obviously, I could have beaten you blindfolded," Fahey teased. "And you can't have missed me that much, you got married."

Did he detect a genuine blush on the face of this woman he'd shared such pain with over the last year, someone who had trusted him so much she had slept with Teppan so a DNA sample could be gotten from Nilsson's semen?

"I did get married, didn't I?" she said shyly. "I'm so happy, Jackson. Benjamin and I had hoped you'd get to the wedding, so you and Chloe could work things out. So glad you two managed it in Spain—I mean, it's going OK, isn't it, you guys are definitely back together?"

"As if I'd ever let go of her again; that stupid, I'm not, Meredith. I'm just grateful she forgives me: The arrest warrant we helped get against her father . . . that morning in the music studio with Teppan and the gun. . . ."

Meredith set a finger against his lips.

"No one blames you for anything that happened to Teppan, least of all Chloe. He might have killed you in that room before he killed himself."

Oddly, the more he thought about that night, the less Fahey believed that was true. Over the last months, he'd relived those hours in the fierce morning sunlight more times than he could count. Teppan hadn't intended him as a victim, but as a prop, just part of the setting before which the world would learn that a) Sebastian de la Coeur was, indeed, gone, and b) that Teppan Nilsson had killed the women Sebastian had impregnated. Two men were meant to die in that room, Teppan had told him, and two men had. Fahey just wasn't one of them.

"Once this open house and the closing on the sale are behind you and Chloe, the baby will arrive and the new, good memories will wash away the old ones, you'll see," Meredith assured him.

She twisted away, picked up the weighty volume next to her on the seat.

"I brought the Herz Bible, as requested, though I doubt C.J. will have much time to look at it. I have papers she has to co-sign, so we can finish setting up the bank accounts that will handle the payments for anything she sells from the house, and a whole raft of documents disclaiming knowledge of the true provenance of whatever has been found on the estate. Don't want someone suing because they're pissed off something isn't the eighteenth-century Bohemian chest they believed it was when they bought it."

Fahey could only imagine all the scenarios Ed Chestack had to anticipate so Chloe would be able to pull off this open house. Fahey could almost hear Chestack, Court of Cruelty's onetime drummer and longtime lawyer, cursing now back in upstate New York, moaning about what a pain in the ass Chloe was. (Not unlike Chloe's complaints about Ed.)

The town car eased into a space next to the moving truck and mini-van Chloe had rented for Daphne and the set designer, so they could dash back to any one of the outbuildings to fetch a last-minute addition to the main house's new décor. Meredith scooped up the Bible, her briefcase, her tablet, and her purse, but she was a few arms shy of being able to carry it all, and the briefcase fell, scattering papers all around. "Shit," she muttered, kneeling to scoop up contracts, memos, pens and what have you.

Conscious that he'd done too much kneeling already this week, Fahey bent to retrieve some of the papers. His glance fell on the names Ronald R. Hamilton and Eric S. Bohlander. "What's this?"

"Something about that bonus track on the new CD."

Meredith took the contract from him, shoved it into the briefcase, then handed it all back to Fahey to carry inside.

" 'Weapons of Class Destruction.' I heard it in the café in the village just now," Fahey said. "Pretty good, though I couldn't place it from any of the albums Court of Cruelty released. Maybe a song recorded but then dropped from one of them?"

Meredith walked ahead, waited for him to open the front door.

"All I know is Ed wants a conference call with Chloe as soon as possible. He said new music makes good financial sense for the de la Coeur estate and the charitable foundation, and that he's willing to sign on, whatever that means."

Chestack had a keen sense of what was good financially for the de la Coeurs, and, by extension, himself. Fahey held the door, allowed Hurricane Meredith to make landfall and, dubious, arched an eyebrow her way.

"I know what you know, Jackson. Just because it turns out Ed is actually my father doesn't mean he tells me any more than he ever did."

"Just means it's harder to say no to him?"

"Precisely. He says set up a call, I set up a call. You know he'd prefer not to deal with Chloe directly until he's sure he's manned the ramparts against her."

As Fahey had learned so well in the last year, there were vampires and there were bloodsuckers. In this crowd, it could be hard to distinguish between the two.

* * * *

"You're out of your mind. A brand-new Court of Cruelty?"

Palms slapped down on the table, baby belly jammed up against the wood, Chloe leaned into the laptop screen as if she hoped to rip open Chestack's throat via video chat.

"A Court of Cruelty reborn," he countered.

"Reanimated, like a bunch of zombies. 'The band that would not die.' Really, Ed?"

"Why not transform Matins and Vespers into a new, twenty-first-century version of the Cruel? Ronnie and Eric have presented an excellent business plan: new music, new records, and new generation of fans. That song, 'Weapons of Class Destruction,' they wrote it the day after Teppan's suicide, while all hell was still breaking loose. You and Kat were dealing with the police and the medical examiner, and no one was allowed to leave the Castle, not even to go into Ithaca on a doughnut run. Listen to the song, and you'll see. No crap allowed, just good tunes worthy of Sebastian and Emilie. Ronnie and Eric will find the best players they can, the best female vocalist, too, if necessary."

Chestack, an early part of the twentieth-century band, clearly had been won over.

"My mother will never sign off on this." Chloe straightened, rubbed the small of her back. Fahey slipped a chair under her, moved behind her to rub her neck.

On the laptop screen, Chestack shook his head. "She doesn't have to. I'm the administrator of the de la Coeur estate and chairman of the board of the winery. I have a fiduciary duty to do what's best for them and the charitable foundation. And, may I remind you, as a trustee of the foundation and a board member of Vineyard de la Coeur, so do you. What we say goes, and I say this is a chance to make all three ventures self-sustaining. She can't overrule us, and why should she? She needs money to live on. This promises to provide that."

Even so, the woman the world once knew as Emilie de la Coeur could raise a mighty stink if she chose to.

"If I sign, then what?" Chloe asked.

"We'll break the news the day of the open house. I'm booked on a flight to Prague in the morning, and Ronnie and Eric are on their way from Stockholm with the rest of the band and the equipment now. Matins and Vespers will be proclaimed the new Court of Cruelty by you three days from now."

Meredith leaned in to show Chloe an ad mockup she'd just sketched.

"She won't show up when she hears about this, and I won't play girl singer to make *her* future more comfortable," Chloe said, sounding like the pregnant, over-tired and overwhelmed vampire Fahey knew his love to be.

"Your mother will show up," he whispered in her ear. "Usually, *you* can count on her, if no one else can."

Chloe turned and kissed his cheek. "More reliable than dear old Dad was, you mean? Hold onto that faith of yours. It will have to be enough for both of us."

Hours passed before the work crews quieted for the night and Chloe finished with the legal paperwork. It was only then, Fahey guessed, that she noticed his absence. "Aren't you supposed to be packing?" she asked on joining him in the bedroom they'd claimed. "The car will be here for you at five o'clock in the morning."

Without lifting his eyes from his computer, Fahey pointed to the garment bag hanging from an intricately carved door made, no doubt, during the days of the Holy Roman Empire of some now insanely expensive Black Forest hardwood. "Slacks, shirts, underthings, socks, it's just a quick trip to Krakow. A jaunt through the tech companies I've contacted, some interviews, some B-roll and audio, and I'm back from Poland in plenty of time for the Big Event."

Chloe stepped behind him, grazed his neck with her teeth, drew a little blood and kissed it away. "So what's this you're working on? It's almost midnight."

"My mate at the Home Office in London did a little digging for me. Turns out Christoph Zwilling, if he was indeed recently married, is not showing up on a sweep of the last ninety days of registry records in Switzerland or the European Union. Not the most comprehensive search, but if he applied for a license under his own name or if paperwork was registered after a wedding, something ought to have popped, I'm told."

She licked along the underside of his jaw, flicked light kisses along its edge. "Hmm, isn't that thirty countries' worth of data, give or take, to sort through? Even your super-hacker could easily miss something. And what if Zwilling got married longer ago than ninety days?"

Fahey twisted, reached up for her face, and kissed her hard. "Good, yes? Now stop distracting me, I've got something else here from my friend, who ran Zwilling through some airline-ticketing databases. An 18 January manifest shows Zwilling flying into Newark, connecting to Chicago O'Hare, then to Las Vegas. Maybe he got married there?"

Chloe squeezed onto his lap, obliterating Fahey's view of the screen. "What, he went to a wedding chapel and got married by an Elvis impersonator? Isn't it more likely that his company had business with one of those Vegas theme hotels, the Palazzo or something like that?"

He patted her bum, pushed her off. "More likely, yes, but I'm curious. So let me do a short spin through the Clark County, Nevada, marriage license records." Fahey tapped, entered log-in credentials he really shouldn't have, and searched for the name Zwilling.

"Here we go: A marriage license recorded 19 January between Christoph Zwilling and a Chiara Nunnally. He's listed as thirty-eight-years old, a businessman from Switzerland, so it's our guy for sure; she's listed as twenty-eight, an actress from Toronto. So let's just do a quick search on her and see what we find."

An internet search shed little light on the identity of the new Mrs. Zwilling, offering up only a March review from a Toronto arts newspaper praising Chiara's performance as Bianca in a road production of *Taming of the Shrew*. Toronto was the show's first stop; no reviews popped from its scheduled subsequent runs in Edmonton and Winnipeg.

"Chiara Nunnally may well be a 'talented newcomer to the Toronto theater scene,'" Chloe said, "but as an actress she sure hasn't left a much of an online paper trail. Any spy sources in Canada, Mr. Bond?"

Chloe pulled the blankets down on the bed and settled under them.

"None that immediately comes to mind, no. I'll do some database-digging tomorrow and see what I can find out about the mystery bride and what's keeping her away from her new husband. Maybe Ms. Nunnally found out about his fling with Katarina in Spain so soon after the nuptials and told Christoph to bugger off. Whatever's going on seems to have him rattled, though, and he doesn't like it one bit."

"A common trait among the Herz boys, impatience. They like to be in control, my father being the classic case."

Chloe patted the pillow next to her, beckoned Fahey to join

her. He powered down the laptop, stripped, and got into bed. He rested his head against her belly, felt the baby seem to stretch within it. He shut his eyes but knew he would not sleep.

He made a mental checklist of all the things that comprised one's official persona: phone number and address, birth certificate, passport, curriculum vitae, driver's license, credit history, military service, voter registration, property transactions, tax and employment records. Even a rudimentary search should have grabbed one of those, though it was possible Chiara Nunnally was a stage name, or maybe even a larger work of fiction. Not that it mattered to Fahey, but it might matter quite a bit to her husband, and hence Katarina, and hence Chloe.

Had Zwilling bitten off more than even he could chew?

Chapter Three

OUTSIDE PRAGUE, MAY 2012

Visitors are flowing into and out of our beautifully, if hastily, staged rooms, as classical music plays in the background. Furnishings are selling and for the prices we ask, without a lot of haggling, almost as if the buyers are trying to be respectful of the belongings Sebastian and Emilie left behind. Honestly, I have no idea how any of these things found their way onto this property, and I'm happy to see them safely escorted off it, thanks to Meredith and Daphne and their credit-card readers. We have gone through two cases of champagne and about a dozen trays of canapés. The crowd is gentle, mellow.

Good thing, because the music is about to start. Matins and Vespers has set up on a platform in what might once have been a ballroom. Ronnie and Ed Chestack have found appropriate black-on-black clothing to coordinate with what Eric, Lars, and the boys are wearing. Only the female vocalist is missing.

Plan B is, unfortunately, me. I'll have to do the only two Court of Cruelty tunes I know well enough to sing in public. I'll also reprise "Cri de Coeur," which had its boffo premiere—notable more for the crowd's surprise than for the magnificence of my talent—at December's Christmas at the Castle concert. Since today's show will be just fifteen songs, only so much of its success depends on me.

Which is fortunate, indeed, because there's no Plan C for this now-much-tweeted debut of the "New" Court of Cruelty. Much like the cheese, we stand alone, without my mother's grace and seemingly effortless rapport with an audience, attributes I never gave her credit for in my need to resent her all those years. Like Emilie de la Coeur before her, Katarina Nilsson is the glue that holds the band together. But evidently not for today's show.

Jackson has been at my side most of the day, knight to my lady as we stride through the throng of vassals, but it's time to leave me to the music. He deposits me on the piano bench.

"You'll be alright? You're looking a little pale," he says, knowing public appearances bring out the worst in me.

"Beyond pale. White dress, with a touch of stage fright, mixed in with a lot of pregnant. What I wouldn't give for some of that champagne right now. You know, a little liquid courage?"

He kisses the top of my head, wraps an arm around my shoulders so I can lean against his chest, nicely muscular under his black (of course) V-neck sweater. "Five minutes till showtime and you haven't hyperventilated yet—that's a good sign. Here comes Meredith. She's doing the mistress-of-ceremonies thing again, yes?"

"Explains the wireless microphone in her hand, yes."

He leans down, tickles his tongue along the shell of my right ear. "Do you know that you get really cranky when you're nervous? As opposed to your usual level of cranky, that is. Here's a kiss for luck." And off he goes, flagging down a server with a tray of champagne, grabbing two flutes before heading for the back of the room and the corner where a scowling Christoph Zwilling stands expectantly.

Meredith taps an earpiece nestled beneath some of her blonde curls, and strains of J.S. Bach's *Goldberg Variations* fade into silence. Ed sits behind the drum kit, which puts Lars on bass and Ronnie on lead guitar and the other sweet Swedish faces on rhythm guitar and organ. Eric hulks like a brooding Norse god at the standing mic closest to me. Voices hush.

"OK, C.J., we're good to go," Meredith whispers into my earpiece. "Ready for some musical melodrama?"

I nod. I am, though that doesn't mean I won't kill my mother next time I see her.

A spotlight illuminates a lone trumpeter at stage right. He raises his herald's horn and sounds the opening notes of Rossini's "William Tell Overture." Meredith proclaims, "Gentlemen and gentlewomen, vassals and nobles, please welcome our musical guests, the New Court of Cruelty!"

Eric grabs the mic stand with both hands and swings it like a broadsword at the audience, then launches into "Born to Slay the King," a perennial crowd-pleaser. He is, like the rebel in the song, a pretender to the throne, in no way the authentic Sebastian de la Coeur, but Eric nails all four verses and the bridge with a passion I've never seen in him before. Ronnie smiles knowingly at me from behind his guitar, his fingers dancing along the fretboard as Lars saws the bass line and Ed pounds snare and stomps the hi-hats harder than a man his age probably should. They can do this and won't sound like posers, Ronnie is telling me: They'll rock it fit to raise Sebastian from the dead.

First impressions are everything, and the vassals approve so far, if the applause and shouting and singing-along are any indication. Thank God, if we must do this, and do it without my mother.

The set list segues into "Inquisition," "Plague of Fools," and the new song, "Weapons of Class Destruction," by which time band and followers are sweating and swaying, and the volume is cranked to break-the-sound-barrier decibels. So when the last chord erupts from Eric's throat and Ronnie's guitar, it is deafening and difficult to dismiss.

Those who have listened, me included, sit for a minute in silence, stunned and reverential. And then it's my turn.

"It's an honor to share the stage with these fabulous musicians and, I must admit, quite a relief that none of you will have enough hearing left for my portion of this program."

The crowd, clearly hearing very well, laughs appropriately.

"The song I'm about to play is 'Cri de Coeur,' which many of you will recognize as a song of my father's, 'Croix de Guerre,' that I reworked. I dedicate it now to the new generation of Court of Cruelty: the band surrounding me and the baby within me. Thank you."

To soft but enthusiastic applause, the piano's first notes resonate from under my trembling fingers and out into the audience. I've done this only twice before, once with both my parents, once with my mother alone. I reach for my ruby pendant, a piece of her Emilie left me when she and Sebastian faked their deaths last year, but I realize I've left it back in London. This time, I really am going solo.

* * * *

When the final note of the final song, "Feudal/Futile," reverberates into nothingness, when the last clap of thunderous applause sounds and the band takes its bows, I follow, waving and blowing kisses as Emilie used to, with Eric trailing me, as Sebastian would have. The overhead spotlights we have installed temporarily go dark; the house lights go up. I can breathe again.

I leave the men to their hand-shaking and back-slapping and fist-bumping. Meredith hands me a glass of orange juice and makes me drink.

"A little sunshine won't kill you this late in the day," she quips.

Funny girl, now she's cracking vampire jokes.

"If you say one word about blood oranges, I'll bite, I swear, Meredith."

She wraps an arm around my shoulders. "You did good, all of you, even my old dad. Look at Ed and Ronnie, they're acting like they're in their twenties again."

So they are. "They had a lot riding on this show, and they pulled it off. The New Court of Cruelty is the real deal. How long before the video goes up on YouTube?"

She pulls her tablet out of the messenger bag slung across

her back. "Another two minutes till the upload finishes and the Communion of Saints begins." Meredith crosses her eyes as she hears what she's said. "I'm quoting Cruel album titles, shoot me now. I really must get back to London and my very normal husband as soon as possible."

I scan the crowd for my very normal fiancé, whose eyes light up the minute he spots me. Jackson waves me over to the corner where he and Zwilling have been ensconced for the last ninety minutes or so. I make my way toward them slowly, my legs feeling as if bricks are attached.

Jackson drags a folding chair from the back row and lowers me into it. "Tired, love? Rest and bask justifiably in your success. Today was just fabulous, you all did such a fantastic job. The house looks spectacular, the band was great, and everyone seems so pleased with it all."

He kisses me heartily. He tastes like champagne, the real bubbly not the effervescence his blood sends coursing through me when I sip from him. He's quite mellow; I wish I were.

Not that I'm inclined to be sympathetic, but Zwilling looks considerably less relaxed than Jackson. Seems well past time he and I were formally introduced. I maneuver Jackson out of my way and approach the future owner of this property. "C.J. Hart," I say, offering my hand, "and you're Christoph Zwilling."

"Call me Chris," he says, his lips barely moving, his hand lightly gripping mine. "Here in this house, it seems like we're all family."

So cute, my possible cousin. Actually, he is quite handsome; undistracted by the chaos of that scene with my mother, I can see now that Zwilling's resemblance to my father is striking. The daguerreotype Jackson found in the barn suggests that Gregor Herz, my father's twin, was just as tall and good-looking; so odd, to see up close a facsimile of them both. But this man means nothing to me, certainly nothing I have ascertained to be good.

"Since my parents' deaths, these people are my family," I respond coolly. "My friends, the band, Jackson, and my child."

Jackson has moved behind me, his back to the wall the better to support me and my baby bulk.

"Is your wife here? Jackson mentioned you thought she might arrive in time."

"She is unavoidably detained, it appears," Zwilling says, offering little to suggest that it upsets him save a curious ripple of his vampire aura. I can't tell whether he's angry or hurt; I'm no more able to read him than I could my father, and Lord knows my mother mystifies me more every day.

Zwilling detects that I'm thinking of my mother and allows me no opportunity to be coy about it. "You don't know where Katarina Nilsson is, do you? I'd hoped you and Fahey were just trying to misdirect me, but I see I was wrong. She really isn't here, or in Sweden, or at the Castle, is she?"

She's managed to befuddle us both, then, that's clear. "Katarina doesn't answer to me or anyone else. I know no one who's been in touch with her since the Casa Cruella show in Barcelona weeks ago—no one except you, that is."

He shakes his head wearily, lifts an arm clad in black leather and rubs the back of his neck. "I haven't seen her since that night. We left the club as the police were arriving. A kiss in the alley and she was gone, like a ghost. I almost don't believe it happened; there's no proof of her anywhere."

The room around us is almost empty now, the crowd dispersed, the band members breaking down the stage and stowing away instruments and equipment. The New Court of Cruelty started the journey to metropolitan Prague as a small Swedish cover band with no roadies to do the packing and hauling for them. Stardom and its privileges might be a ways off, as Jackson seems to realize. He gives me a peck on the cheek, abandons me to this awkward conversation, and rushes up to lend a hand.

I head for one of the makeshift bars set up at the perimeter of this large space, peruse the selections, pour a ginger ale for myself and a scotch for Zwilling, who looks less like a vampire than a millionaire businessman who cagily bought this house but gave away his heart a bit precipitously. Consoling him seems the only thing to do—I'm worried about Kat, too, after all—so I hand him his drink and move over to the last row of folding chairs. He takes the seat I designate in the row in front of me.

"It's been a rough few months for Katarina. Her husband did commit suicide, after weeks of being in the news because of the sex tapes and the dead bodies found on this property. I was surprised when she urged me to come to Barcelona for the show there—I hadn't heard from her since she left the Castle just after Teppan's death, so I'm not surprised she's gone silent now. Kat has a lot to work out, and, though maybe she's not aware of it, you do have a wife."

Zwilling downs his scotch in one swallow, stands and turns toward the exit.

"She knows about my wife," he says, "and my wife knows about her. I believe I have no secrets from either of them. I see no point in deceit or subterfuge. The surest way to win what we desire starts with knowing ourselves and acting accordingly, a lesson my father learned too late."

What was it, I wonder, that his father desired but failed to win?

* * * *

The Herz Bible, which Meredith has brought with her from London, sits open before me. I've been through some of the genealogical records already, gleaned what I can from my father's notations and those entered by others, his mother and grandmother, I suppose; there is something feminine about the eighteenth- and nineteenth-century handwriting.

Jackson's laugh tinkles behind me; he leans over, kisses the top of my head, hands me a dish of applesauce.

"Must you immerse yourself in the Herz family lore when Jesus knows you're exhausted and about to burst with that baby? Meredith's gotten everyone fed and tucked in; we should be too, love. I have to be on a plane to Copenhagen tomorrow, and I was hoping for a bit of sip-and-sin tonight."

That's right, he's leaving again. For how long this time, is he even coming directly back here or heading to Brussels for some BBC face time? The next few days I'll spend emptying out this house and packing up what's in the barn and the outbuildings and getting them into storage or shipped to Aspect Ratio. So much to do in the next two weeks before I close on the deal with Zwilling, so much to do before the baby comes. Do I even have two weeks left until then?

I wave off the applesauce. I need Fahey, not fruit. "You're right, I've had enough of my family for one day. Go up to bed. I'll be right behind you."

Jackson circles back to the semi-functioning kitchen; I hear him open and close one of the mini-fridges we've rented, then start up the stairs, whistling as he goes. A few heartbeats later, his phone buzzes and the whistling stops.

"Chloe, hurry! You need to see this!"

I find him sitting about midway up. He pats the space beside him and hands me the phone, its small screen filled with news alerts, from the BBC, CNN, Reuters and others, about the crash of a private jet in the North Sea. He gives me a minute to read through them, then switches to his text messages, to the one he's just received, from Detective Gippel at Interpol.

"Mid-air explosion, eight aboard, plus two crew; survivors unlikely," it reads. "Passenger manifest lists Katarina Nilsson. Security footage shows her arriving at the small airfield and waiting for the flight."

I look up at Jackson, unable to form words. He folds his arms around me protectively. "Gippel would have watched the footage before texting, you know that. He'd recognize Kat and would have picked her out from among the people passing through the security checkpoint."

My mother, alive one minute then, poof, gone? Just like that, after a century and a half, maybe longer?

Cold rises from my core; tears well and fall. Jackson's embrace tightens, he rocks me, whispers soothing syllables, wraps me against the solidity of his body, against the firm, steady beat of his heart. He lives, he breathes, he hurts for me, and so he tries to draw into himself the pain climbing through me. My pulse thuds in my neck, I can feel its percussive echo inside my head; a pounding too quick, too hard, a rush of adrenaline and stress hormones and who knows what else convulses within me, scratches at my consciousness trying to break free. My fingers snake around his forearm; it's only when I feel wetness that I realize I've clawed him and drawn blood.

"I'll make some calls, see what I can find out," Jackson says. "All we know is that she was at the airfield, apparently booked on that jet. We don't know that she took her seat." He wants to believe that, for my sake.

I shake my head, will my thoughts to reach him: *Just sit here with me, let someone else get the story.* My heart is in my throat. I never knew what that meant until now—it's like paralysis, words frozen inside me. Really just one word I want to scream over and over: No. . . .

He kisses my hair, kisses my forehead, kisses my eyelids, and takes my face in his hands.

"You know they're searching for her. You know they'll try to find her."

But he knows I know what that means. I feel him imagining a debris field, luggage, papers, airplane parts strewn across miles of open water. It could be days before anything is discovered, but before too long someone will intone the words he won't put into thoughts, for fear I'll feel those too: Missing, presumed dead.

Some primal need to breathe again forces oxygen into my lungs; my autonomic nervous system pushes it back out in a spasm of coughs. Jackson rubs my back, small, slow circles that eventually relax me, settle my respiratory system until it resumes its normal rhythm. He lifts his wrist to my mouth, shivers as I slice a vein there and drink, just a little, just enough. As soon as I finish, I sense him trying to shake off the lethargy, trying to regain his wits enough to stitch a sentence together. Because he has to ask, he needs to know: "Is it possible an explosion could kill her? She's a vampire."

The baby twists within me, as if turning to hear my answer, except I don't have one, not for Jackson, not for Avalon, not for myself.

* * * *

The day my father killed himself, I felt the precise second the bullet penetrated the parboiled mass the morning sun had made of his brain; it was as if the lead had pierced my skin and skull, as well. I recognized the exact moment Teppan's tainted spirit passed out of his body, as if a piece had been ripped away from my own soul.

Despite the twenty-four hours I've now passed waiting for that feeling again, expecting to sense it any moment, it doesn't come. Isn't the blood bond she and I share stronger than that? Sebastian may have sired the vampire in me, but Emilie carried me, nurtured me inside her, and protected me in ways I couldn't even begin to understand until she took that most extreme step of all and repudiated him, the vampire she created, at least in part to safeguard me.

Of all people, I should know if she's dead, shouldn't I?

Jackson walks into our bedroom, coffee-black hair curling and damp from his shower, towel slung around his taut waist, my sweet, handsome love. He tosses his shaving kit atop assorted clothing and zips his suitcase shut, looks over to me and the computer bag standing near the window alongside me.

"Screw Copenhagen and the bloody assignment, I don't want to leave you. I should be here with you at a time like this."

As always, he thinks he can fix things.

"If you waited for my every crisis to pass, Jackson Fahey, you'd never work again. You told your boss you'd finish the reporting for the euro economy project before the baby was due, and you're what, a half-dozen interviews away from being done? So you'll go, you'll finish those. I have all the details here to distract me, and Meredith will be with me. I'll be OK."

He flings himself onto the mattress. "The grief is so thick in this house, love. Ronnie Hamilton crying. Chestack without bluster, quietly sitting with the Matins and Vespers boys, doing what he can to comfort them. And poor Eric, what must he be thinking?"

Through the window, the exterior spotlights half-illuminating, half-shrouding him, I watch Eric pace the driveway. Occasionally he looks skyward, as if he expects Katarina to fall to earth where he stands.

"He's thinking about the Casa Cruella show in Barcelona and how he never got to tell Kat how much he loved her. He thinks that he let his jealousy drive her into Zwilling's arms and that the last thing Kat saw was his anger. He would have loved her forever if she'd wanted him to."

Jackson sits up, no doubt wondering about our own issues with forever and what is and is not possible.

"Did Kat ever say, Chloe?"

So much always went unsaid by my parents, especially my mother.

"I know she'd be terribly upset that Eric is hurting and that she's the cause of it," I reply.

I have to believe that's true, that she'd feel that way about us all. She just wouldn't let us wonder indefinitely.

Would she?

Chapter Four

OUTSIDE PRAGUE, MAY 2012

The flight from Copenhagen to Prague was less than two hours long, and the trip to the suburban village nearest the de la Coeur estate usually took Fahey only another ninety minutes via airport shuttle. But a relentless rain meant traffic crawled on the main motorway out of the Czech capital. After midnight, pressing onward to the house was less than appealing, so he booked a room for the night at the little hotel in the center of the village and texted Chloe that he'd be back come morning.

"Avalon and I will miss you, but that will just mean bigger hugs. Sleep well," she replied. "Oh, and if you bring chocolate croissants with you tomorrow, I'll love you forever."

Again with forever, the possibility of which was quite real for her, less so for him, and so Fahey tried not to contemplate it at all. They'd have whatever time they'd have, unless somehow more turned out to be possible. That mystery was beyond him. It was enough, right now at least, that Chloe sounded good. He didn't know how her vampire grief manifested, it was something he'd avoided with her father's death since Sebastian, as Teppan, had done a good job of almost killing him, too.

Without bothering to go up to his room first, Fahey walked into the hotel bar for a drink, to unwind after too many hours in the air, then on the road. His eyes adjusted to the dimness, and he noticed a couple kissing in a shadowy corner.

Good for them, he thought. How many nights, in how many foreign places, had he finished a workday just that way, with how many foreign misses? Too many, before Chloe. This late, this tired, he was hard-pressed to remember any of their names.

Floating like a sunny island in the middle of a dark ocean was the bar, white fairy lights under the shelves reflecting the color of the bottles, mostly shades of blue and green like the sea itself. Beached up on shore, so to speak, ignoring the bartender and the football match on the big-screen TV above him was Eric, looking only a few shots shy of a full bottle of something. Fahey was surprised to see him, but nonetheless took the stool next to him, flashed two fingers at the barkeep and gestured at himself and his oblivious companion.

"Fancy meeting you here, Bohlander. Drink with me until my bed beckons."

Eric eyed the bags Fahey piled onto an adjacent stool. "Walk on that road in this rain, and you'll end up as dead as Katarina," he slurred. "No taxis in this town, Fahey."

The bartender, biceps thick as a stevedore's evident under the sleeves of a red shirt, placed two fresh glasses in front of them and poured two vodkas. "In the old days, Court of Cruelty fans had to stay here if they wanted to stay nearby," the man minding the booze said in what sounded to Fahey like an American accent straight out of Boston. "Story goes that the de la Coeurs paid off the local council to keep taxis out. You wanted to see their house, you walked the nine-plus kilometers up and back. Not my type of music. I never bothered."

Eric snarled, downed his vodka, dragged his hand across his mouth and at least two days' growth of blond beard. "Court of Cruelty was a great band, you fucker—fuck you, it *is* a great band. But if I never have to see that house again, I'll be happy."

Shrugging, the bartender left them to whatever debates, musical or otherwise, might ensue.

Fahey sipped his drink, let the alcohol burn his throat, the pain exquisite. "Checked in here as well, are you? Are Lars and Anders and the rest here?"

Eric stared, as if he couldn't remember the names of his comrades, let alone that Matins and Vespers had arrived as a cover band and would leave as a Court of Cruelty reboot. When the stupor lifted, he muttered something in Swedish then, Fahey supposed, repeated himself in English.

"Still at the house. Couldn't stay there," Eric slurred. "They'll find me, put me on a plane, send me back to Stockholm. Not much good for anything else, they know that."

True enough, still Fahey didn't like the idea of Eric's grieving alone. Something about the possibility of Katarina's death cut too close to the bone for Fahey, and not just because she was Chloe's mother—more like it was yet another portent of his own mortality. He and Eric had that in common, yet here Eric was, mourning Kat's loss in a way neither of them could have predicted.

Eric waved the bartender over for a refill. The man looked at Fahey, who nodded. "He's a friend. I'll see that he sleeps it off safely." He pulled out his phone, texted Chloe that he had taken Eric under his wing at the hotel, then went off in search of the loo.

Re-entering the bar from the other side, his eyes now more accustomed to the darkness, Fahey recognized at least one-half of the couple in the corner, less snuggled together now than seeming to argue: Zwilling and a brunette Fahey presumed was his bride. He walked to their table, pulled a chair over and joined them, stretching his long legs, still stiff from the trip, in front of him.

"Small town, you never know who you'll run into, eh, Chris? Introductions, please, or should I just jump in?"

The woman turned for a better look at Fahey, winked and extended her hand.

"I'm Chiara. You'll have to forgive Christoph, he's distraught. A friend has died, or we assume so, in a plane crash."

Zwilling grabbed her hand before Fahey could shake it. "Jackson Fahey, my wife, Chiara Nunnally. Happy?" he asked, glaring at both, rising as if he planned on leaving. "Fahey introduced me to Katarina Nilsson in Barcelona, blame him for what I did that night, since you're looking to find fault. I have no intention of apologizing to you again. What's done is done, you'll live with that and more before we're through. I'm going up to bed."

Chiara covered one of Zwilling's hands with both of hers, a gleaming oval ruby on the right, a square diamond on the left, and gazed up at his looming height. "Don't go," she murmured, softly but loud enough for Fahey to hear. "I'm sorry I upset you, it was childish of me, you're right. What's done is done." Zwilling brought her hands to his lips and sank back into his chair, soothed, it appeared, by the touch of her and the sound of her voice. Could it be, if what Fahey saw were to be believed, that love was the source of this beautiful woman's power over a vampire who, in their short acquaintance, had seldom shown himself willing to give ground?

Zwilling smiled at his wife.

"Apologies all around, darling?" she said, hinting.

"I'm sorry," Zwilling said. "I know the news has been distressing to all who knew Katarina." He glanced over his shoulder to where Eric lay sprawled over the bar, snoring. "Bohlander came in after us. I don't think he even realized I was here in the same room, so consumed was he by his sorrow."

Chiara moved a finger to Zwilling's mouth. "Shh, we don't want him to know now either. There will be no repeat of Barcelona here if I can help it."

"So you do know?" Fahey was surprised Zwilling had been honest about that with Chloe.

"Oh, yes, Mr. Fahey, I know—the YouTube video was everywhere. Not exactly how I thought my marriage would begin, but we can't help who we love, can we? Or who they love."

What story had Zwilling dished out to explain his liaison with

Kat that night? Fahey wondered too: Did Chiara Nunnally know Christoph's secret, the one about being 147 years old, give or take, and destined to live forever, barring solar self-immolation like Teppan or mid-flight explosion like Kat?

As if peering into their minds, Zwilling looked from Fahey to Eric and back again. "Bohlander blames himself for what's happened to Katarina, thinks she never would have left him if he hadn't been so jealous. He's a fool, of course, she would have, probably very soon. She was ready to move on. Coming here to perform with the band, whatever its name, would not have changed that."

"And you know this how?" Fahey asked, knowing he poked at his peril.

"Bohlander was not who Katarina wanted," Zwilling spat out. "Was I not a vivid enough demonstration of that?"

"Christoph, enough!" Chiara scolded. "Jesus, what is it about this Nilsson woman that makes you behave this way? She was a less-than-one-night stand to you, unless all your so-called honesty with me has been anything but."

Now that was an angle Fahey would love to pursue. He knew he should back off, but seeing Zwilling so provoked was enlightening. "I'll speak for Eric, since he's in no shape to rebut your assertion. Eric and Kat have been very close for more than a year; their future together, or not, is theirs to work out. None of us can know just yet what has happened to her. In the meantime, she is his to grieve, Chris, not yours. Best to remember that."

Zwilling's eyes blazed to black, then red. He reached across the table, grabbed Fahey by the front of his leather jacket, and growled. Chiara fastened her ruby-emblazoned hand onto his arm, applied pressure until Zwilling released Fahey and lowered himself back into his chair. She turned his face to hers, kissed his lips lightly, then whispered, "Christoph, Mr. Fahey is right. Calm yourself, darling, I am here."

And once again, the new Mrs. Zwilling's vampire-taming abilities subdued her husband. The blaze in his eyes extinguished to a more-mortal brown, and he kissed her gently, as if he had forgotten everything that just transpired.

What was it about this woman, Fahey wondered, that she could work such magic? He risked incurring more of Zwilling's wrath but had to know. Never taking his eyes off Zwilling, he asked her, "Talk about Beauty and the Beast, how did you ever come to be with this one, Chiara?"

She directed a dazzling smile Fahey's way, winked a sparkling hazel eye. "He is a beauty, isn't he?" she joked, pulling an actual smile out of Zwilling. "Christoph travels a lot for business, I travel a lot for my career; he went to the theater one night, saw me in a play and stayed after the performance to meet me. But I suspect you already knew that I was an actress. Just as I've seen you on the news, Mr. Fahey. I've worked on and off in Europe in the last two years. You might have seen my candy commercial. All that chocolate was so bad for my waistline."

From where Fahey sat, there wasn't a damn thing wrong with her waistline, or anything else. She was lovely, curved and feminine and sexy.

"She was in that racy Roman Empire television series everyone was talking about, the one with the full-frontal nudity, female and male," Zwilling said, churlish again, as if looking inside Fahey's head. "Soft porn almost, more of my wife than I'd like to share with others."

"No, no, I can't let you get away with that," she said, laughter drowning out his complaint, right hand waving in protest. "We met after it aired, Christoph, and you admitted that's why you came to the theater that night in the first place, because you saw my name in the advertisements. All that exposure worked in my favor, no? I'm yours now, aren't I?"

Chiara, it seemed, was determined to charm her husband into sociability and keep him there. Fahey scanned his memory but didn't think he'd ever seen the TV show they referred to. Just as well, perhaps.

She stifled a yawn, checked a gold watch bracelet on her

wrist. Light from the candle on the table caught the crimson iridescence of her ring. She pushed back her chair to stand. Zwilling quickly rose to help.

"It's almost two o'clock in the morning, darling, let's wish Mr. Fahey a good night. I have a noon flight to Toronto, then a two-hour layover before switching for Vancouver, too exhausting to ponder." She smoothed nonexistent wrinkles from her slim black skirt. "It was lovely to meet you, Jackson. Take good care of your friend; he's so lost." She stared at Eric's broad back, for a moment looking as if she wished she could comfort him as she had her husband.

There were so many questions swirling about Fahey's head after the encounter. Blissful newlyweds, yes or no? Iron vampire will versus smart, intuitive woman? Could that marriage be saved? Fahey didn't know how he'd carry it all upstairs and Eric, too.

* * * *

A bleating woke him. No, more like yodeling. It took Fahey a few minutes to realize it was Eric, singing in the shower, sounding more sober than he'd been earlier, thank goodness. At least he wasn't vomiting anymore, that sort of vocalizing Fahey had heard enough of.

He rummaged through his bag, found his emergency extra-day boxers and socks, reached for his black jeans, still in a ball on the floor at the side of the bed, his mobile half in/half out of a back pocket. Scrolling through his news apps, he found repeated bulletins about bodies having been found from the private-plane crash, about a recovery effort underway off the coast of Scotland, between Aberdeen and Edinburgh. Fahey checked his texts, located the one he'd been hoping for from Detective Gippel, his helpful new source on the inside.

Without preamble, it read: "Some bodies—flight attendant based on bits of uniform, the rest probable passengers—discovered in a piece of fuselage severed from the rest of the plane by the force of the blast. Working theory is that the explosion decompressed the passenger compartment and everyone was pulled out, front to rear. No complete bodies, identification problematical. Fahey, you should come."

Water still ran in the shower; no grieving Swede could hear him speak. Fahey punched Gippel's number, counted six rings before he picked up. "Are you there, in Scotland?" Fahey asked.

"*Naturlich*, I have volunteered my services and yours too. You know Katarina Nilsson more than well enough to identify her if facial recognition is possible."

It might not be, after an explosion and almost four days in the water, which was warming with each passing day as summer neared.

"I can't do that, conflict of interest professionally and, well, you know. . . ." Fahey allowed Gippel a few moments to put it together.

"Who then? Her husband is dead."

"Eric Bohlander, he's still here in Prague. The band was scheduled to leave today anyway, I'll persuade him to travel to Scotland instead."

"You must accompany him, Fahey. Identifications traumatize. People sometimes see what they wish to see."

Fahey heard Gippel's unspoken warning: what they wish to see might differ from what is there before them. "We'll need to book a flight, who knows what will be available. I'll text you the particulars as soon as I know them."

Gippel coughed; Fahey envisioned him lighting up a cigarette as he did. "And Miss Hart," Gippel finally rasped. "You'll undoubtedly fill her in on the particulars, as well."

"You may be certain of it, Detective."

* * * *

Chloe would not be swayed. "I'm going with you, without you if I have to," she shouted over the sound of the shower as Fahey washed. "You can't possibly believe I'm going to rely on Eric to make this ID any more than Gippel will. I have to see the bodies, see what they've carried out of the water, and what that tells me. We're talking about my mother here."

He'd checked out of the village hotel immediately, practically jogged back to the de la Coeur homestead, one hungover musician barely keeping up. While said musician packed a bag and arranged for his instruments to return to Sweden along with his New Cruel band mates, Fahey raced in to tell Chloe about the trip, stripped down, and threw himself under the hot water. Had the heat of her reaction been applied to Fahey's shower, he would have been thoroughly scalded by now. He poked his head around the shower curtain.

"I know it's your mother, damn it. I know what's at stake. But two plane tickets to that part of Scotland today will be hard enough to score, Chloe; three could be impossible. Let us go, and if Eric thinks one of the bodies is Kat, I'll text, and you can get on the next flight out."

"Private jet!" she shouted, the challenge in her voice unmistakable.

"You're always telling me you have no money, you'll pay through the nose. We're bound for Dundee. Whatever possessed them to set up a makeshift forensics unit there, I'd love to know."

All of which, he realized, made a private jet a much better, much more efficient way to go. Which, of course, she had figured out way ahead of him.

Chloe grabbed the edge of the curtain.

"Live by the sword, die by the sword, Jackson, though hopefully not over the open waters of the North Sea. There was a reason Kat chose a private jet to get back to Prague—it was the most direct way."

"Or was it the most direct way not to get back to Prague but leave the impression that she intended to? It's possible she didn't board, that one of the eight passengers wasn't her but someone else." Fahey cut off the spray and stepped out, dripping. "The explosion, she couldn't have known that would happen. She wouldn't have engineered it, would she?"

Chloe handed him a towel. "Take ten lives to build a new one of her own? That's a type of monster I've never known her to be."

But what Chloe knew of her parents for three decades had been a lie. Of what, given that deception, could she be certain even now? As the question formed in Fahey's mind, he knew she saw it, heard it though it went unspoken.

He wrapped the towel around her, pulled her closer to him, simply wanting to protect her but of course growing harder as her softer, lusher body neared. She laughed, the vibration against his damp skin such a turn-on he reached a hand under the terrycloth and cupped her buttock to lift her against his so-not privates.

"You're getting me wet, Jackson."

"That's the idea. I love you. You're irresistible. I'd like very much to show you how much right now."

He pressed lightly against the curve of her stomach, no bigger than a soccer ball at almost full term. "I'll be gentle," he promised, lifting her dress, looping a finger into her panties, then into her. He backed her up, braced her against the door and positioned her above his cock, supported her weight and eased into her, slid through her moistness; advanced then retreated, almost withdrew.

He felt her tighten around him, her muscles grip his penis, her teeth graze his nipple then bite into it. He surged as she sucked, bucked as his blood flowed out of him and the euphoria of that loss overtook him. When he shuddered and spilled inside her, she rocked on him, against him, shivered then stilled. His heart pounded in his chest, against the red flower-print fabric separating his skin from hers, tiny poppies shimmering as his vision blurred.

Fahey lifted Chloe off, settled her legs around his waist, slid down the length of the door to the gray slate floor, startingly cold against his overheated posterior. He let the lethargy of the bloodletting overtake him. Chloe snuggled in his arms; Avalon rippled against his midsection.

How long they sat there, Fahey didn't know, didn't much care, there was never enough time to be with Chloe like this, to just love her and glory in what she meant to him. There was always another plane to catch, another assignment to complete. Like today.

"Of course, you'll come to Dundee," he finally said. "How could I not want you beside me there with Eric? And how could I not be there for you? I can't imagine what you're going through, not knowing, or how gruesome it might be when we do."

Chloe feathered kisses along his left pectoral; he started to go hard again, tried half-heartedly to fight it, to make his brain take over. Seeming to understand, she gathered her dress from around his legs, shifted and knelt on the floor between them.

"Jackson, you can't protect me in this. I may be the only one who can detect whether any of the bodies belongs to my mother."

"And whatever reaction you display, Gippel will be there to witness, no matter what official identification Eric makes."

Gracefully, she got to her feet, readjusted her clothing, reached out a hand to help Fahey up.

"Julian Gippel has already reached certain conclusions, based on the DNA evidence you and Meredith collected for him in December. He knows Teppan was Sebastian, knows my father didn't commit suicide until that sun-scorched morning with you at the Castle. What's he going to do, expose the big secret now, after his murder investigations have closed?"

The mirror reflected a defiant Chloe, but it was an act, Fahey knew—his odd alliance with Gippel made her wary. So much of her life and livelihood, the whole industry that continued to revolve around the band, depended on that one big lie: that Sebastian and Emilie de la Coeur had killed themselves in April 2011 because Emilie was dying of cancer and Sebastian couldn't bear the thought of life without his adored wife. Precarious, all of it.

"Wasn't much of a leap for Gippel to conclude Katarina is

Emilie. That's why he showed up at the barn, and you know it, love. He won't let it go until he proves it."

"So maybe the Cruel's whole unstable mythology crumbles, and we're trapped beneath it. But what if he just wants to satisfy himself that he's right? I'll take that risk, Jackson."

Chloe took Fahey's hand, stroked his knuckles slowly, sadly. "Let's go. If there are any answers to be had in Dundee, only my mother can lead us to them."

Chapter Five

DUNDEE, SCOTLAND, MAY 2012

The North Sea's tang assaults me; the salt irritates my eyes and throat. Perhaps I am sensitive to it in ways the others around me are not, the merely human beings who wander the rows of tables in this makeshift morgue with me, looking at bits of burned and brined flesh for signs of a loved one now presumed dead.

My discomfort is beside the point, as am I. With each minute I pass among the grieving, each sensory hint I collect, one thing becomes clearer: that the loved one I seek is not here.

Katarina Nilsson, once known as Emilie de la Coeur and before that Eugenie Verlaine Herz, is not here in this hangar-size tent, on that I will stake my immortal life and soul. However long ago she was born, however long ago she became what she has been for the last century and a half at least, she did not die in that plane as it burned and crashed. Someone died in her place, though. Who, and more important, why?

Jackson and Eric and I number among the two dozen or so ushered in today by Scottish authorities, called to view the ten bodies retrieved from the water or to support those who, officially, have the right to view them. We have moved as a group, at first too apprehensive to do more than acclimate ourselves to the sterile environment of metal tables and plastic sheeting, the whine of the air conditioning in our ears, the chill forcing us to clutch our meager spring jackets around us. Even those of us searching for a woman walk by each of the ten bodies, including the five assumed to be men solely because of the length of the bones that remain. In most cases here, body is a relative term. Not a single complete corpse has been discovered—what was not incinerated struck the water with phenomenal impact. Five men, four women and a child, a boy about nine. Eight passengers, plus a pilot and a flight attendant. As I walk by each of the ten tables, I breathe deeply, like a bloodhound, in hopes of picking up clues suggesting who the person under each plastic shroud was, in hopes of differentiating which scents are common to all ten and which peculiar to only one.

I walk slowly behind Eric, keeping a respectful but close distance. On our third circuit, he pauses at a clipboard in the second row of tables indicating a female whose height approximates Kat's. He asks a morgue worker to lift the sheet covering the woman's face. Before the worker can comply, a hand stops him.

"This could be most upsetting, Mr. Bohlander, and may, indeed, not tell us anything at all. Did Mrs. Nilsson have any distinctive physical characteristics that might help us identify her? The forensics staff have very little to go on, you see. An arm that once was broken, for instance, or a leg? A nose?" asks Detective Constable Annaliese MacKenzie, the police officer assigned to us. She has been our law-enforcement shadow since we arrived, presumably because our potential casualty was the only pseudo-celebrity among the passengers, and MacKenzie needs answers for any questions that might be directed her way.

Eric seems confused by the question. Everything about Kat is distinctive as far as he is concerned; he loves her, he longs for her to be standing next to him now. Instead, he's looking at me, as if I can somehow articulate on his behalf how special Kat is. I can, which he knows, but that's something never openly acknowledged between us. Now is no time to start.

"I didn't know Katarina all that well," I say. A lie. "Sorry."

Distinctive physical characteristics? I run the inventory in my head: ever-so-slightly longer, sharper canine teeth; vivid green eyes that now appear pale blue; auburn roots under nearly platinum blonde hair. Nothing, in other words, likely to have survived fire or force. What would her destroyed face tell us if it were the one under the sheet?

I breathe in, searching for the only fragrance my mother wore, the faintest touch of lavender—my first memory of her, that scent, not that it would be detectable to the normal olfactory sensors after four days of immersion in salt water. No matter, even my heightened sense picks up no lavender, just the smells of soap, deodorant, shampoo, hairspray, also gasoline from the plane and a sulfuric odor, perhaps from a bomb. But there's something else, too, something noxious, though, that's not quite right either.

MacKenzie signals the morgue worker, grants permission for the sheet to be lifted. The sight is grisly, the woman's face and neck and shoulders have been charred, her features flattened; what hair remains spikes from the base of her skull as sparse blackened tufts. Eric sobs, sinks to the gray concrete we stand on. "*Min Gud, min* Katarina!" he shouts.

Can he actually believe what he's saying? Knowing my mother as he did, knowing what she was and how he let her drink his blood all those months? I look for Jackson, standing with Detective Gippel at the nearest door, not needing to see the cigarette to know Gippel has one in his hand. Jackson looks our way, sees Eric's form prone on the floor.

"What happened?" he asks, dropping to his knees before Eric.

"Mr. Bohlander has identified this woman as Katarina Nilsson," MacKenzie says, and looks to me for confirmation.

"I suppose it must be," I reply, bowing my head. What else can I possibly say?

"Her DNA isn't on file in any of the databases we accessed," MacKenzie explains. "We'll take Mr. Bohlander's word as definitive, in the absence of any conflicting claims of identification." She, too, kneels beside Eric, who has been revived by whatever sharp scent an orderly is shoving under his nose. "I am so sorry for your loss, sir," she whispers.

She does seem to be. This isn't easy for anyone. How much more difficult for those whose losses, unlike ours, cannot be denied?

As she departs, MacKenzie crosses paths with Gippel, exchanges a few words with him before she heads for the office area set up in one corner of the tent.

Gippel moves closer but stays outside our small circle of grief, watching Eric, watching me. Awkwardly, I maneuver into a sitting position on the floor alongside Eric, the table bearing the dead woman supporting his back now, tears staining his jeans. Jackson averts his eyes, an uncomfortable witness to this odd sorrow. I am crying too, now, because I can't bear to see Eric crumble like this and because I understand that, for him, this is the end. I slip my arms around his broad shoulders; Eric slumps into my embrace and wails. There is no coming back for Katarina Nilsson, she is as dead as Emilie de la Coeur, at least officially. And this time, the evidence of her demise is tangible, thanks to Eric.

Is he carrying out the last details of a plan they made together, or maybe one he imagines Kat might have made? No way to ascertain that now. Best to assist Eric in collecting the body and laying the woman who lies here dead to her eternal rest.

Some minutes pass before I allow the orderly, with an assist from Jackson, to help Eric to his feet and over to a temporary examination area. A woman wearing a dark blue hijab and a white lab coat leads Eric behind a screen. Jackson follows. I watch them from my spot on the floor next to the table, trying to soak up that odd smell, to translate it. It's caustic, but not in the industrial sense; not medicinal, but something like it. It smells of sickness.

Well-worn brown shoes appear before me, a hand lowers into view. Gippel offering me a boost up. Back on my feet, I head for a table set up with urns full of coffee and boiling water for tea. I fill a cup with water, select a bag of Irish Breakfast, tamp it into the water with a plastic spoon, and hand it to the liaison from Interpol.

"What happens next?" I ask Gippel, prepare a cup for myself, and settle into a metal folding chair nearby.

"The doctor will evaluate Mr. Bohlander for shock and assess his mental state. She will give him something to calm him. He likely should not travel tomorrow."

"That makes sense, but it's not what I meant. What happens next with the body—Katarina, that is?"

"Bohlander will be free to take her back to Sweden, or the authorities will help with a cremation here, if he and Mrs. Nilsson had no prior arrangements." Gippel bites into a shortbread cookie he's taken from the refreshments table, waits for my reaction.

"Nobody my age plans for their death," I protest. "OK, Teppan Nilsson shot himself, but that was different. Suicide is different. I have some experience with that."

He sips, swallows, smiles—just a small, smug one.

"Post-mortem examination indicated Mrs. Nilsson may have been terminally ill. *Naturlich*, the forensics team could not say with certainty, but lymphoma perhaps, based on some chemical residues." Gippel points to the clipboard hanging from the table, crushes his empty cup, and bids me *auf wiedersehen.*

Eau de chemotherapy drugs and cure-resistant cells—*that's* what I smell. The woman we have just identified as Kat Nilsson was effectively dead before she ever took her seat on the private jet, and my mother knew it. Somehow, that's a comfort.

* * * *

The key slips easily into the door that opens my flat, as if it last left this lock four hours ago instead of almost four weeks. Like the vampire vagabond I am, I have traveled here under my own steam, running from Dundee to London. This after leaving Jackson to accompany to Stockholm a much more serene Eric—

better bereavement through chemistry, you could say—before he doubles back to Copenhagen to finish one last on-camera interview, finally, for his BBC report on Europe's economy outside the eurozone.

Just as I left it, almost as I initially found it, my flat is a collection of rooms I have never felt at home in. Rarely used furniture, barely scuffed floors—the only decorating I've done is to hang a few pictures, mostly black-and-white photographs, original Sebastian de la Coeurs, circa 1980s, brought here from my gallery in a lame attempt to have some good memories of my father, to honor the talent he was in spite of the bastard he could be. I am especially fond of one image: a young couple kissing at night on the steps of Barcelona's old Gothic cathedral. I love that church because it reminds me of my first home, the Castle, where I grew up with Emilie and my Daddy Bastian.

My last minutes in this apartment were spent saying a hurried farewell to Will Baumann, who left with only enough time to avoid running into Jackson as he reentered my life. Dear devoted Will, who kept me going when I wasn't sure I wanted to after my father badly wounded Jackson, then killed himself. Will, whose brewpub T-shirts I wear now to grub through dusty rooms during my Czech sojourns, to Jackson's annoyance. Will's special essence of cinnamon and craft beer still hangs in the air here.

But there's something else, too. After my experience in Dundee, I'm learning to trust my nose, though this is more a feeling than a fragrance. Someone, or maybe something, has been here, and recently. I retrace my steps to the door, exit and come back in again, from the front hall to the living/dining area, to the inner hall and the bedroom and the bath. There's something, a disturbance in the air.

No, a disturbance in the light, a wavy weirdness I've sensed only in space a vampire has occupied. Not my mother, though the only thing I'm sure of is where she isn't. Zwilling, then. Every inch of the flat shimmers faintly with him. How long ago, and why? I do a quick scan: Nothing seems to be missing; the kitchen cupboards are as bare as always, save for a box of saltines and a tin of Earl Grey teabags. Folded laundry sits on the dining table, a little dustier than when I left yet otherwise unchanged. On my second loop through, as I turn from the hall to look back toward the bedroom, I finally see what's gone: a framed picture of my parents as they last appeared onstage as their true selves; that moment, captured through vampire-proof digital photography at the start of the Christmas at the Castle show in December, when they impersonated Teppan and Katarina Nilsson impersonating Sebastian and Emilie. The vassals went nuts, screaming their appreciation as though Jesus himself had returned as he promised, *resurrexit, sicut dixit.*

A fan sent me the picture, with a note telling me how much he missed my parents and wishing me only happy memories of them. It was tucked into the back of the frame. I sink to the floor and try to catch the tears before they start to fall. Avalon kicks, just a little swipe but enough to remind me that preternatural strength and speed don't mean I can run hundreds of miles without running out of gas.

"Being sad is no excuse, I get it, baby."

I pull myself up and check the fridge. Aha, a wedge of white cheddar that's gone only a little blue around the edges. I fish around for a knife, give the cheese a shave, and take the box of saltines down from an otherwise empty cupboard. I plug in the electric kettle and make myself a cup of the Earl Grey. And when I've fed the hungry beast within, I flop onto the bed and stare over to the faint poster-size outline on the wall, seeing Zwilling instead vowing that he, too, was born to slay the king.

* * * *

Aspect Ratio is my real home. I'm more myself here on the gallery floor, in its cramped office or back in the storeroom, than almost anywhere else. Benjamin Kwesi, my business partner, greets me with a brilliant smile and a genuine hug of affection, unresentful of the burdens I've placed on him these last months. Now that Daphne is untangling the remaining details of the move of the Prague house, I can hang here until the sale closes, staying on the receiving end of all those shipping containers and crates and boxes, unpacking and keeping an inventory, and leaving Ben to charm the customers and sell the art.

His hug is bruising. He first came to Aspect Ratio as my bodyguard, after all, after men in masks abducted me, beat me and broke my arm, sparing Meredith a thrashing but not the trauma. Ben leans back and gives me a once-over.

"Fabulous to finally have you back here, C.J.—but not for long, I'm guessing. That little girl looks about ready to make her debut."

I give him a gentle squeeze and a kiss on the cheek, soothed by the Ghanaian rhythm of his voice.

"I can't promise not to give birth in the storeroom. We'll just hand Avalon a clipboard and a tablet and put her to work. God knows, there's enough to do."

"And we'll get it done, you mustn't worry. I have already moved most of the older inventory into storage next door, so you can work here where I'm close enough to help you and also mind the gallery floor. Meredith is in New York, so we may actually accomplish something. I love her beyond all reason, but my wife is a whirlwind at times."

Benjamin is a master of understatement, from his impeccably tailored suits, to his precise bookkeeping, to his dry wit about the tumult around him, Meredith's big personality being the least of it most days. This gallery is his baby as well as mine; I'm the negligent parent.

"Tell me what I need to know, Ben, and we'll get to it."

Online sales since the Prague open house have been better than hoped for. Traffic into the gallery has been up, too; the newly arrived pieces held out of the Prague event have done well, as have works featured in our March "Bohemian Legacy" show. I can't wait to get back into the business of introducing

London to worthy artists and collectors who are not named de la Coeur, but cash needs to flow just a bit more reliably for a bit longer.

He puts on the kettle, unwraps some sandwiches he's ordered in for us, and settles down into a chair, leaving the space behind the desk for me.

"Ben, we should reconfigure now that we have the additional space next door: create discrete offices for each of us, or a larger single office we work in simultaneously. What do you think?"

Mr. Practical doesn't miss a beat; he is, as always, one step ahead of me.

"I think Daphne's set designer friend might be able to help us with that. At least one of walls in the storeroom could come down, and we could put in better lighting, paint the place. Do it on the cheap, but nicely. We do have a few vintage pieces here we might put to good use; if the gallery corporation buys them from the de la Coeur estate, we could likely take a tax write-off. But before we embark on a renovation, we should consider upgrading the security, especially for the exhibit area and the reception space next door. I know we're not as liquid as we should be, but there have been three apparent intrusions recently. Each time, the front-entrance alarm sounded, the motion sensors went crazy, but the cameras got nothing. Twice on a single night, back in January, it also happened, but there had been a storm and power disruptions, so I did not give it a thought. I'd like to have the security consultant come in tomorrow, so we can both hear what the options are."

"Show me the rooms where the motion sensors went off." I need to put myself in those spaces to see if they do the same vampire-shimmer thing.

"You're sitting in one," Ben says and points to the safe. "The sensors here went off all three times last week, but I opened the safe to check afterward. No cash taken, all checks accounted for. The velvet boxes are there, with the pendants inside. Everything is as it should be. . . . You have your father's family Bible, yes?"

I point to the messenger bag braced against the side of the desk.

"I was going to return it to the safe. Maybe I shouldn't, though really, who would want it?"

Of course, I know exactly who might want it, but Ben isn't aware of the whole de la Coeur history. He married into this family via Meredith; if he decides he has to know the rest, he'll ask.

"Run the security footage for me." I move away from the computer, picking up a curry chicken salad sandwich as I do. "The recent incidents and the ones in January. Maybe I'll see something you didn't."

Ben rolls his chair toward the desktop's keyboard, humoring me. We spend about an hour looking at footage from the four nights the alarm and motion sensors registered intrusions: the first in January and three more recent events. I think I see some disturbances in the light, but the beams of the high-intensity security lamps that activated with the alarm, combined with the low-resolution video, make it difficult to be certain. Were those the indistinct movements of a vampire?

The buzzer sounds at the front door, and Ben heads out to the gallery's public area. I stare at the computer screen, rewinding and fast-forwarding each sequence, as each repetition leaves me less certain I'd know a vamp caught on video if I saw one.

But I sure know one when I hear him, especially when his voice rises and reverberates from only a room away.

"I must see Ms. Hart. The matter is most urgent. Here is my business card, you will recognize the name."

"Christoph Zwilling, Gregor Zwilling GmbH, architectural fittings and fixtures," Ben says, reading the words on the card. "You will understand, sir, that my partner has just returned to London after a grueling ordeal at the plane-crash recovery site in Scotland and is exhausted, given her condition. She is not taking appointments today. Come back tomorrow."

"Clothilde!" Zwilling shouts. "Do not play games with me, cousin!"

"Cousin?" Ben asks. "Of course, you must be a relative of Sebastian de la Coeur. The family resemblance is quite strong, please forgive me. I am Benjamin Kwesi, Chloe's partner. I'll fetch her."

"I'm here, Ben." I touch his elbow from behind. "Christoph, I wasn't expecting to see you until we closed on the Czech house. This is a pleasant surprise."

"Do not lie to me, Clothilde. You are neither surprised nor pleased by my visit," Zwilling says as he pushes past me and makes his way toward the office. "We'd like privacy, Kwesi, there are some details my cousin and I must sort out."

Zwilling pushes ahead toward the office. Ben moves to block the spot where the exhibit area narrows into the hall, making clear there's no way he's leaving me alone with anyone.

I throw Zwilling a nasty look. "Aspect Ratio is as much Benjamin's as mine. Don't you dare presume otherwise."

"It's time for you to leave, Mr. Zwilling," Ben says.

"Ben, I can handle him. Why don't you call it a day? I'll lock up." I smile and focus on breaking through his need to protect me. "You should go."

He starts to protest then realizes he can't refuse. He nods, moves past us to collect some things from the office, and leaves through the rear door. The lock clicks into place behind him.

I take a seat at the desk, close out of the video surveillance replay, make a mental note of the way Zwilling disturbs the patterns of the dim light in my office, then finger the buttons of a remote-control unit. Overhead, light blazes through the room. Zwilling blinks, glares.

"Was that little scene necessary?" I ask.

He sits in the chair Ben recently vacated, shoots the cuffs of his no-doubt bespoke white silk shirt through the sleeves of his no-doubt bespoke navy pinstripe suit coat. "We are family, as you have surmised by now. Our secrets are not yours to reveal to outsiders, at least not at great personal risk to yourself."

"And the threats begin, just when we were getting acquainted.

Not what I might have expected from my father's nephew. I had been led to believe the Herz men were raised with the manners of gentlemen though they were lower-born. My father said that served him well when he went to the Hapsburg court; it helped him stand tall among his supposed betters."

Zwilling laughs, an ugly, icy sound.

"Your father was no gentleman, though he wore the trappings convincingly enough. So many people were fooled right up until that nasty business with the sex workers in Kosovo and their dead babies—his dead babies. Even you, I'd venture to say, were taken in by Sebastian de la Coeur's elegant façade, while I scarcely knew my Uncle Stefan or any of the other Herz men. I was just seven years old when, after my father's death, your father paid my mother to leave our home on the condition that we never return. We went to Switzerland, where she married Gregor Zwilling, who raised me as his son. I never saw any of the Herz family again, never saw my grandmother again."

Sebastian said his mother blamed him for destroying the family. Was that why? At least Zwilling knew them for a few years. Court of Cruelty was my only family, Gloria Dennehy the closest thing I had to aunt or godmother or grandmother, the guys in the band, uncles of dubious character. Is my financial rescue part of a strategy to control me, as my father controlled Christoph's mother with money? If he cannot slay the king, is the princess next in line?

"What is it you want?" I ask, voice steady; I dare not reveal any of myself to this man. "What's here in this gallery you want so badly you've broken in to get it?"

He throws back his head, his eyes red-ringed black holes in his face, a visage so fearsome yet so familiar—the face of my father in full vampire fury the night I was miscarrying Avalon's twin, the night he might have . . . no, I can't go there now.

"Tell me what you want," I demand again, "and I'll tell you the fastest way to go to hell."

He rises, stretches to his much greater height, leans over

the desk and grabs my chin. "I want the pendants," he growls. "Every time I come for them, they vanish."

What is he talking about? The pendants are in the safe, I've just seen them. They've been there since the day I got back from Barcelona, the day after Christoph and my mother precipitated a riot and a public sex scandal.

"The pendants? My parents' bequest to me, rubies and gold worth thousands of dollars and priceless at the same time? You're crazy. No way I'll give them to you."

Zwilling rips a ring from his finger, pounds it onto the desk between us.

"Does anything about this look familiar, cousin? Examine it, your answer is important."

I open a drawer, retrieve a loupe, and pick up the ring. Two small red stones reflect the overhead light.

"Expensive probably, but I don't know jewelry, I couldn't say what the going rate is for rubies or garnets—or whatever they might be—of this size. It's lovely. An heirloom?"

"A gift from the woman I love."

"She must love you too, the ring is beautiful. But what does it have to do with me?"

"Let me have the pendants, and we'll both have our answer!" he bellows. "Let me have them or I'll tear that baby from your body and gladly watch it die!"

I rear up before him, flash my fangs, grip his wrist and slash my nails through his skin to the tendons, which I could tear clean through.

"Threaten to hurt this child again and I will rip all the flesh from your bones. I am the child of two vampires, while you are merely the creation of one. Do not underestimate my strength. My father once did, to his dismay. If you want a further demonstration, I'll be happy to oblige you."

He shakes me off his arm, licks blood away. His eyes gleam with rage, but he backs up, wipes bits of torn skin from his finely tailored trousers.

"Those pendants are the scourge of this family."

"What? Like a curse?" I laugh. "You'd attack my baby, the future of this family, for some links of shining metal and a couple of brilliant rocks?"

He picks up the ring, returns it to his left hand, works it past the knuckle of his little finger, and positions it side by side with his wedding ring.

"I believe," he begins hoarsely, "that if we dismantle the pendants we will find these small stones are chips taken from the portion of the rubies their settings conceal. My father made the chains, he would have fashioned the settings in a way that would hide any imperfections."

Gregor Herz made the pendants? Was he the one who imbued the stones with a magnetism so powerful they could make two people fall in love, as my mother swears they can? Did Zwilling's wife capture his heart with it as my now-missing mother captured my father's long ago? Where he sees an answer, I see leverage.

"Tell me about this curse. It won't get you the pendants, but I might agree to hire a jeweler to disassemble them and determine whether the gems in your ring came from the larger rubies. If they did, you have your answer. In return, I want you to finalize our deal for the Prague house and forget you ever knew me. Leave me and my loved ones alone."

Zwilling calculates; I hear the wheels turn as his anger recedes.

"The pendants hold many answers, and I swear I will have them someday. I will not negotiate that with you," he says, his voice calm again. "You are inquisitive, cousin, still a researcher at heart. Study the stones, examine that Bible your father left you, and you will understand why I hated him and why those necklaces are mine by right."

A part of me hated Sebastian, too, toward the end, but Zwilling doesn't need to know that.

"I'm still waiting to hear a reason why I should give a damn."

"You have twenty-four hours before the pendants disappear again."

"They've never been gone," I protest. "I've known where they were all along."

"Is that so?" he counters dismissively, in a tone one might reserve for a child. "That security upgrade your partner has recommended, I'd see to it immediately, cousin."

* * * *

Benjamin is erudite, with an undergraduate degree in art and a graduate degree from the London School of Economics. He's also 6-foot-5, weighs 250 pounds, and did a turn as a sniper with the Ghanaian army. He has protected individuals and cargo; he knows people who know people. When I ask, he, of course, knows a jeweler who will discreetly dismantle my parents' pendants and determine whether the stones have ever been altered.

Shortly after noon the following day, the jeweler arrives from the Hatton Garden diamond quarter with a briefcase full of small precision tools. Tension coils through me as I watch Ben open the safe and retrieve the velvet boxes. The pendants are, to my relief, where they should be. I pace the hall outside the gallery office; more than once, the jeweler casts a nasty look my way through the open door.

"He can't work if you're hovering, Chloe. Unpack some boxes or take a walk." Ben points toward the storage area at the back of Aspect Ratio, pulls his mobile phone from his pocket. I give in and head toward the storeroom. Not three minutes later, my mobile rings—it's Jackson calling from Copenhagen.

"What the hell is going on? Why is Ben is calling me about security enhancements and Zwilling turning up at the gallery. Tell me there's no connection."

"Wish I could. Zwilling's obsessed with the pendants; he's tried to break into the gallery several times to steal them, in fact. Yesterday, he walked through the front door instead and made nasty threats to get them."

I can hear Jackson's heartbeat accelerate; he can guess at the kind of chaos Zwilling is capable of, having been on the receiving end of my father's ire.

"Do not engage him, Chloe. I'm booked on a flight there tomorrow, but I'm due back in Brussels Monday for ten straight days in the studio. This is really not the time to mix it up with him, not alone."

As if he could protect me from my irrational vampire cousin.

"He broke into my flat, too; this is some kind of vendetta. He says the pendants cursed our family—yes, he admitted who he is. He says that Gregor Herz made the pendants, and that they're his by right. They hold answers he's intent on having, and he warned that I should study the Herz Bible. Also, a ring he wears has ruby chips in it that he thinks came from the pendants; he says the woman he loves gave the ring to him."

A loud laugh just about pierces my eardrum.

"Won't Christoph be disappointed to learn that those rubies only lure you to a woman—it's the woman herself who keeps you obsessed. I've felt that pull, it's irresistible. But I've also met his wife. I can see where he might think Chiara has bewitched him."

"You've met Chiara?"

"At the hotel in the village, the night I stayed there with Eric. She and Christoph were in the bar. He's enchanted by her, that's clear. Keep your distance, Chloe love, he may not be thinking clearly. Remember how I was?"

Tormented by an unrelenting physical need for me, a desire that would not be sated—I remember all right. Sebastian and Emilie intentionally struck a gold-and-gem-encrusted match to light our sexual inferno. Who's to say Zwilling is wrong about the source of his?

I blow Jackson a kiss, end the call, and crouch with my tablet alongside an already-opened packing crate in the storeroom, one filled with my mother's costume sketches for the 1990 *Blood Sacrifice* tour, their first swing through Eastern Europe after the fall of the Berlin Wall. Or was it *The Rack* tour in 1992?

The costumes were as similar as the torture theme, as I recall.

Later, when Benjamin and his jeweler friend interrupt to confirm that the rubies in the pendants each have similar, irregular flaws hidden by their settings, the scent of lavender rises around me, like a welcoming embrace.

Or, as Zwilling might describe it, like a lover's kiss.

* * * *

Something startles me awake. I'm cold and very wet and lying on a floor. Where am I? It's bright, the light nearly blinds me. I can see around the edges of it, but I can't focus on what's straight ahead.

Crates surround me. Packing material has settled into faceless scarecrows. Am I in the storeroom?

Pain rips me, ribs to groin. Oh, Christ, my water has broken. The baby is coming.

"Benjamin! Ben!" I shout, hoping he'll hear me in the office or the exhibit space. I listen for footsteps, but there are none, he must be gone.

Yes, definitely gone. I remember now. Ben left hours ago, and I stayed on working, despite his objections. I squint, look for the clock I know is hanging near the door to the hall, but I can't see past this iridescent white fog in front of me. Is it because I haven't had blood in a few days?

Where's my phone? I have to call a cab and get to a hospital. No, not a hospital, what if they need to cut the baby out and they can't slice through my vamp skin to make an incision? I feel my way across the floor, one arm stretched out so I don't crawl into a wall, but still I clip something blunt with my forehead, a baseboard maybe, and let fly a string of four-letter words. How is it I suddenly hurt everywhere?

Wait. Someone's out in the hall. I can sense motion near the door. Not Ben, I know the sound of his bulk moving through the gallery. But if not Ben, who?

"Jackson?" I'm desperate; I can't have this baby alone.

"We'll find him." A woman's voice, familiar but not.

"Who's there? Kat?"

A soft sigh. "She's dead, isn't she?"

"Emilie?"

"Also dead, as far as I know."

Another pain. I try to breathe through it, try to remember every bad chick-flick depiction of childbirth I've ever seen, but I can't, so I count: one, two, three, four, five, six, seven, eight, nine, ten, eleven . . .

"Good idea," the woman says. "I've called a taxi. We're going to take you someplace safer to have this baby."

"Why can't I see you?"

Instead of an answer, arms encircle me, and warm fingers brush my matted, sweaty hair from my face.

She helps me to my feet and down the hall; the door to the alley opens. A taxi pulls up, and the driver lifts me into the backseat. Despite the darkness, I can see him just fine. Some minutes pass before I hear locks engaged, an alarm code entered, and the woman gets into the backseat beside me, sending a slightly sharp, slightly sweet fragrance over the taxi's damp smell. I force myself to sit upright, though I am dizzy and an ice pick is wedged into the small of my back and a basketball is forcing its way down through my private parts. I stare at the silhouette sitting next to me, a face framed in a blue hijab, a face that I can't quite bring into view.

She eases along the seat, settles my head against her shoulder. I breathe in lavender and something else, lemon. Her scent and mine.

"Mom?" As I drift off, I know it must be her.

Chapter Six

LONDON, LATE MAY 2012

Explicit directions notwithstanding, Fahey felt unaccountably lost as he set foot on the sidewalk and two dozen cameras took aim at him. That morning's text from Chloe—or, under the circumstances, perhaps simply from Chloe's phone—had asked him to come here directly from the airport and spout some proud-papa lines to the press he would find waiting for him. He hadn't recognized the address and knew better than to question some things too closely. But why was he standing on a Bankside street not far from the Tate Modern, in front of a pub that wouldn't open for several more hours, to collect his fiancée and newborn daughter and very publicly hasten them to a hospital?

American Revolution, Craft Beer from the Colonies, letters across the pub's front window declared, stars and stripes festooned behind them. Suddenly, all became clear.

"Fuck me," Fahey muttered. "No, fuck him."

Where did she run to have their baby? To Will Baumann, of course. Baumann had always been there for Chloe. As for himself, the same could not always be said, despite Fahey's best intentions.

"Jackson, Jackson, you're a new dad! Tell us, how does it feel? How are Chloe and the baby? Boy or girl? Have you seen a picture yet?"

Questions came at him right and left. He waved, flashed his best TV grin their way.

"*Give them a good story,*" Fahey reminded himself, as he always did before the tape rolled.

"I'm over the moon, naturally. I've been on an airplane the last few hours, flying from Copenhagen, so I missed the big moment. But I've got a baby picture here."

Fahey held his phone up to one of the video cameras and allowed Avalon her first fifteen seconds of television fame.

"I'm told all is well with Chloe and our daughter. Obviously, I can't wait to get up to see them."

"A girl, that's brilliant, Jackson, congratulations!" shouted a Sky News correspondent he'd dated a few years back, long before a certain vampire-in-the-making had entered his life. The reporter pushed her way closer to Fahey, shoved her microphone in his face—a bit too aggressively he thought, given they'd once enjoyed a lovely week's holiday together.

"Please, Jackson. All the UK is dying to know: Did Chloe really give birth in this pub? Ouch."

He smiled an especially savage smile her way, turned toward her video guy, and lied through his teeth.

"The owner is an American friend of Chloe's who has rooms up on the third floor. When she returned to London a few days ago, she found her flat had been burgled and was understandably reluctant to stay there alone so far along in the pregnancy. Her friend Will Baumann graciously allowed her to stay here. Very fortunate for us that he did, wouldn't you say, Claudia?"

He turned his back on Claudia and the rest of them and banged at the pub's front door. Waited for Baumann to open it and step through, clap him on the shoulder in a hail-fellow-well-met charade that Fahey had no choice but to play along with.

"Just a second, Jackson: Isn't Will Baumann the man you punched at the Christmas at the Castle benefit in New York back in December?" Claudia asked, all innocence. "Will, weren't you and Chloe Hart a couple for a while?"

A crowd of passers-by had gathered on the sidewalk behind the throng of press, which was perhaps the only thing keeping Fahey from pounding heads against the door frame, his and Baumann's.

"Pax, Brother Fahey," Baumann whispered. "Your girls are upstairs waiting for you."

Baumann pushed the door wider. Fahey pushed past him and stopped, realizing too late that he had no idea where his girls were. Baumann shut and locked the door behind them, pointed right.

"None of this was my idea, friend. Chloe showed up at the kitchen door about eleven o'clock last night. First place I think of when I'm about to give birth."

Baumann led him to a narrow stairway and up four flights.

"Good cardio workout, you know, even if you're dripping amniotic fluid."

Fahey looked down at the treads. Baumann laughed.

At the top, he put a key in the lock, bowed, and indicated Fahey should proceed.

"The bedroom's just ahead, you can't miss it. Coffee?"

"You've done enough already," Fahey grunted.

"I'll go downstairs then. You should have everything you need for a while, diapers and wipes and some emergency baby formula, some extra undershirts and baby nightgowns. I think I got everything on the list Chloe handed me. Once the pub staff arrives, I'm heading over to her apartment for some sleep. It was one wicked rough night—your little sweetheart made quite the entrance."

"Remind me again I wasn't here, and I won't feel guilty about smashing you one," Fahey growled, appalled by his jealousy but unable to tamp it down.

Baumann shrugged.

"You're not the only guy who loves Chloe, but you are the guy she loves. You want to waste your time worrying about me, Jackson, be my guest."

A few feet away in the bedroom, Avalon fussed, and Chloe made goo-goo noises about baby bunnies and baby bears. Behind Fahey, Baumann closed the door to his flat. He was right, of course, Fahey had more important people to worry about, including one he'd been waiting months to meet.

Sitting up, baby clutched to her left breast, Chloe was blowing kisses across Ava's tiny head.

"It tickles," she said, looking up at Fahey with those gorgeous green eyes he loved so. "She's tugging on my nipple—I expected that might be uncomfortable at first. I didn't expect that her hair would tickle my skin. It's funny and a little weird, but wonderful too."

Fahey sat at the edge of the bed, leaned over and kissed Chloe then settled back to watch the baby nurse.

"Is she getting anything, Jackson? Can you see?"

He could.

"Little dribbles of white at the edge of her mouth, looks like milk to me. Is there a towel or something handy? You're about to get a bit sticky."

"On the dresser. Will picked up a few cloth diapers along with the disposables."

Fahey fetched one, assessed what needed covering and tucked it in as Chloe lifted the baby.

"I'm supposed to let her nurse as long as she wants, so she can get the hang of it. This is the third time already this morning. Maybe later you can read the directions to that electric breast pump over there and sterilize those small bottles Will bought." Chloe pointed in the direction of what looked like miniature satellite dishes attached to a charging dock. "Once we fill them, you'll be able to feed her too."

He sat on the bed again, closer this time.

"Did you know you'd be able to breastfeed? You never said . . ."

"Apparently, both our little hybrid and her mother are trending human on Day One. I decided to give it a try after Will got us cleaned up, and Ava latched on right away. Good thing—

it's not like I've been studying up on how to do this."

"Will helped deliver the baby, helped clean the two of you, helped you start nursing her. Handy sort, isn't he, available to offer assistance in all kinds of unusual situations?"

Chloe became very interested in Avalon's ear. Avalon became very disinterested in the breast and started to whimper, milk flowing over her tiny lips.

"Put a diaper on my shoulder, Jackson. Burp time."

Up the baby went, her head cradled against Chloe. Jackson peered around to look at her. Little blue eyes opened, and he fell in love. He leaned in to kiss her baby forehead; she belched in his ear.

"That's Daddy's girl," he said. "Direct, just like a Fahey. No dodging the important stuff like your mother, the princess de la Coeur."

"It's not dodging the question when you already know the answer. This was always a possibility, Jackson, that the baby might come at an inconvenient time, in an inconvenient place. Will was my best option—my only option, really. If you want to resent that fact, feel free, but there it is."

Avalon's mouth went slack; her eyes fluttered shut. Chloe, yawning, handed Fahey the baby. "Lay her in the carrier over there please, then help me into the shower. I have to look my best for the cameras when we show our little bundle off to the press."

Their daughter tucked into her makeshift crib, Fahey lifted Chloe and carried her into the bathroom, trying to be gallant, trying not to be an ass. "So we're going to do the whole celebrity Mummy and Daddy thing, are we?" He tightened his arms around her, kissing the soft spot below her ear, the spot that made her melt under normal circumstances. Oh, how he wished for those right about now.

Chloe sighed, offered her neck for him to nuzzle, reading his mind or more probably his body, now pressed rock-hard against her bottom, the need to abstain from such endeavors for the moment unappreciated.

"Hmm, yes, my love, we're going to do the celebrity thing. How much do you suppose *People* would give us for exclusive rights to our 'De la Coeur Daughter Gives Birth in a Room over the Pub!' story? Oops, journalistic ethics, no pay-for-play magazine cover for us. Oh well."

Fahey set her on her feet. Chloe raised her arms, and he pulled a stained American Revolution T-shirt over her head. "Hiding from Zwilling in plain sight, snug in the security of the worldwide gossip machine, will have to be enough for us. But we won't have to hide for long, I hope."

Nude, Chloe stretched, her breasts swollen with milk, a slight rounding of her stomach the only other sign she'd recently given birth. Fahey groaned. She leaned in and licked his neck, nipping it for a quick taste before stepping into the stall, turning on the spray, yanking at the curtain.

"We can't hide long enough," she said over the blast of the water.

* * * *

A thin blade pierced the leather of his jacket and nicked his midsection. So swift its movement through those layers, just seconds between the moment Fahey stepped into Chloe's flat and the dagger's subtle puncture of his skin. A circle of blood stained the gray cotton of his shirt, he watched as it began to spread, then lost sight of it as the door slammed behind him and an arm circled his neck, choking him back against a wall of chest muscle and that sliver of cold, hard steel.

"You are late, Jackson Fahey. You make me wait all day here. I do not like to wait," the man with the iron chest and the efficient little knife rasped in an accent that might have been Russian, might have been Ukrainian. Fahey kicked back with all the force his new knee provided, landed boot heel into shin bone. The guy with the knife cursed in some Slavic tongue, pushed Fahey forward and landed a blow just behind his right ear that forced him to his knees. Fahey willed himself not to black out from the pain.

"Late and stupid, Jackson Fahey. You make me want to kill you, but my boss, he said don't do it." Iron Chest grabbed a fistful of Fahey's hair and yanked him to his feet. With the knife, he encouraged Fahey farther into the center of the room, between the sofa and the dining table. Fahey stumbled, regained his feet, and heard moans rising from the floor.

"Shut up and be a man," Iron Chest roared in the direction of the moans. "I give you a job. Do it or die."

A man slowly unfurled his body and pushed himself up from the floor. Fahey saw the gun in the man's shaking hand before he saw the American flag on his sweat-and-vomit-stained shirt. It was Will Baumann but not, his blue eyes unnaturally bright.

"Oh, good, give someone who'd like me to disappear permanently a loaded pistol," Fahey complained. He hoped Baumann would recognize his voice and think better of whatever task had been assigned him.

From behind, Iron Chest once again wound his hand in Fahey's hair, stretching his neck back painfully.

"I give him gun and some crystal meth, maybe enough to keep him awake twenty-four hours to watch you, eh. But he already not sleep for two days and not eat, so he get sick to stomach and just lay there, so maybe he not stay awake at all. Who can say? Next time, I bring food, I learn lesson. But I let him keep gun. It will be fun for you, no, Jackson Fahey? Who knows what he will do?"

The grip on his hair slackened, and Fahey eased his neck back to vertical.

"If you are smart, Jackson Fahey, better to not piss Will Baumann off, or make him lose balance and fall with gun in hand."

Fahey felt the man's hot, rancid breath against his skin.

Baumann paced the length of the living/dining area. Fahey listened as he stomped down the hall, stared as Baumann returned, his jeans wet at the crotch and down one leg.

"So if I'm lucky," Fahey said, "Baumann wanders around

pissing himself until he comes down from this uber-buzz he's on. If I'm not, Baumann kills me so you don't have to. Who the fuck are you, and what do you want?"

Baumann stopped in the kitchen, took aim at Fahey, and shrieked with laughter when Iron Chest jerked Fahey's head back again. Baumann began drumming on the counter with the gun, and Fahey wasn't sure which was more unnerving, the cackling or the butt of the pistol thudding.

Iron Chest moved alongside Fahey, twisting his hair more tightly. "You answer *my* question, Jackson Fahey, and maybe we let you go. Maybe we let the wise-guy journalist go free to see his beautiful baby girl? What you think, Will Baumann?"

Baumann quit drumming and resumed his circuit through the flat, opening and closing doors as he went.

"Who are you and what do you want?" Fahey repeated, a bit more deferentially this time.

Iron Chest shoved Fahey toward a chair. "You sit," he ordered, and commenced binding Fahey's wrists behind him with plastic cable ties, then each leg to a leg of the chair. "Better, eh? Well, better for me, easier to keep eye on both of you."

He bent suddenly and planted his face before Fahey's. Nearness did not improve his looks—a bad comb-over of greasy, once-blond hair, a serially broken nose, and rumpled clothes that smelled of boiled meat. "You can call me, Igor. Is funny because I work for the vampire, right?"

Dracula jokes, wonderful. Fahey couldn't imagine a more ludicrous way to die.

"Very funny, yes. What can I do for you, Igor—that is, what can I do to get rid of you?"

Igor shrugged. "You give me pendants, I go. But I leave Baumann here to take care of you, so you don't call cops and try to be big hero."

The pendants, of course.

"I don't know where they are. Has your boss, Herr Zwilling, checked the safe at Aspect Ratio today?"

The gallery's name brought Baumann staggering back toward them. He paced rings around Fahey's chair, stumbling into Igor and forcing the bigger man to retreat to the door.

"Aren't you afraid he'll shoot you instead, Igor?" Didn't seem like the best strategy to Fahey, drugging a man, then arming him.

Another shrug. "I die, I die. Give me pendants and maybe we all live, OK?"

"I don't have them. Chloe doesn't have them with her either—all she took to the hospital was the baby and herself. If they're not here and they're not at her gallery, maybe they're at Baumann's place?"

Igor shook his head. "No pendants there. We know this."

How they knew was a matter that could wait, Fahey figured. "Tell Zwilling he's hit a dead end, then, there's nothing I can do to help him."

From a back pocket, Igor retrieved a mobile phone, snapped a photo of Fahey, then one of the now perpetually moving Will Baumann, and tapped out a text. Barely a second passed before the phone rang. Igor answered it immediately, and muttered, "*Nyet*," repeatedly before the call cut off.

A Russian-speaker from Ukraine, Fahey concluded, though where Igor was from made absolutely no difference to his continued survival.

Igor quickly stepped to the counter and grabbed a dish towel before Baumann noticed. He wrapped it over Fahey's mouth and around his neck, gagging him with the damp, sour-smelling fabric.

"You and Baumann, you play buddies," he said, and hurled the phone past Fahey's head. Fahey heard the door shut behind Igor, heard a key turn in the lock.

From somewhere toward Chloe's bedroom, the phone rang repeatedly, the ringtone a horns-heavy version of Court of Cruelty's "Inquisition." Baumann smiled, recognizing the music, then looked startled, as if he knew he was not himself, that something wasn't right.

He lurched into the kitchen, dropped hard to the floor behind the counter. The gun went off.

"Will!" Fahey tried to shout, raging against the foul rag in his mouth. The man had just helped Avalon enter this world—the first hands that held his daughter had been Baumann's.

Fahey shifted his weight in the chair, shimmied it forward a few inches, then a few more, but not far enough. He pitched hard to the left, rolling the chair over onto its side, dragging it and himself along the floor. He propelled ahead a little more, aiming for a spot where he could at least see around the counter, determine where the gun was, whether Baumann was conscious.

A smash of wood against wood halted his progress. A table leg had caught in the legs of his chair, entangling him in straits of dining furniture, effectively wedging Fahey between the table and the counter, bringing another chair down on top of him. He was buried under too much, too far from the corner to be able to see Baumann.

What little he could see made Fahey wish he hadn't. He closed his eyes against the sight of blood flowing from the kitchen.

* * * *

The crash of a door roused him. The thin whine of an infant's cry answered the collision of powder-coated steel with drywall. Helpless on the floor, where he had lain impotently for what must be hours, Fahey vibrated with Chloe's frantic need to find him.

"Jackson! Please be all right!" she shouted. Then she stopped. She was behind him; he couldn't twist his head sufficiently to see her face, but he could sense the panic building in her.

"Oh my God, I smell so much blood! It's Will's—Jackson, where is he?"

She kicked through the labyrinth of toppled furniture and deposited the baby carrier and a screeching Avalon next to Fahey. Chloe ripped through the cable ties lashing his wrists behind him and righted the chair. Fahey shook some sensation back into his arms and tore the gag from his mouth.

"Behind the counter."

She vaulted over the last of the chairs and sank out of sight.

"Oh my God, oh my God . . . he's not breathing, Jackson."

Fahey maneuvered the chair over a lip of carpet onto the kitchen floor but couldn't see much. He smelled the blood, imagined it seeping from Baumann's skull. He heard pounding, envisioned Chloe sitting on Baumann's chest, banging on it to restore a heartbeat.

From his newly upright position, Fahey stretched to reach a phone on the counter, Baumann's, he guessed. He tapped "Emergency" on the touch screen, tapped in the flat's address, told the voice that answered: "My friend dosed on crystal meth and fell. A gun went off. I think he's dead."

Fahey leaned as far to his right as he could with his legs still tied to the chair, saw Chloe alongside Baumann, her shoulders heaving as she wept.

"Please hurry," he implored.

Chloe rolled away, sat up against the refrigerator, and cradled Baumann's head against her chest, his blood staining her shirt, her blood tears staining their cheeks. Ava wailed. Fahey levered his upper body until he got a grip on the closest knife in the block on the counter, pulled it out, and sawed through the cable ties still binding his legs to the chair. He tried to stand, felt his legs go out from under him, managed to sink down onto his rear and slide over to the baby. He lifted her from the carrier, rocked Ava in his arms as her mother rocked Baumann's lifeless body against hers. The heat of Chloe's grief seemed to sizzle through the chill of the flat.

Sirens blared, first in the distance, then closer. Feet pounded up the stairs, and ambulance personnel and police surrounded them. Officers quickly took in the makeshift plastic handcuffs still attached to the chair, the welts on Fahey's wrists, the blood streaming across the floor, the depression at the side of Baumann's skull, the bullet wound, the wild disarray of the room, and the screaming newborn amid all of it.

Fahey hauled himself to his feet and pulled Avalon's carrier over to the sofa, to give everyone space to work. He freed the baby from her nest of blankets, located a small bottle in the folds, and tucked the nipple into her mouth. Ava fussed at the unfamiliar texture, but eventually sucked and dozed, oblivious to the hurt around her. He closed his eyes and wished he could let exhaustion carry him off, as well.

Instead, Fahey recited the circumstances of the previous evening: finding Igor and a cranked-out Baumann, his twitchy fingers wrapped around the trigger of a handgun; being lashed to the chair by Igor when he could not supply the pendants or their hiding place; the phone call Igor made before leaving his prisoners on their own.

"Find Igor, you'll know who's behind all this. He left his phone here. Maybe there's something you can use."

No one rushed to take that advice.

"You didn't see Baumann fall?" a plainclothes officer inquired for the third time.

"I couldn't, I had maneuvered only so far before the chair toppled and I got wedged in among the dining furniture. I heard a thud against the floor, that's all, and then no more."

"How do you know Baumann took crystal meth?"

"I personally don't know. That's what Igor told me."

"How long since this Igor person left?"

Fahey gestured to the watch on the policeman's wrist. He turned the watch to face Fahey.

"Six hours, seven at most. Long enough I would have swallowed my gag whole if it meant I could call for help; long enough to wish someone would come amputate my arms, they had been tied behind me for so long."

"Can you describe the man? Did you see his face?"

Fahey stood and handed the baby to the police officer. "Fifty maybe, shaved head, no neck. About five ten, stocky build. Now I really must use the toilet. It's been hours."

In the bathroom, he lingered longer than he should have. All that had happened replayed in his head, and Fahey wished there were a god he still believed in.

When he forced himself to return, a bag containing Will Baumann's body was being borne away and the last of the paramedics were leaving. Chloe was on the sofa, nursing Avalon, tears falling as she did. He looked from her to the open door.

"The police will be back with a crime-scene unit, but they couldn't say when, so I gave them my key. I need to get out of this place, Jackson, and never come back."

Fahey sat next to her and kissed away a tear. "I know Will meant a lot to you."

Chloe flinched, as if his words had burned her. What did Baumann mean to her? Their relationship evolved all those months Fahey stayed away. Will Baumann had been his shadow, stepping into a space the minute he moved from it. If Fahey hadn't come back into her life when he did, might she have chosen Will over him?

He tried again. "OK, I have no idea how much Will meant to you. But I know you're hurting; that's all I need to know. I'm so sorry, truly I am."

"That bastard went after two of the people I love most in this world. I can't let this go, Jackson, he needs to be punished. He needs to feel my wrath the way Will felt his."

By he, Chloe meant Zwilling, of course. Not Igor, who likely would be found only when his large corpse washed up on some Eastern European shore, brought to justice for his crimes by the man who'd paid him to commit them.

"That's not you, Chloe, you're better than that, better than Zwilling. Let's find a hotel room and get our bearings; then we can figure out what the next move is."

Fahey suspected logic would do little to sway her, but he had to try. The blood ties between her and Zwilling were already stretched taut. How long before they tore?

She looked at him, sadness welling in those eyes Fahey adored.

"I'm better than him, you say. How can that be, Jackson, when Zwilling and I were cut from the same cloth? Who knows what I'm capable of? I don't, and can you honestly say you're not afraid to find out?"

He couldn't. No matter how much he wished it weren't so, Fahey could never quite forget that Chloe was her wretched father's daughter, child of his human *and* vampire natures.

* * * *

Something woke Fahey, his ears ringing despite the absence of sound. He was in Chloe's bed, still at the flat, but she was gone, and the baby was too. Panic rose like bile, its acid nauseating him. A cold sweat filmed his forehead and his neck. He pulled on his jeans, wrapped his belt around his hand, buckle-side out, the itinerant journalist's makeshift weapon of choice.

Out to the hall, he walked, the only light ahead the glow of the television, its volume muted. Shadows shifted in the void beyond, followed by an almost inaudible click, click, so low Fahey wasn't sure he'd actually heard anything.

"Shh, little girl, it will be alright, the nasty hiccups will go away. Mommy will rub your back till the bubble is gone, promise."

His eyes adjusted, and Fahey saw tiny arms and legs waving. Avalon wasn't buying it. He dropped the belt, leaned over and reached for his daughter. "Let me walk her a bit. Maybe a change of scenery will help."

Chloe gingerly handed the baby up, watched as he settled her into the crook of his arm and paraded across the floor. "She knows her daddy will take care of her."

"I'd lay down my life."

"It won't come to that. I won't let it."

Chloe walked past them, kissed their cheeks, picked up the courier bag she'd dropped at the front door hours earlier. "I've booked us a hotel room—the address and the confirmation number are there on the counter. I told them we'd be there before dawn, to avoid the press. I'll meet you there as soon as I can."

Fahey put his free hand on her shoulder. "Where are you going?" he asked, but he guessed what must be in the bag and where she must be heading.

"I'm taking the pendants to Aspect Ratio."

"I thought you didn't have them."

She shrugged off his hand. "I didn't, not until the cab ride from the hospital tonight. How I came to have them again isn't important."

No way that was true; Fahey detected the hand of an unseen de la Coeur minion. He hoisted the baby properly onto his shoulder; she burped and immediately moved her bowels. Fahey could feel her small body shudder against him.

"Then why leave them at the gallery now? Do you want Zwilling to take them?"

"What good would withholding them do?" Chloe argued, her voice thick with guilt. "Nothing was worth losing Will."

Fahey moved behind her, brushed a soft kiss across her neck. "The pendants have a power you shouldn't relinquish so readily. They brought your parents together. They brought us together."

She smiled wistfully; he could see it as clearly as if she were facing him.

"It's harder every day to remember the woman I was then. I know you love me, Jackson, but it's in spite of who I am now."

"And Will loved you differently?" he asked, hearing his voice strain with the old resentment.

"Will only knew one Chloe, the one who almost killed him."

"You mean the Chloe who carried him to Zurich to save his life?"

She pressed a kiss along his jaw and one on Avalon's forehead. "Zwilling can have the pendants," she said, moving toward the front door. "I won't fight that fight, I won't lose anybody else. I should have done better by Will."

This, Fahey recognized, was her bid for atonement.

"Hold on, let me come with you."
But she was already gone.

Chapter Seven

PRAGUE, MID-JUNE 2012

If we were in the US right now, it would be Father's Day. How appropriate, given that we are here to dispose of one of dear Daddy Sebastian's remaining messes, etched forever in my memory as the House of the Unmarked Graves. Do they even celebrate Father's Day in the Czech Republic?

Not that it matters. This particular Sunday morning is the only one that accommodates the schedules of the many parties that have to be present for the closing on Gregor Zwilling GmbH's purchase of my parents' estate: Ed Chestack, who has flown in from New York; Izak Sobel, a longtime de la Coeur attorney who has navigated the real estate waters here for us since the company's offer was tendered back in February; Jackson, who will be on a plane for Brussels at dawn; and myself, due back in London later tomorrow with a retinue consisting of Avalon and Daphne, who has agreed to baby-sit today while she packs clothing and other odds and ends she has accumulated during her month in the outskirts of Prague.

Here at Sobel's law office, we have arrayed ourselves along one side of a richly carved, impressively polished conference table; at its head sits the modern, twentysomething Czech equivalent of a notary public, impatiently tapping her tomato-red nails on the mahogany, her laptop powered up.

The seller is ready. The buyer, however, is unaccounted for.

"He's late. Why did I know he'd be late?" Chestack mutters. "He's been dicking us around from the start."

Sobel rebuts that assertion, leveling what I recognize from our past encounters as a string of Czech vulgarities at Ed and Americans in general, especially American musicians and their rich, spoiled children, by which he means me. He stands, stacks and restacks each pile of documents before him, seeming quite eager to wash his hands of all of us.

Jackson arches an eyebrow at whatever part of the tirade he has understood, then settles back into his chair, obviously wishing he were napping back at the hotel.

Another vampire migraine settles on me, with full-blown aura of zigzagging lights before my eyes and olfactory hallucinations; I've been having these weird headaches, smelling weird smells, since we returned to Prague three days ago, as if I'm fated to not see or think clearly while I'm here, when I need most to be on my toes. But I am, unlike the rest of this group, very good at waiting. Before inheriting Aspect Ratio, I conserved antique, sometimes ancient, textiles. Nothing teaches patience better than restoring a tapestry weakened by age. You learn to bide your time, to let the stitches guide your way to a new strength. So this delay doesn't faze me. I have been anticipating the moment when Christoph Zwilling finally reveals what it is he wants, and I reveal to him, to Jackson, to myself, just what price he'll pay for Will's death.

It's all I have thought about the last two weeks, since the day Will died and I placed the pendants in the safe at Aspect Ratio, which is where they remained until I removed them to bring them to Prague, to this meeting. The gallery's beefed-up security system detected no intrusions in all that time, but I have no doubt Zwilling knows exactly where the pendants are. He claims they are his, after all, a sort of reparation.

Why doesn't he just take them and get it over with? I really don't care anymore. Let's call them my gift to him and his bride, who Jackson tells me has just received kudos for a limited engagement as Lady Macbeth in Vancouver. I long to hurt her, thus hurting my cousin through a person he loves, as he has wounded me by taking Will. But I won't do that. This dance will never end unless I end it.

The lawyers are debating some common point of Czech and US estate law when the Zwilling contingent arrives: my stern, impeccably attired cousin; an elderly gentleman who is likely the family's loyal legal retainer; and a petite woman dressed in a black sheath and a cream-and-black-striped blazer. Chiara Nunnally, I suppose, though I can't fully see her, the headache's aura fills the central part of my visual field. Jackson quickly gets to his feet, extends his hand across the conference table to her. Yes, it must be Chiara.

"Herr Gassner's flight from Switzerland arrived late," Zwilling says curtly, frowning at his attorney. "Let's not waste any more time." As if another minute to exchange pleasantries will kill a multimillion-dollar transaction months in the making.

Papers shuttle from one side of the table to the other, brows furrow, confidences are whispered, heads nod. I watch from within my migraine shell, sign what needs signing, listen but say nothing, as Chestack has urged. He knows how angry I am at Zwilling, how it's all I can do to keep from plunging a metaphorical stake through his heart. Ed, too, wants this deal done with a minimum of fuss, which he's certain I'll provide if he doesn't reel me in. If I didn't know better, I'd say Ed arranged for my headache.

All goes swiftly, the lawyers and the notary make quick work of it; in a little more than an hour, the property my parents owned for almost a century is no longer my problem. The notary verifies the transfer of funds to our account from Zwilling's, stamps the appropriate governmental stamps on the documents, then floats out on a cloud of perfume that makes me gag.

"I don't know what I expected, but that seemed rather civilized. No fangs dripping blood, no Igor," Jackson whispers.

Across the table, a throat clears. "Igor Danshov has just been arrested by the Metropolitan Police in London for administering the drug that helped kill Will Baumann," Zwilling says. "He surrendered to the authorities earlier this morning." He raises his phone, displays the text message from his office heralding this bit of news.

Rage I've kept bottled up swells within me, tries to knock the headache aside but can't fully succeed. "Bastard!" I jump to my feet and lean over the table as far into his face as I can get. "You've got the estate, and now you've rid yourself of some annoying collateral damage. Your Uncle Stefan would be so proud.

"Yet the things you declared you wanted most, Christoph, the things you condoned a murder for, go unclaimed. I practically delivered them to you; I all but surrendered my parents' legacy to you, as well as my good friend and my dignity to your greed. How dare you try to appease me with some kind of sham justice when it's you who should be behind bars?"

Zwilling stands. Jackson scrambles to his feet on our side of the table, about equal in height and weight but lacking my cousin's viciousness. Chestack and the other attorneys freeze, sensing a fight three men over sixty should stay out of.

Suddenly, the fragrance of lavender wafts my way, disorienting me. I look around, knowing who it cannot be, who is clearly not in this room, when I feel a presence at my back, a hand on my shoulder. "Let's go to the little girls' room," a voice says. "Best to escape the rising testosterone tide."

My head pounds. I sway from the pain. I'm a vampire, for God's sake, I'm not supposed to be troubled by human weakness anymore.

"Chloe must be exhausted, between a new baby and her friend's death and this idiotic campaign for those pendants. Christoph, call a ten-minute cease-fire," Chiara demands. "Jackson will agree, won't you?"

Jackson nods, as does Chiara's husband. Apparently satisfied we won't return to find them dead on the floor, she leads me out of the conference room, down a short hall to the restroom, which is, thank goodness, equipped with a fainting couch. How apt, since I feel as if I'm about to do just that.

"Lie down, close your eyes. I'll find a towel or something for a compress," she says softly. "The feeling will pass in just a few minutes, I'm sure," She sounds so convincing.

I feel moist paper gently laid over my eyelids, cool but not uncomfortably so. My hands, so cold I've had them jammed under my armpits, now rest on my stomach, warmed by Chiara's breath. "Just lie here and rest," she says. After a few minutes, she whispers, "Come back to your parents' house tonight, for dinner. There will be no tricks, no threats. I'll make Christoph behave."

"Why should I believe you?" I ask.

"You brought the pendants here today," she replies. "You know why."

I swear, I don't anymore.

* * * *

We arrive at the manor house just before six o'clock, though no one specified a time. "It's still cocktail hour at our hotel," Jackson says, in hopes of avoiding this engagement.

"Nice try, but I'm not drinking, I'm nursing." I clutch Avalon to my chest protectively.

"You're bringing the lamb into the lion's den, you do know that, don't you, love?"

"At least we know where the lion is. What if there's another Igor, waiting to strike when I'm not nearby? Daphne can't protect this baby, and neither can you, not if Zwilling chooses to hurt her. Only I can."

Jackson takes Ava, lays her in her carrier, belts her in and tickles her tiny feet, clad in little purple-and-pink-striped socks. "Sounds to me like control a la Sebastian and Emilie."

He's absolutely right, of course, but right now that's irrelevant. Tonight, where I go, the baby goes, period. End of argument.

"Not too late for us to escape," Jackson tries again, but he knows he can't win. Thus, as we pull up to the house, we are a party of three joining Mr. and Mrs. Zwilling, our new best enemies. Ah, family. I feel the freakish headache building again, and the aura forming in front of my eyes, all violet and white and blue. Damn.

Chiara answers the door herself. Did I expect servants?

"Welcome back, Chloe," she air-kisses my cheeks. "And you brought the baby; I was so hoping you would." She air-kisses Jackson and bends to peer into the carrier. "What a sweetheart, how perfect she is! I can't wait to hold her."

Jackson smiles over at me angelically, as if to say, "Can't wait to see you restrain yourself when she tries," and follows our hostess into what used to be the library. Well, it still is, though the furnishings are less ponderous, and the space seems more feminine now than it was when I saw it three weeks ago.

"Please make yourselves comfortable. There's some of that good Czech beer we had at the hotel, Jackson, and wine, of course, and some flavored sparkling water. Help yourself." Chiara points to the bar cart in a paneled corner. "I don't know where anything is yet. Christoph had a few things loaded in this afternoon, but I'm still exploring this big old place."

I settle into a petite wing chair newly upholstered in peach linen; I pet the fabric—it's good quality. Jackson puts the baby carrier on the floor at my feet. "Let's see if I can find that beer and something soft for Chloe. Where is Christoph, by the way? I hope we're not too early?"

She waves off the suggestion. "Wouldn't matter. For a man as precise as he is, he battles the clock constantly—probably because he's always trying to pack too much into every minute, always on the phone with his people in Zurich. If I hadn't seen him actually sleeping, I'd think he never did."

"Sounds like someone I know," Jackson offers, then winks at me.

Chiara does too. "Just as I suspected: Chloe and my husband

are more alike than they might like to admit."

And what would she know about that?

On cue, my cousin enters, tall, ramrod straight, dour as ever. Even dressed in jeans and a sweater the soft gray of a baby squirrel, he looks like one mean son of a bitch.

"Clothilde," he says, bending over to kiss my hand, "it's so good to see you back in your parents' home, my dear."

I do not react to his attempt to annoy me by using that name. I won't give him that power.

"I see you have brought your daughter, as well. Interesting."

"Just keeping my family close and my enemies closer, you might say." This time, I do glare at him—a reminder, no, a warning that he should in no way underestimate what I will do to safeguard those I love.

Hard to know whether my message is received. He strides over to the bar cart, extends a hand to Jackson, who shakes it then holds up a bottle of beer. Zwilling declines, points to a bottle of red wine. "Some of that, please, the Montepulciano d'Abruzzo, it's more warming. This room is decidedly chillier than I'd like— and I am not referring to the temperature."

"Whose fault is that, cousin?" I ask sweetly.

"Jesus, love, won't you even pretend to be civil here? Play nice." Jackson moves behind me, a gesture of solidarity, but conditional solidarity.

"The same goes for you, Christoph," Chiara demands. "There are differences to air, yes, but also peace to be made. You alone are responsible for the hostility Chloe bears toward you. Fix it."

I tap three ibuprofen tablets out of a bottle from my courier bag, which has become a makeshift diaper bag, as well. The smell of baby lotion that rises from it makes me sick to my stomach. I down the pills with a swig of the pomegranate-flavored water Jackson has brought me.

"You'll want some food along with those. Come along, Chloe, Jackson can get the baby. We're having a light, cold supper, salad and sandwiches. Let's get something into you now." Chiara hands

Avalon and her carrier to Jackson then offers me a hand up out of the chair. "Follow us, gentlemen. Christoph, be a dear and pour me a glass of that wine. I, too, am feeling the need for something to dull the pain."

Zwilling obeys, Chiara's six-foot-something vampire puppy. If I look at his teeth, will I find that she's filed down his fangs?

She leads us into the smaller formal dining room, where the table has been laid with a plain white cloth, white china, and appropriately simple glassware and cutlery—the same things my crew used here in recent weeks. Several baguettes are arranged in a wine cooler. Platters of cold meat and cheeses, fruit, and sliced vegetables are surrounded by mustards and some dressings for the crudités. Petit fours stacked on a china tower shimmer under a dusting of sugar.

We arrange ourselves much as we did in my lawyer's office, though the table that separates us is much less imposing. Jackson and I are on one side, Avalon's carrier on a chair between us, and Chiara and Zwilling are on the other side, childless. Will they stay that way, I wonder, or has he inherited my father's ability to reproduce in a more than human way?

She hands me a plate with two slices of crunchy brown bread, several slices of cheese, and a handful each of white grapes and strawberries and makes two identical plates for herself and her husband. Jackson, who probably hasn't eaten all day, unashamedly piles a bit of everything onto his dish—living with me, he's learned to take food when he can get it. I lift a slice of what seems to be Jarlsberg to my mouth, chew, and swallow; why not enjoy some tasty, empty calories?

Zwilling, like my father, goes right for the fruit, licking juice from a strawberry in a way that's disturbingly reminiscent of that night in an Edinburgh hotel with Teppan Nilsson, my vampire coming-out. He drinks his Montepulciano and sets his glass down hard on the table.

"I must begin by offering my condolences to you, cousin, on the death of your friend Will Baumann. I know you believe me to be guilty of his murder, but I assure you I gave no such instructions to Igor Danshov. He was told simply to force Baumann to hold a gun on Jackson and to do whatever small inducing might be required for the threat to both of them to be easily perceived. Igor's enthusiasm overruled his common sense."

Jackson touches my hand. "It's true, Chloe, Igor told me he'd miscalculated and given Will too much meth; he said Will had already vomited once before I arrived at the flat."

"Is that supposed to comfort me? Someone—you, Christoph— should have seen to it that Igor stayed there with Will and Jackson, instead of leaving Will with the gun and Jackson lashed to that chair. Both of them could have died, and today you would be responsible for two murders."

Zwilling raises his hands, a gesture of surrender. "Igor Danshov's mistakes are my mistakes, it is true; I might well have more blood on my hands right now. But I compelled Igor to turn himself in to the London authorities, so he might suffer the consequences of his actions. Killing him myself, as I was sorely tempted to do, would have done nothing to punish him for Baumann's death. In prison, he will suffer, I will see to it."

I feel for my bag, lift two velvet boxes from within it, and place them on the table between Zwilling and me. When I reveal them, the rubies sparkle with light from the chandelier overhead, sending pain piercing through my eyes and across my forehead. "You wanted these pendants so badly, a man died because of it. Take them, I want nothing more to do with them."

Chiara watches her husband, waits for his answer. As does Jackson. From an inner room of the house, I hear a clock ticking off the minutes of Zwilling's hesitation.

"Here they are, *cousin*. Are you trying to tell me you no longer want them?"

Zwilling gathers the boxes toward him, touches the gemstones, feels the texture of the gold chains his father forged. Then he slams the boxes shut and pushes the pendants away.

"This is not just a whim on my part, not just vengeance."

"No more *Born to Slay the King* fantasy?" Jackson asks dubiously, recalling Zwilling's claim as he introduced himself back in April, before the concert in Barcelona.

"As I told you that night, Fahey, the king is already dead. His sins live on to condemn him."

"Enumerate them," I demand. "Tell me what my father did to you that I'm expected to pay for now."

* * * *

Zwilling refills his wineglass and drains it. He looks from me to Avalon, then back.

"As a boy," he begins, "I heard people whisper about my father's death. Our town, not so far from where we sit, was very small. People would say that it wasn't an accident, that the fire that burned Papa's forge was set deliberately, and that Papa himself had set it. I often ran home to my mother and cried in her arms. I was only six years old when Papa died."

The gossip mortified Grandmother Herz, he says, she was certain that the bishop would order her son Gregor disinterred from sacred ground as a suicide.

"When a year had passed and my mother's mourning was over, our grandmother said we must leave. When they thought they were alone, I heard the family blame Stefan for causing my father's drinking and Papa's rages at Mama, and now, the family would be humiliated, and punished for whatever it was Stefan had done and for my father's stupidity in letting it torment him so."

When I was a child, I yearned for the grandparents and aunts and uncles everyone else had. I don't think I would have liked my Herz relatives very much.

"The family chose its reputation over you," I concede.

Zwilling clenches his fists. "Yes, the high-minded Herz family, whose only claim to quality was that Stefan, their eldest son by mere minutes, was a musician in the Hapsburg court and had married the widow of a wealthy diplomat. They had no time for their second son's wife and child. My mother stood up to them, told them if they wanted us gone so badly, Stefan should be the one to find us a new home and pay for our passage."

"And Stefan called Marie Beatrisa's bluff?"

"Of course, he did," Zwilling says, seeming embarrassed by his mother's naivete. "He found a widowed merchant with a ten-year-old daughter in Zurich and shipped Marie Beatrisa off to be his bride. In my mother's version of the story, your father bragged that he had found another Gregor to replace the first."

Sebastian, or rather Stefan, was no saint, but that doesn't sound like him.

"Why would he taunt her like that?" I challenge Zwilling. "Stefan had nothing to gain by it. Actually, he had nothing at all to gain by helping your mother settle somewhere else. Maybe he simply wanted to help her."

My cousin's face blanches with a white-hot anger he struggles to contain.

"Then why did my mother never forgive him for sending us to Zurich? She wielded Stefan Herz's wrongs against her like a club and beat the rest of us with them for years afterward. We were all Stefan's accomplices against her, she said: my father for killing himself; my stepfather, a successful merchant, for never being the man she thought he should be; my stepsister, for merely living in her house.

"Nine years later, on the day Gregor Zwilling died, my stepsister stole every piece of gold in her father's safe and ran off with a soldier she'd met at a friend's birthday party. My mother was penniless with no one to rail against except me. I was sixteen years old, left to run the business myself if we were going to eat. And because she blamed Stefan for making her marry Gregor Zwilling, my mother also blamed him for her second husband's death."

"You blamed Stefan too, don't deny it," Jackson interrupts. Zwilling, Chiara and I all turn toward him, as if only now remembering he is here with us. "Is that why you became a vampire, Christoph, so you could destroy Stefan Herz?"

Jackson has used the "V" word. The gloves are officially off.

"Yes," Zwilling barks. He pushes away from the table, seizes the empty wine bottle and throws it to the ground, shattering the glass. Jackson dives between the baby and a flying green shard. The commotion startles Avalon and starts her howling. Jackson hunts under the baby's back for her pacifier, coaxes it between her trembling lips, hums "Three Blind Mice" until she settles down, then picks up the carrier.

"It's time for us to go, Chloe, Ava and I, that is. Stay if you like, but I'm out."

"Halt!" Zwilling roars, his voice shaking.

Chiara plants herself directly in front of him. She takes his hands in hers, raises them to her lips, kisses them. "Christoph, go gently. Lose Chloe now, and you lose her forever. It will be war. How long will you allow hate to rule you?"

It's painful to watch Zwilling grapple with the beast inside and tame it back into the careful, controlled man he pretends to be. It's hard to know how much of the human is left. Maybe I'll be like that in a century myself. Maybe Chiara is right about our being alike.

My cousin reclaims his seat. His wife melts into the space next to him, her hands wrapped around his left arm, her eyes shifting warily from him to me. My headache recedes, I can almost see directly ahead, but Jackson senses I'm still not right. He hands me the baby, gently pushes me down into a chair behind him, and kisses both me and our daughter. He wants the truth from Zwilling too, and he won't stop until he's finally heard it. Jackson pulls his phone from his back pocket, selects a number, turns to show me, then makes the call.

"I left a message for Julian Gippel earlier, informing him where we'd be tonight and how to proceed if he didn't hear from me in two hours. That's now. He's been in Bratislava, just an hour or so away by air. For all I know, he got on a plane the minute he heard from me, he might be in Prague already, given how Interpol smoothes the way when one of its men is investigating a murder. Gippel takes a particular interest in Chloe, of course, having directed the murder case against Teppan Nilsson, but Will Baumann was an acquaintance of his, as well, did you know that, Chris? So it seems you have a choice: Tell us what this is really all about or tell Gippel why you let your man Igor kill Baumann."

"As if you cared whether Will Baumann lived or died. Really, Fahey, we all know better, even Clothilde. He loved her. If anyone had motive to kill Baumann, it's you, not me."

Jackson puts the phone to his ear, poised to carry through his threat. "Now, we're making progress. Talking about motive, let's talk about your expressed desire to kill Stefan Herz, or Sebastian de la Coeur."

Zwilling's irises pale a bit, from the black of charred flesh to their usual shade of brown. I see my father's eyes, or more accurately, my Uncle Gregor's. He shakes Chiara off.

"I became a vampire because I could, because the opportunity presented itself. Nothing more than sheer lust for a woman, which led to lust to be with her forever when she promised it. My mother was finally dead; more than three decades of listening to her rant about my father, about his brother, about his brother's wife and the pendants that evil woman had used to seduce her husband had come to an end at last. If I had known where my uncle was, I might have killed him then, but it was much easier to disappear in those days. No need to fake one's death. Seventy years passed before I realized Stefan Herz was still alive."

Jackson's body blocks my view of him, but I don't need to see Zwilling's face to know that fake-death crack is directed at me. Julian Gippel is on his way, of that I have no doubt; another shot at the de la Coeurs and their secrets is too juicy for him to pass up. I need to know where this story ends, immediately.

"OK, I get it, cousin: Your mother thought my father was every manner of bastard imaginable, and so did you. Not enough for you to want to kill him, though, was it? Or, if it was, not enough that you didn't wait another thirty years to get your act together. Really, Christoph, you do know how to hold a grudge."

"Really, Clothilde," Zwilling says, mimicking me, "do you honestly think I was stupid enough to go up against Stefan and your mother, the woman who wrecked my parents' marriage? Both were vampires with the combined strength of a century more than I possessed? I needed leverage, and suddenly they—as Sebastian and Emilie de la Coeur—laid it at my feet with the deception about their deaths. Sebastian very nearly brought exposure on himself and your mother, and never gave a thought to what exposing you might mean. That he lost everything is more than he deserved. That he lost it by his own hand is regrettable. The right to kill *my* father should have been *mine*."

Did he say what I think he did? I push Jackson out of my way, until I can stand as face-to-face with Zwilling as the dining table will allow. Jackson grips my left arm but doesn't try to hold me back; it's a gesture of solidarity, not censure. I look quickly over to Chiara, anticipating a similar show of support from her, but she is pale against the room's candlelight, her white skin stark against her lovely brown hair, her hazel eyes fixed on the velvet boxes at the center of the table, as if she, too, has come to believe the pendants might ignite with ruby energy and finally reveal their secrets.

"Your *father*?" I ask when my voice returns at last. I feel Jackson at my side, his hands on my shoulders, steadying me. "What are you talking about?"

Zwilling smiles—Sebastian's smile—the charming, seductive smile of a con man who's played his mark, in this case, me. I am his leverage, and not just by default now that my father is dead. I always have been.

"Upon my mother's death, Gretchen Herz, wife of Thomas, the youngest brother of Stefan and Gregor, sent me a letter. I did not read it for ten years, until I received word that she, too, had died. In the letter, Gretchen said Marie Beatrisa had sworn Stefan was the father of her only child. My mother swore to her husband's family that Gregor was cold and drunk and violent after he learned Stefan would be marrying Eugenie Verlaine, the woman who had commissioned the pendants. My mother swore, Gretchen said, that Gregor beat and raped her every night for a month afterward, and that before his marriage Stefan visited her often to offer his love and comfort. When she learned she was pregnant, my mother said, she feared for her life if Gregor learned the truth.

"The family didn't believe her, Gretchen wrote, but my mother swore the proof of it was in the Herz Bible, which my grandmother had passed on to Stefan as her eldest son. Gretchen speculated it was also to remind Stefan how he had destroyed his brother and shamed his family. But who knew the truth of any of it then? Who knows now?"

Chiara's chair clatters to the floor as she quickly stands. "When were you going to tell me this?" she asks, more accusation than question.

Zwilling seizes her by the wrist. "When were you going tell me about your own lies? Did you think I'd never recognize you for who you really are, Katarina, my poor, dead love?"

"Mom?"

Of course. Who else could fool me and Zwilling this long, this completely?

Chiara rips free, staggering her much-larger husband as she rushes from the room. As she passes me, I hear Emilie's voice in my head: *I'm so sorry.*

"What the hell is going on here?" Jackson shouts after her. The noise wakes the baby, whose considerable volume outdoes her father's.

A look of ignorance is all I can offer.

"Avalon's hungry and wet—and pissed off, like everyone else in this house. I need to tend to her." I scoop my courier bag from the floor with one hand, grab the baby carrier with the other.

Jackson leans in, brushes his lips across my cheek, whispers, "And it gets better: Gippel is here. He just texted me."

A good time to make myself scarce and take care of baby business. I press my lips to Jackson's, soundlessly urge him to stay safe, and make my way out of the dining room, following the path Chiara took. Avalon shrieks in her highest register, tosses her head from side to side, demands her dinner. The squeal pierces my pounding skull, but the ache is different: Finally, there is no aura, no flashing lights.

After the events of the last few minutes, pure, unadulterated pain is refreshing.

* * * *

I follow the main-level hall past the kitchen, easing down a dozen steps to a laundry area I remember having a table, for folding clothes, and a bench. I feel for the wall switch and flip it; a lamp hanging over the table illuminates a small circle around us, but only just, so faint is the light it sheds. I hoist the carrier onto the table, release my very unhappy daughter and set her at my right breast before I even think about sitting down.

Hardly a minute passes before the lightbulb sputters and dies, leaving Avalon and me in darkness. The baby relaxes, as if the dim light was more upsetting than no light at all, though more likely it's just a fuller belly doing the trick. Why ask why? She's peaceful—that makes one of us.

Footsteps sound on the stairs; I figure it must be Jackson coming to fetch us. "Hope you brought a candle to guide your way, sweetheart."

Within my mind, a female voice replies: *"I don't need light to see, or words to speak, but I do need you to listen."*

Fragrance floats toward me, clean, like newly laundered sheets, but with a touch of lavender. Always lavender, as if my mother had been in residence here all along. Can she really have been in front of me all day without my even suspecting it was her?

"I have to leave here," she whispers. "I can't stay, not while Christoph is this angry. What happened to Will, I didn't anticipate. Endangering the rest of you would be inexcusable."

That's an excuse in itself, quite the cop-out. "Explain this to me, Mom: Why would you marry him? You must have known who he was, he looks exactly like Gregor Herz."

From the shadow, she materializes, tears streaking a face that's been so lovely, so long. I see her as Chiara, but also as Emilie, as I adored her but also resented her for so many years: distant and impossible to fathom.

"Love makes you stupid, Chloe, surely that's not news to you. I was lonely; I fell in love with the wrong man, nothing more."

Nothing more? "Sorry, I won't accept your evasiveness—or your selfishness—any longer. You owe me, you owe Will Baumann, the whole story."

She recoils, as though I've slapped her. God knows, I want to.

"Not now, I have to go. He could lash out again." She takes a step closer, kisses my cheek, bends down to kiss her grandchild, but I pull the baby away, tighter against my body. Avalon whimpers her displeasure.

"Don't think I can take care of myself, Emilie? Of course not, it's all about control with you. As Eugenie, you used those pendants to manipulate Stefan into marrying you, didn't you?"

She rests her hand against my arm, the one that supports Avalon's little body against my own. I try to twist away again, but my mother won't allow it.

"Knowing Daddy, it's not impossible, is it? Stefan could have slept with Marie Beatrisa and fathered Christoph."

"It's not impossible."

"But you don't know, do you?"

"No, I don't."

Frustrated, she backs away. "The pendants, Mom? What do they signify to Christoph? What does he hope to prove?"

She runs up the stairs. My headache surges anew, but where the aura once floated I see four words suspended in the air between where I sit and the place where my mother briefly stood.

"True love begets love," they read, the emphasis clear.

Does she even know the meaning of the word true?

* * * *

"Chloe, are you down here? I've been looking all over . . ."

I fold the sides of a dry diaper on Avalon's midsection, press lightly on the tapes to fasten it. I roll the soiled diaper and used baby wipes into a ball and drop them into the plastic bag I remembered to bring with me.

"Stay where you are, Jackson, there's no light. We're coming up now."

He smiles when he sees us, as though we're the only light he needs in his life. My mother is right: Love does make you stupid.

"Here are my girls." He kisses my cheek then the baby's, clearly pleased by something other than our reappearance.

"What did we miss?"

Jackson's smile grows wider. "Gippel with a warrant. Christoph agreeing to surrender himself to the Metropolitan Police for questioning day after tomorrow. No drama, same story: that Igor Danshov's only orders were to wait for me at your flat but that he found Will Baumann there and got carried away. Christoph says he'll cooperate. No point in not."

"And Chiara?" I ask.

Jackson puts an arm around my shoulder. "Haven't seen her. Would I recognize her if did?"

He takes the baby carrier and guides us through the hall, past the small dining room, to the front door and toward our rental car. As he loops the seatbelt into position and secures Avalon in the back, I allow myself one last look at the house I spent months working to get rid of.

"Won't miss this place, will you, love?" Jackson opens the passenger door for me.

"Not for a minute. No wonder my mother didn't care if I cleaned it out."

Some things are better forgotten.

Chapter Eight

PRAGUE, MID-JUNE 2012

One good thing about being a key figure in a criminal case: You were encouraged to stay put. Which meant the spotlight cast on Fahey and his life amid Sebastian and Emilie de la Coeur's extended family had become a career asset rather than a liability.

He was a victim in the abduction/assault/involuntary manslaughter case against Igor Danshov now wending its way through magistrate's court, murder charges having been deemed by prosecutors too difficult to prove. His presence required in London for now, Fahey's bosses at the BBC had deemed the time appropriate to make him host of a weekly news magazine. He simply could not resume his regular duties covering the European Union in Brussels until legal proceedings were at an end, they argued to their superiors.

So Fahey and Chloe and the baby were living together in a lovely flat near the Kensington High Street, not too far from Chloe's gallery, not too far from the television studio. With help from Daphne and her set-designer friend, Chloe had found some secondhand pieces that were, in truth, better than anything either of them had had in their previous apartments. A few touches of classic Court of Cruelty memorabilia, a finely wrought frame for her Grandmother Roget's quilt, plus a small office area for him in the living room (with sufficient wall space to hang several of his awards for videography and news reporting), and within two weeks of their return from Prague, the place was warm, inviting. It was everything Fahey had missed without realizing during the last year in Belgium.

More each day, Fahey wanted Chloe to agree to a wedding date. But marriage was a sore subject as long as her mother was disinclined to contact her. Oh, there were Chiara Nunnally sightings in Canada and the US; she was keeping busy with the Shakespeare repertory company. But nothing suggested that a reappearance, let alone a reconciliation with Zwilling, was in the offing, so Fahey thought it best not to press. Anyway, he and Chloe had their own vampire issues to resolve. He was thirty-four years old, a good age to be forever, if forever was a possibility. They watched Avalon for signs she was anything other than a happy, normal human infant. If Chloe was any measure, they could be watching for decades. Better to dwell on something more immediately controllable.

It was a philosophy dear also—it seemed—to the prosecution barrister, who had spent that afternoon prepping Fahey, examining every aspect of his behavior toward Will Baumann in minute detail: How did he feel about Baumann on the day of his death? How did he feel about Baumann's relationship with Chloe, both that day and in the past, when they were intimate? What about Baumann's assistance the night Avalon was born— did Fahey resent that? Was Fahey projecting his hostility about Baumann onto Igor Danshov? The defense would argue that it was possible, and thus Fahey might be deemed an unreliable witness to the events of that evening. On and on, it went, until Fahey felt as if he, rather than Danshov, were the accused, which was, naturally, the barrister's intent, so he'd be ready for anything at trial.

For Fahey, these days of preparing and anticipating and waiting were a welcome respite from the usual racing around.

He and Chloe had actually lived together, in the same city, for eight consecutive weeks, getting to know their daughter, getting to know each other again. No one had died, nothing had been stolen, no new scandal had erupted. Even Zwilling's statement to the police had been accomplished without incident, according to the prosecutor; Zwilling had come to London as ordered and departed when he was cleared to do so.

Chloe was immersed in her too-long-neglected duties at Aspect Ratio, taking the baby to work with her in the afternoons. Fahey was grateful for the peril the morning sun posed to vampires. It meant spending each morning with his girls until it was time, again, for a deposition or another re-creation of the crime scene at Chloe's old flat before he headed off to the studio. He'd learned, too, that if he intended to have regular meals at all, he needed to eat them out alone or bring food home. Truthfully, he'd eaten better on assignment with the BBC in Afghanistan. Maybe he'd take up cooking, once Avalon required a more varied diet than breast milk and mushy cereal.

It was Tuesday, a short day for Chloe at the gallery, and when he arrived home she had just settled Ava down for— they could only hope—three or four uninterrupted hours. The baby was eating more, sleeping longer. Fahey leaned into the crib, pried a tiny fist open with his index finger and watched again in amazement as his little girl clutched it. Her eyes fluttered open, looked up at him then closed again. Fahey pressed a kiss on her forehead.

"It's my turn to feed her tonight; don't you dare let me sleep, C.J."

Chloe stepped up behind him, locked her arms around his waist, and pressed her lips against his back. "I make no promises. When I'm done with you, you may need all the rest you can get."

He twisted to face her. "Sleep *is* overrated, don't you think?" He crushed his mouth to hers, lifted Chloe and carried her to their bed, where he quickly peeled away her clothes. She unbuttoned his shirt, raking her teeth down his chest before sinking them into his left pectoral for a languorous suck that made his head spin and his cock hard. He kicked off his slacks and pulled her on top of him, thrusting high and hard, gripping her hips, slamming her down until they were both sweaty, until their hearts pounded and their tongues danced. Then she lowered her head and bit into his upper arm, sucking on the vein, milking it as she milked his penis with her body and he came, spilling into her. Her muscles spasmed around him, her body shuddered against him as her teeth disengaged and she climaxed too. He flipped her onto her back, and they rested a little while, until they were ready to repeat.

Later, when thought was again possible, Fahey wondered at the perfection of these moments together. He'd take it, if it were all he could have. He would manage to live with his limited allotment.

"Bliss," she sighed. "You. Me. Now."

"And here I thought I was the only sentimental one."

She rubbed up against his thigh. "Just the one who's not afraid to appear sentimental."

"Or, love, maybe I'm just the one not waiting for another shoe to drop."

She bit his left nipple, tugged on it until she drew a tiny drop, and licked the sting away with the blood. "So many dropped shoes—enough for a regiment."

He wrapped a leg and an arm around her, trapping her against him. "Hush. Bliss, remember? You. Me. Now." He licked along the slope of her neck, tasted the saltiness of her along with the sweet. "That's all any two people can ever count on."

Her hair, longer than he'd ever seen it, spread dark across his skin. It felt like silk, like satisfaction, as she nodded, sweeping his pectorals, his ribs, his abdominals with it before lifting her head to look at him. "I wish I could say you were wrong about that."

Fahey kissed the tip of her nose. "We'll just have to wait and see, won't we?"

She stretched contentedly and bit him again.

* * * *

He was running toward the Serpentine, well into his second mile and dodging a group of tourists leaving Kensington Palace, when his phone vibrated against his hip. Fahey ignored it, but the vibrating persisted. He stopped to catch his breath. "Eric Bohlander," the caller ID showed. "Must talk," a text read.

"Eric, old friend, how goes it?"

A gruff snarl. "Ain't Bohlander, just his phone. Knew you'd never call *me* back—well, not without thinking long and hard about it, and I needed to get in touch urgent-like."

Ronnie Hamilton, de facto leader of the New Court of Cruelty and a name well known in circles in which weapons and Lord knew what else were bought and sold illicitly. Fahey generally tried to keep a wide berth, but the man had a way of making himself hard to ignore.

"I can't imagine why you'd urgently need to talk to me. I surely can't recall the last time I wanted to talk to you."

"Yeah, yeah, I'm a right bastard, but I can't call your girl direct, Fahey. That prick Zwilling's probably hacked her phone, and Chloe needs to know there's trouble afoot. Her mother's here."

"Where's here?" Far away, Fahey hoped, but he didn't feel particularly lucky. "I'm in London, you know."

"As am I. New Cruel's playing the Little Goth Club day after tomorrow—your holes in the wall today, stadium tour next summer, that's the plan. Anyway, about three nights ago, Bohlander ties a drunk on at a pub in Stockholm after rehearsal; Lars and I find him hooked up at his flat the next morning with a curvy brunette, but he's acting really cagey about it. Says she's a singer, says she'd be perfect for the band. You see where this is going, right?"

Jesus, Mary, and the saints, Fahey wondered if they'd all

lost their minds, Chloe's mother tops among them. "She didn't hide who she was?"

Ronnie laughed so hard, Fahey swore he could feel the phone shake. "Doesn't even try with me—I spent forty years with Emilie de la Coeur and the big family secret. She's fucking here, in this city, and she's fucking with the boy just when we got him straight again after that business with identifying Kat's body. Without Bohlander, we're screwed, Fahey. Took forever, all those Matins and Vespers gigs, but she taught him how to *think* like Sebastian on stage, how to react like Sebastian on stage."

"And Eric knows who she really is?" Fahey was still trying to figure out how Chiara had succeeded in fooling her vampire husband for months.

"We were in Sweden, auditioning singers, and who should turn up but Miss Chiara Nunnally. So yeah, Bohlander knows. She fed him some nonsense about her needing to lie low, needing him to take care of her, which of course he was keen to do. In return, she said she'd hang around long enough to do the gigs we've got lined up and help the New Cruel get established. She snookered Lars and Anders and the rest without batting a vamp eyelash, so here we are, back in London."

No way was Fahey inclined to step into that. "You're on your own with Chiara and Eric, Ronnie. If the New Court of Cruelty crashes, don't expect Chloe to save the day."

"You might not see it, Fahey, but your girl will: The Emilie we used to know, the one who always calculated the odds, is gone. Sebastian took risks, he almost burnt the house down I don't know how many times, but that woman was steady as a rock. This woman, she's completely lost."

With that insight, Fahey lost the call. A text buzzed in with an address for Fair Trade Hummus in Cheapside, not far from the late Will Baumann's brewpub. Ronnie's girlfriend, Fahey recalled, was a chickpea broker or something like that from Lebanon whose business was on the ground floor of a new townhouse he could only guess the price of. Big enough to accommodate a rock band, for sure.

Fahey sprinted home, quickly showered and changed, and decided to pay a visit after all to the once-and-future queen of the Court of Cruelty. Could he make things any worse?

Before he set out, he sent two texts—insurance, Fahey reasoned, in case her majesty became extremely displeased with him.

The first one read: "Did you know Chiara was in London?"

The second contained only names: "Teppan Nilsson. Christoph Zwilling."

* * * *

Fair Trade Hummus had a doorbell; so did M. Gattus, as in Martine Gattus, onetime fashion model, longtime squeeze of the New Cruel's lead guitarist, Mr. Hamilton himself. Fahey leaned on her bell until Eric Bohlander's handsome features appeared on the video intercom.

"What do you want?" Eric was neither surprised nor happy to see him.

"Can't I just visit a friend?"

Eric scowled from his remote vantage point. "Fuck off. This is my choice, and she's my woman."

The intercom went blank.

Fahey leaned on the bell again. A heartbeat later, the door opened, and Eric pushed through the entryway, pushed Fahey back toward the street. "Don't give me any shit about being her puppet. What does that make you, Jackson?"

"You're right, none of my concern. Don't fool yourself, though. She's not yours. She wasn't a year ago, and she isn't today. If she belongs to anyone, it's Christoph Zwilling."

Eric raised his middle digit and stalked away.

Fahey stepped through the entrance and climbed until he saw a door standing ajar at the top. He knocked. Anticipating there'd be no answer, he walked in. From the end of a long hallway, he could hear music, Mahler, he thought, and followed the sound, moving toward ever brighter light. An artist's loft, with the quintessential grid of windows.

Chiara stood at an easel, a box of charcoals on a table next to her. Long chestnut-brown hair pulled back into a ponytail, she wore black yoga pants and a tight purple and gold T-shirt with lettering on the back that read: "The Reign Resumes. New Court of Cruelty 2012." Nice packaging, Fahey thought. He'd buy what she was selling. If he didn't know better, that is.

"Why are you here?" she asked, her eyes never leaving what she was working on. Fahey leaned in for a look: a clinic scene, maybe, or a hospital. A man sitting on a gurney, his head bowed; a woman in a white lab coat holding his hand.

"I might ask you the same question," Fahey replied.

"Get out, Jackson. No one invited you."

Ronnie didn't count, evidently. "Strange to see you here in London with the band. Their singer died, but you wouldn't know about that would you, Chiara? I don't suppose you ever met Kat Nilsson." Fahey knew she wouldn't appreciate the sarcasm but decided he didn't give a rat's ass what she thought.

She turned from the easel, smiled sadly. "I did, in fact. The woman on the plane, her name really was Katarina Nilsson. We met at a Matins and Vespers show last year in Sweden, right before Emilie and Sebastian's suicides were announced. It was one of our first shows, Eric and I, and one of our worst. Absolutely dreadful, Katarina informed me afterward. We looked a lot alike, she and I—almost twins, except for the cancer, she joked. She had just learned her lymphoma was likely terminal. We became friends."

She stopped. Fahey waited. "Do all your friends die for you?" he finally asked, his voice harsh.

She blinked back tears.

"The day the plane exploded, Katarina was traveling to Prague in my place, so Chiara could come via another plane, under her own passport. I arrived first at the airport, walked past the security cameras near the taxi area, so there would be a record that I, as Kat Nilsson, had been there. Katarina walked in the main terminal doors wearing different clothing. She waited in a restroom for me, and we switched. She was the one who walked through the security checkpoint and got on the plane."

"Hold on," Fahey said, interrupting her. "Why would she agree to that?"

"Katarina planned to kill herself; she'd arranged for the necessary drugs through a contact in Slovakia, and I—as Kat Nilsson—needed to disappear. This trip was going to solve both our problems. Kat would miss the show at Chloe's open house in Prague, then be found dead a day or two later. The explosion on the plane wasn't part of the plan. . . it just happened."

Sobs tore through her, and she sank to the floor, pulling easel and sketch down with her. Fahey bent to right them, recognized the scene from that day at the makeshift morgue in Scotland, recognized the man in the drawing as Eric. And the woman—it was clear to him now who the doctor had been.

He couldn't imagine what comfort he could offer; she wasn't responsible for the blast that destroyed the plane, she couldn't have saved any of those lives, though she seemed to think otherwise. So he watched her cry, then watched her pull herself together.

"What now?" He stood, offered her a hand up.

She declined his help. "The New Court of Cruelty needs a girl singer. Turns out I do a pretty good impersonation of Emilie de la Coeur."

"And that's it, that's your plan? What about Christoph?"

"*Go, Jackson.*" The words *echoed in his head.* "Don't make me do anything else I'll regret."

He made no move toward the exit. "If you wanted to kill me, dear almost mother-in-law, I'd be dead, wouldn't I? You've had ample opportunity."

She looked him up and down appreciatively, possibly

remembering how she and Sebastian had dragged him into their daughter's life in the first place, or maybe just recalling how much he looked like Sebastian, Fahey couldn't say. Though when she lifted her eyes to his, he saw Emilie's iridescent green eyes there rather than Chiara's hazel gaze.

"Christoph isn't Sebastian; he has no sentimental attachment here. Don't be foolish enough to think you can fix things this time," she warned. "You and Chloe both, stop trying."

Something slammed into Fahey's chest, an invisible battering ram forcing his body backward, propelling him along the hallway he'd come through, down the stairs, to the sidewalk in front of the townhouse. The door slammed shut on its own.

The ribs along his left side ached; the bruising would be noteworthy, he was sure.

Better to stay just a little afraid of Chiara Nunnally, Fahey reminded himself.

* * * *

"The Book of Judith." Chloe was sitting cross-legged on their new sofa, the Herz family Bible open across her lap.

Fahey threw his jacket onto the coffee table, loosened his tie, pulled it over his head. He sank down onto the cushion next to her. "Classic revenge story, as I recall: Patriotic widow takes off invader's head, right?"

She threw her arms around his neck, pressed her lips hard onto his. "You know it? I'm familiar with Judith from my art history courses at Cambridge, and of course from tapestries I've worked on from Catholic countries. It's not necessarily standard in the Protestant Old Testament, yet here it is. The only thing in this Bible that even suggests it might be the mark Marie Beatrisa referred to is a tear that looks intentional in the margin next to Judith 8:16."

She pulled away and pushed the heavy book over onto his lap. The room was dark; Fahey could barely make out the words: "God is not man that he should be moved by threats, nor human, that he may be given an ultimatum."

"What do you suppose Marie Beatrisa was trying to say? The God and human thing—is it possible she knew your father was a vampire?"

Chloe stood, stretched. "Or was she saying Stefan was playing God by giving her no choice but to marry Gregor Zwilling?"

From the rear of the flat came faint whimpers. Chloe walked toward them, returned a few minutes later with a bundle of baby. Fahey set the Bible aside, put his arms out for his daughter. Avalon's eyes fluttered open; she yawned and sort of sighed and fell asleep again. He kissed her forehead, settled her up against his chest.

"Here's what I think: It means absolutely nothing." Chloe burrowed into a corner of the couch. "All Marie Beatrisa wanted was to piss off her in-laws. She had no idea Stefan and Christoph would outlive her by a century and spend who knows how long trying to find some hidden message in a random Bible verse she saw fit to rip up a bit. Classic revenge tale, indeed."

"So it's a just a blind alley, and we still don't know for sure if Stefan ever was Marie Beatrisa's lover, let alone the father of her child."

Chloe nodded. "Am I supposed to believe my mother when she says doesn't know either? She spent almost 140 years with him—when he was Stefan, and Sebastian, and Teppan, and who knows how many others. Am I supposed to believe she was oblivious to all the rumors within the family and my father's obsession with this Bible?"

Stefan had carted the Bible around all those years, from Europe to America. Then again, Chloe, like her mother before her, cherished her Grandmother Juliette's quilt as if it were a treasure. The de la Coeurs kept things; Fahey had sorted and catalogued hundreds of objects at the Czech house alone. As far as he could tell, for them, holding onto something didn't signify it was important.

"I believe Chiara," he said, surprising himself. "I believe she didn't know."

On the coffee table, his coat began to vibrate, swiveling as his mobile rang in the right pocket. Chloe retrieved it, looked at the caller ID. "A blocked number," she said, and handed the phone to him, exchanging it for Ava.

"Maybe a source," he said with a shrug as she walked from the room. "This is Jackson Fahey."

"Per your earlier text, I will see what connections can be made. It could perhaps take several days. There will be forms to complete; the official specimen must be discovered among the evidence amassed during the investigation of the bodies found at the de la Coeurs' Czech property. The unofficial specimen is at hand."

"And the third?"

"A post-arrest swab."

"Contact me when you know more," Fahey said, and the call cut out.

He refused to believe some things couldn't be fixed. He preferred to be a fool who died trying, thus Fahey texted a particular number for the second time that day.

"Trade?" he asked.

Chapter Nine

LONDON, LATE AUGUST 2012

"Fight the fear!" the bouncer at the door exhorts, and stamps my hand with the small purple image of a medieval keep. "The Cruel shall prevail!"

Will it, though? As he steps aside, chain mail swaying over his rippling bronze muscles, I wish my gallery partner/former bodyguard Benjamin were here, to balance my fear with some fight. But I am alone as I descend a familiar flight of steps into the Little Goth Club. Loudspeakers blare something from the early Court of Cruelty catalog, maybe from *Miserere Nobis*, m*f*y parents' first electric album, a mid-Seventies blast of overproduced synth rock and nonsense lyrics from an assemblage of musicians that hadn't yet settled on a sound. Have mercy on us, indeed.

It's almost half past ten, the set is thirty minutes late starting, yet the typically restless vassal types who cling to the Cruel seem pretty chill, quaffing flagons of ale and chalices of whatever the cheap house red is. I haven't had wine in months; I'm dying for my first post-pregnancy pour. Leaning in between a couple of men in leather vests, I wave twenty pounds at the bartender and shout, "Merlot," over a bass line my father composed. He snatches the cash, fills a glass for me, and hands it over.

One of the leather backs turns and offers me his stool, but

I'd rather stand and watch the crowd, so I carve out a little space for myself. For a Thursday night, it's a pretty tight squeeze, every square inch occupied. In fact, banners sway overhead, proclaiming, "Occupy Camelot!" On a table near the stage, CDs are stacked high—it's the New Cruel's first EP, half a dozen songs Eric, Ronnie & Co. are calling *Divine Insurrection.* I sip at my wine, which tamps down my paranoia a bit, enough that I stop replaying the last time I was in this place, when I stood mesmerized by the sight of my father onstage in his Teppan Nilsson persona, offering a more visceral interpretation of the music he created. He was a charismatic, manipulative bastard, my dad.

With a few more sips, I'm more mellow and I see another reason for my Teppan overload that night: There are mirrors all around, on the walls, on the supporting beams, on the ceiling; cracked in some places, stained in others, but intact enough that the action on the stage and everywhere else repeats and repeats, funhouse-style.

At my elbow, I sense a presence. If I look up, the mirrors might grant me my fervent wish for Jackson to appear, fresh from this week's installment of *Europulse,* the live news magazine he hosts each Thursday night. He's made no promises to come, but I know he wants to be here. Who could resist, when the promise of mayhem is so great? Between Matins and Vespers and the New Court of Cruelty, we've had exploding aircraft, coitus-inspired rioting, pre- and post-performance suicide.

I could resist, that's who. I could be home with my baby right now instead of revivifying the legend of the de la Coeurs.

"Bored, sweet Clothilde?" my cousin, or possibly my brother, asks in his unmistakable German-tinged English.

A cool breath shivers along my neck, as though a block of ice has taken human form.

"You would be bored at home, as well, my dear. The vampire in you strains against domestication; it was inevitable. You wear the stress like an ill-fitting coat; it weighs you down, like that pendant."

"One of the pendants you've decided now you don't want." Obnoxious son of a bitch stares at my chest; the ruby I wear goes cold against my skin, as if reacting to his insult. "You know nothing about me, Zwilling," I say softly, controlling my voice, the better to control my pique. "Don't presume you do."

He moves off to the side, where I can see him directly, and a smile tries to form on his lips. "It's what gets us into trouble: We bore easily, little one. Eternity can be a very long, empty stretch without variety. You'll see."

"You'll excuse me if I don't report back." I hiss, giving him the slightest view of my fangs. His half-smile widens to full. Somehow, I keep my hands away from his throat.

My homicidal reverie is interrupted by a chord blasting from the electric organ onstage. The organ's notes swell to fill the room with a tune the crowd recognizes immediately. Some stand automatically, respectfully. Others scramble to their feet. Anders leans on the notes, stretches them into a slow processional as Chiara, wearing a purple halter maxi-dress, a white feather boa, and a regal gold coronet, strides majestically to center stage. Ronnie, followed by Eric, Lars, and another tall young Viking I'm not sure I've met, flank her and vocalize in imperfect harmony:

God save our gracious queen!
Long live our noble queen!
God save the queen!
Send her victorious,
Happy and glorious,
Long to reign over us:
God save our queen!

Applause erupts from the audience. Chiara gives a swivel-hand royal wave and bows to acknowledge her subjects before ripping the crown from her head, throwing it to the floor and stomping on it. Lars, now behind the drums, taps out a military beat that segues into "La Marseillaise." My mother's soprano floats gently above it.

Allons, enfants de la Patrie
Le jour de gloire est arrive!

Someone yells, "*Vive la France!*"

"*Vive la difference*," Jackson coos into my ear. Warm lips caress it; teeth and tongue nibble and lick; warm arms encircle my waist and tighten; the pendant sizzles at my cleavage. The French national anthem never sounded so erotic, and I squirm appreciatively against Jackson's groin. As he laughs, his body rubs against mine just as gratefully. He pinches my rump, sighs. Right time, wrong place.

"A little Sex Pistols, a little Emilie de la Coeur fomenting discontent among the body politic right off. I thought the New Cruel had a new singer," he whispers hoarsely. He turns me to face him, touches my forehead with his as if I'm the one who nourishes him instead of the other way around. He's exhausted, but he's here, to do this with me, if I need him. My eyes stray to one of the mirrors surrounding us, to a reflection of Zwilling, who's moved farther up the bar. Jackson follows my glance, tracks the reflection of my cousin, steps around me in that direction and, to my surprise, offers his hand. Zwilling shakes it as his wife reiterates, "*Aux armes, citoyens!*"

The music abruptly shifts forward a few centuries, and the band asserts the call to arms with a new, instrumental appeal, heavily percussive in a blues rhythm the organ embraces. Anders pounds out the pain of governmental oppression; Ronnie, on lead guitar, wails with a taut ferocity I remember from my childhood, imbuing the strings with rage enough to garrote an enemy.

Eric, the handsome, straddles a kneeling Chiara, lifts his pure white shirt over his head, waves it like a flag of victory, but she slips from beneath him, leaps to her feet, whirls suggestively across the stage in front of the other players, until at last she lowers herself demurely onto a bench, legs crossed at the ankle like a schoolgirl.

The music ebbs; she waits a beat, then tosses her boa into the crowd. Rowdies in the front wrestle for it, until she shouts, "Hush!" and the room does.

"Don't do it again," she scolds the offenders, warning them with a gaze so sultry it might blister the paint from the walls.

"Better," she says.

"Listen," she commands, then takes that melody they know so well for an *a cappella* American spin.

> *Let music swell the breeze*
> *And ring from all the trees*
> *Sweet freedom's song*
> *Let mortal tongues awake*
> *Let all that breathe partake*
> *Let rocks their silence break*
> *The sound prolong*

Anders fires off a final thundering note on the organ and cuts it off just as violently.

"You," Chiara points to the faces lifted before her. "Are you ready for the revolution?"

Lars hits the high-hats, and with the clang of the cymbals they're off. Eric launches into "Weapons of Class Destruction," anthem of the New Court of Cruelty. Vassals jump and gyrate and scream enthusiastically. I push away from the bar toward the steps, for some air, for a broader view, if possible, of the spectacle. Jackson follows me. Zwilling, I notice, moves closer to the performers, to his bride, my mother, who seems able to command the affection of her kingdom, no matter which version of herself she presents.

"They're good; Ronnie's polished them till they shine," Jackson says. "And she's, well, she's fabulous, like Emilie and Kat, maybe the best of both."

Suddenly, he grips my shoulder from behind and drapes an arm around me, nearly toppling us both, he can barely stand.

Perspiration drips from his face as he steers us toward the wall; he sinks to the floor, rests his back against the cool brick, closes his eyes, and lets the wall support him. "Haven't eaten since I left the flat this afternoon," he admits when the dizziness and weakness pass. "Live-broadcast days are a bitch."

Poor man, if I don't kill him, his job just might. Once I regain my footing, I snatch a half-full plastic bottle of cola from the drinks ledge that encircles the club. "Emergency! I'll buy you another," I shout at the aggrieved owner of said soda.

He takes one look at Jackson's pallor and shouts, "No worries!"

None, except perhaps risking disease by swapping saliva with a tattooed vassal.

Jackson sips at the soda, scoots himself off the rather sticky floor onto the club entrance's bottom step. I wave off the about-to-protest bouncer. "Give us a minute and we'll be gone, OK? He's just a little woozy."

Jackson puts his head on my shoulder. "If I were a vampire, this wouldn't be happening."

"If you were a vampire, you'd have other issues," I remind him, ignoring the issues of life everlasting versus life less so he and I now dance around daily, thanks to his new London assignment.

Our cola-drinking bar mate reaches in with a full bottle. "Take it with you, he might need more. Happy to help Sebastian and Emilie's family where I can," says the man, a large red-bearded Scot, or so I guess from his accent. I stretch up and kiss him on what I can see of his cheek.

Jackson downs half the new bottle as well.

"Let's go," I insist. "I've shown the de la Coeur flag, seen all I need to see. We'll get some food into you before you really pass out; you're too big for me to carry home." He smiles weakly; we both know that's a lie, that I could easily get him back to the flat, but it's good to maintain some of his manly illusions. Hand-in-hand, we start up the stairs until I feel a formerly green stare boring a hole through me. I turn around and see my mother watching me from a dark corner of the stage, pulling at me.

Why should I hang around? What's the point? She has refused to talk to me for weeks now, keeping me at arms' length yet again, so we can't discuss matters she clearly would like to leave undiscussed.

Jackson observes Chiara watching me, and me watching her. He unlaces his fingers from mine, kisses them. "I'll be all right. Stay," he says, and slowly makes his way up the stairs alone.

* * * *

As blood-sucking predators go, I am a rank amateur. I don't hunt, and Jackson's episode means he needs to build up his strength a bit. So I will go hungry at least until tomorrow, maybe longer. Unless . . .

Men park themselves next to me, sensing whatever pheromone I emit, volunteering to service me whatever way I choose. Giving up their blood is probably not the first thing that occurs, though. It's not as if I'm dressed like a nun tonight: It's August in London, the season of high heat, so I'm wearing a pink tank top that's a little tight across my milk-engorged breasts (thankfully they don't leak, a most welcome vampire superpower) with a short, clingy black skirt, and four-inch black pumps without stockings (no blisters, no pinched toes, more vampire plusses). If I wanted to, I could have a full meal, appetizer through dessert.

One prospective suitor gives up his barstool; another starts a tab and the barkeep pours me a fresh merlot. It shimmers through the glass, bloodlike but not quite. These willing males are tempting, but there's Jackson to think of. Things were awkward enough with Will on the periphery of our lives, why complicate things further and risk pushing him away again? I don't know if I can make Jackson immortal without killing him—I get to create only a single vampire life, and it's unclear whether our baby counts as that one. If I can't change Jackson, will he stay? Will I want him to?

Big questions, with no ready answers, certainly not tonight.

As they sidle up to me, the gray-haired men are deferential; they know I'm their monarchs' daughter, which seems to spare me the smarmy pickup lines I might otherwise be treated to in this severely woman-poor crowd. Younger guys who don't know leer a little; they patter on a bit about how they'd heard the band would be good, and it is. Through the remainder of the first set and the thirty-minute lull before the next, I discourage about a half-dozen of them. Thanks for asking, it might be more than tasty, but no thanks, gentlemen.

A sound tech is testing microphone levels for the band's second set when I feel a tap on my shoulder. A man points to a table with good sightlines of the stage.

"This spot is yours, Miss Hart, I own the place. Can't believe no one told me you were in the audience. My apologies, I was busy in the back."

He has a Southern accent, sixty-five if he's a day. Trim and very good-looking with thick gray hair, and virile enough to make a younger woman momentarily reconsider her need for blood and other things. He reminds me of Zeke Segal, the original Cruel's late, great guitarist, Emilie's onetime lover, and my frequent childhood playmate. The man grins as if he knows what I'm thinking, as if maybe he's thinking it, too.

"Anyone gets inappropriate, signal someone to find me, Miss Hart. Ronnie Hamilton will never let me forget it if I neglect you."

He knows Ronnie. So maybe he actually knew Zeke and my parents, but I decide not to ask. A waitress brings over a merlot and a tall club soda.

"Whatever you need, don't hesitate to ask," the Little Goth Club's owner says before disappearing into the late-night crowd.

Who should reappear but cousin Christoph, raising a bottle of Belgian ale to his lips, the little rubies on his finger flashing as he does. Uninvited, he sits.

"You're like a bad penny," I snarl.

"With all these men vying for your attention, I must act as your protector," he snarls in response.

"I am not without certain skills, as I believe I have demonstrated."

"So you have, Clothilde, but you are a new initiate to our select society, and I am not aware that your sire taught you much more than the basics. I could show you how to make these men oblivious to your charms, or to do so selectively, keeping the ones you want near."

My education is lacking, it's true. Certain things just kept getting in the way, among them my sire's murdering several women and wanting me in his bed, too. When Zwilling's attitude changes, from haughty to I'm not sure what—something less hard—I realize I've failed to close off those thoughts. He's heard them.

"I had forgotten. Things may have been more complicated for you," he says, greatly oversimplifying.

"Some things were complicated for you too, though not in the same way." I owe him that acknowledgment. Our childhoods were odd; our adult lives haven't deviated much from that.

We sit quietly for a while, sipping at our drinks, ignoring the bustle around us as the crowd anticipates the band's return. And the longer we sit, the greater my need to ask Zwilling the questions his wife won't answer.

I go for the big one: "How did you not know about Chiara?"

He hurls his ale bottle over three tables and into a trash bin, adeptly missing the club's patrons, wait staff, and mirrors.

Hit a nerve, have I?

"I was too intent on shielding my own nature from her, on maintaining the façade of humanity for a woman I believed to be human. I wanted Chiara as I had not wanted a woman in years. I exhausted myself, keeping the mask in place so I could woo her and win her the way any man might. She is older, more powerful than I; she must have waited until I rested to let down her guard and regain her own strength."

"So she blinded you, and you blinded yourself?"

"Yes. Love makes one act irrationally."

They agree on that much.

"Love makes us stupid; Chiara told me that at the house in Prague when the truth came out. She realized who you were— you look just like Gregor Herz—and what you were, and still she fell in love with you, enough to marry you."

He drags his hands through his hair, scrubs down his face. "You saw us in Barcelona, we nearly combusted, and nearly took everyone else with us, that's how hot we burned. I recognized at that moment who Chiara really was. Two vampires can kill each other if there is no love—and almost kill each other if there is. When vampires mate, we mate for life, for good or ill, it seems."

For better or for worse. Sebastian and Emilie had that; I want it for myself, for me and Jackson. But it's easier to challenge Zwilling than to think about my own problem.

"So tonight, you're here, you can't take your eyes off Chiara, but you don't say a word to her? Didn't take you for a coward, cousin."

Zwilling lowers blood-red eyes to mine. "She lied to me. She used the pendants to manipulate me."

"You lied to her, and you used the pendants to intimidate me and get revenge. She should have told you the truth, yes, but you took it too far. No one ended up dead because of Chiara's dissembling. You may not have murdered Will Baumann, but he's dead because of you just the same."

He bangs the table, bouncing it about a foot off the floor. "She knew the rumor that Stefan Herz was my father."

"And she swears she doesn't know if it's true. You can't claim the moral high ground, there is none. Settle this thing or stay out of her life and mine. We will manage quite well without you."

Zwilling rises from his chair, all six feet, three inches, just like his father, just like my father. And like Sebastian, looking for all the world as if he fears nothing.

* * * *

The last encore has been sung. The house lights are up; the bar tabs have been paid. The organ and drum kit have been hauled off the stage, the amps and microphones disconnected.

Zwilling vanished a while ago. The woman he loves has neither come out to find me nor summoned me backstage to see her. I'm about to leave when Ronnie lowers his lanky form into the seat opposite mine.

"She's not herself, you know, hanging onto Eric like he's the bloody beacon who will light her way. No help for him as long as she's here; no help for her if she doesn't talk to her rich businessman husband. And why am I in the middle of this? Because the bloody band's all I care about."

"Good job then, be proud of what you've accomplished in such a short time." I stand, tug my skirt lower, and make a move to go. But Ronnie's quick for his age. He steps in front of me to block my route to the door.

"Meet us at Martine's. Talk to her."

"No." I mouth the word and just as soundlessly command him to let me pass. He sketches a bow and steps aside, laughing off my attempt at compulsion even as he complies.

My flat is a good forty-five minutes away on foot, only ten if I run. I kick off my high heels, hang them from my thumbs, stretch a little and take off at a slow jog. I miss my three miles each morning; getting them in pre-dawn is difficult, and later in the day is worse, between the baby and the gallery and Jackson and the "never before noon" sunlight thing.

So I decide to go for a real workout, via a more roundabout run by the Thames—about ten minutes down to the river, thirty to the Millennium Bridge, then about twenty over and up to our posh new neighborhood. There will be some people out at this hour, wondering who the crazy girl is. Don't care.

Near the Embankment, I see her, sitting on a ledge, a three-quarter moon reflecting her shape in the water. She's substituted a white crocheted shawl for the feather boa, maybe a little something she whipped up with her finest needles just for tonight. She stands, knowing I'll stop.

"What do you want?" I ask, leaning over, a little out of breath, though it passes almost immediately as my vampire metabolism engages.

My mother thinks a minute. "Fresh air, fresh perspective perhaps, just like you. Let's walk."

I set a fast pace. "You didn't talk to Zwilling tonight. Why?"

"What would I say? That I'm sorry for ruining his past, and I won't be responsible for ruining his future?"

She's serious. All that French-Canadian convent-school guilt, after so many years. "You ruined his past how? Explain that to me."

"With this." She fingers my pendant, once hers. "Two drops of blood, mixed with instantaneous attraction and physical proximity, that's all it takes to fate a couple. Fix a man's attention on the stone, my mother said, draw him to it, and his attention will transfer to you. Like alchemy, transforming rock into desire. Who could guess it would be so simple, and so dangerous?"

"Grandmother Juliette taught you that?"

"I made Gregor Herz fall in love with me, Chloe. I meant no harm, but I was reckless and emboldened by my power and pitted the brother who had little against the brother who had more. I didn't count the consequences. I came to love Gregor for his kindness and his gentle soul, but I stole those from him along with his heart. The family said he went mad when he learned his brother was engaged to marry me. Marie Beatrisa told them Gregor raped her in his jealous rages, but it was my fault. I hurt a woman I'd never met, and then hurt an innocent child. I don't know why Gregor ultimately killed himself, but I must be to blame for that, too."

Longstanding sibling rivalry, parental indifference, spousal infidelity, maybe clinical depression, all the other factors that helped mold Gregor Herz seem lost on my mother.

"Daddy bears some blame if he did, indeed, sleep with Marie Beatrisa, as she claimed in that letter."

Chiara gazes at the Thames, its current sluggish in the summer heat. The night is clear; the stars sparkle on the water, yet I doubt she's even aware of them.

"Stefan didn't send me to Gregor. I went on my own, to help him financially. Gregor resented Stefan's success and would never have taken money from me had he known my plans for the pendants. I'm the one who set us all on the road that led here."

"Stop it. Stop absolving Daddy of his sins!" I want to shriek at her.

"You made Stefan a vampire," I manage to say instead, "but he became a son of a bitch on his own."

"Marie Beatrisa *never* claimed Stefan forced himself on her, and I know he never guessed Christoph might be his," she counters, blood tears welling in her now-hazel eyes. "You knew his ego, your father would never have sent his son away; he would have set her and the boy up in a house and supported them."

Crying is not something I've seen my mother do very often. She is stoic to a fault, and I faulted her for it for a long time, calling her cold and unfeeling. I regret that now.

"Tell Zwilling what you just told me. What's done can't be undone, including falling in love with him."

"He's a vampire, Chloe. He'll never let this go."

"You want the man, fight for him."

I put my arms around her, comfort her as best I can, until she insists that I run along home. But as my strides take me farther away, I hear these words in my head, in her voice.

Take your own advice.

* * * *

Flickering from the television are images of a soccer match. Real Madrid, of course. It's still his favorite team after all those years in Spain.

Jackson has crashed on the sofa. Food containers litter the coffee table: chicken curry, broccoli and brown rice, judging from the little bits left. A half-full can of ginger ale and some candy wrappers round out the evidence of dinner. I drop my shoes under the table, gather up the trash, carry it to the can in the kitchen.

I locate the remote under his left elbow and gently work it free. One eye the color of dark chocolate opens, then the other; his gaze focuses, he recognizes me.

"Sorry, I didn't mean to wake you."

"Barely slept. It's too quiet without the baby here. Mustn't ever leave her at Meredith and Ben's again." Jackson yawns, scrapes fingernails along the black stubble on his face.

"They're her godparents."

"I can't believe you let Meredith practice playing mommy with *my* daughter. But I suppose if *you* could learn . . ."

So funny, and so cute when he's sleepy. I melt down onto the edge of the sofa.

Jackson runs a hand up my arm. "I'm too tired to move. Let's stay here, plenty of room."

I give him my vampire stare, waggle an eyebrow for effect. "I don't know, looks a little cramped to me."

Jackson slips his other hand under my skirt, up into the moisture he finds there. "We can arrange ourselves very comfortably," he assures me, and with a minimum of fuss, we do just that. He grips my hips, lowers me onto him, thrusts until he's high and snug inside me.

"Paradise," he sighs. "I could stay here forever."

There must be a way.

Chapter Ten

LONDON, MID-SEPTEMBER 2012

His taxi had no sooner deposited Fahey in front of the magistrate's court when the press ambushed him.

"Jackson Fahey, now that Igor Danshov is dead, do you think the authorities will prosecute Swiss businessman Christoph Zwilling for killing Will Baumann?"

Wait a minute, what?

Fahey put his head down and pushed his way through the line of reporters, some of whom he had known for years. "No comment," he muttered every few feet, until he was in the vestibule of the building, more or less protected by the guards staffing the metal detectors. When he was waved through, Fahey sprinted up the central courthouse stairway to the prosecutor's office, where credentialed press had set up another, if less frantic, offensive line. He spotted his recently less-than-friendly old flame Claudia staring at him, no doubt calculating whether she could charm him into a statement for Sky News.

He decided to let her try.

"Jackson . . ."

"Over there, Claudia," he pointed to a corner away from the press cordon. "No mics, no cameras, just you and me."

"But on the record."

"We'll see," he said, moving closer to the prosecutor's door.

"All right." She whispered something to her video guy, ducked out of the line and walked backward, daring anyone but Fahey to follow her.

"I told you she'd get him to talk, they were together for a while," a correspondent groused to his cameraman and everyone else in the hall

"So much for discretion," Claudia snapped. "Thanks, Jackson."

"Tell me about Igor Danshov. What the hell happened?"

She looked incredulous. "You really don't know, do you? They found him dead in his cell this morning. His throat had been cut clean across, my sources say. So the question now is: What happens with Christoph Zwilling? Do the authorities drop whatever immunity deal he might have gotten and prosecute him for something like conspiracy, or do they just call it a day because the bad guy got his?"

"Zwilling's not a bad guy?" Fahey looked at his watch; he was due inside now for a meeting with the prosecutor.

"Let's see, I represent the citizenry of metropolitan London. I don't want the public to think a nice man like Will Baumann, just helping an old girlfriend, isn't safe in this city, do I?" Claudia batted her eyelashes, casting herself in the role of the girlfriend. "Don't I want to say justice has been served? Leaving aside, of course, the fact that people end up dead if they're connected to C.J. Hart. You have such a handsome back, maybe you should watch it better."

"I didn't think you still cared. Thanks, love." Fahey blew a kiss as he dashed for the prosecutor's door and slipped inside.

"Bastard!" he heard Claudia shout.

He checked in at the desk, and a junior prosecutor assigned to the case scurried his way, hustling him into a conference room. There was a lot going on, the junior said, it might be a while before someone got to Fahey, but they needed him to stay, just in case. "First, the forensics unit was burgled overnight, six months' worth of files and samples taken, then Danshov was found dead. Everyone's in a bit of a panic; the press will have a field day when it all comes out. All they know about so far, we think, is Danshov, because someone at the detention center leaked that."

Stolen forensics the same night as a prison killing? That had a certain ring of plot rather than coincidence, at least to Fahey.

The prosecutor stormed in, looking like he hadn't slept or shaved. "Coffee," he ordered his assistant, and slumped into the chair next to Fahey. "I assume you've been brought up to speed on the events that have ruined this lovely late-summer Tuesday for us all."

Fahey shrugged. "I know about Danshov and some stolen forensics files. Is there more?"

"More? How about no chance of implicating Christoph Zwilling in Baumann's death? Rumors to the contrary, we made no deal with him, we just couldn't hold him on the little evidence we had: Danshov's contention, refuted by Zwilling, that he was hired to intimidate you to persuade Miss Hart to hand over some jewelry at the center of a family dispute. What's gone now as well is the toxicology done after his arrest that showed Danshov was as high that night on crystal meth as Baumann. That might have given us grounds at the very least for a conspiracy case against Zwilling, who does not deny Danshov was working for him as a messenger. Oh, and there was a lab report linking what was in Danshov's and Baumann's bodies to a type of methamphetamine cooked largely in Switzerland and distributed through a network based in Zurich, where Zwilling's company also is based. All circumstantial, but still."

The prosecutor took a breath, loosened his necktie, massaged no-doubt aching temples. "Without it, we have rubbish. Roundabout financials show payments to Danshov from the drug network, for whom he was a bit of freelance enforcer—notably a case in Poland last year in which he almost beat a man to death, but the man declined, on his recovery, to press charges. There was also some not necessarily reliable information putting Gregor Zwilling GmbH on the periphery of an operation that laundered cash for various Russian and Eastern European mob figures over the last few years, though the extent to which that activity was either known to or condoned by the company's management is unclear."

Not necessarily reliable? Meaning from Danshov himself. Fahey had no doubt that Christoph knew and/or condoned what went on in his business. In his experience, vampire enterprises were nothing if not diversified. Why not methamphetamine and money laundering as well as architectural detail work?

"Someone on the inside killed Danshov. Who was it?"

The prosecutor almost smiled. "That part's just too easy: a minor-leaguer from Gdansk, awaiting trial for moving heroin, brother of the man Danshov nearly killed in Poland. Turns out we should have segregated Igor in a protective block. Only shocker, in retrospect, is that it took so long for the brother to get to him. Anyway, Fahey, you're done here. Sorry to have wasted your time and Miss Hart's."

The junior returned with the coffee, likely one of many the prosecutor would consume over a day of embarrassing statements to the press and job-endangering reports to his superiors. Fahey located a rear stairway, made his way down to street level, and walked two blocks to the nearest Tube station. Before he moved through the turnstile, he checked his mobile: an outraged text from Chloe, who had heard the news; seventeen new emails from fellow journalists seeking his thoughts on the unexpected developments; and an eighteenth, with neither identifiable address nor subject line. Fahey opened it anyway.

"As you requested," the email read. Attachments, three of them, surreptitiously sent by Julian Gippel via an address

Fahey doubted could be traced back to him. Within them, lab results Fahey was now quite certain could not be replicated.

* * * *

From a table at the rear of a fortunately rather empty coffee shop, he watched the Crown Prosecution Service's televised news briefing about the morning's discovery. A prison official explained that Igor Danshov was slain at the detention facility where he had been awaiting trial on involuntary-manslaughter charges in the death of London brew master and pub owner Will Baumann. (The report cut to video footage of Danshov being transported to a court hearing last month, then to a head shot of Baumann.) The official went on to explain the high-profile nature of the case (cut away to more video, this time of Fahey and Chloe entering the court for that same August hearing). A deputy chief crown prosecutor fielded questions about the just-made decision to close the case without pursuing charges against Swiss businessman Christoph Zwilling (with video of Zwilling avoiding reporters' questions this morning in Zurich). Zwilling had purportedly hired Danshov to intimidate London gallery owner C.J. Hart, his cousin, in connection with a dispute over family jewelry left to her by her parents, deceased rock stars Sebastian and Emilie de la Coeur.

Standing behind the deputy chief crown prosecutor were the man whose office Fahey had recently left and his junior staff. The briefing lasted ten minutes, and when it was over, it was hard to tell which of the five attorneys of varying rank looked the grimmest. A case that had seemed so simple had fallen spectacularly apart, and as the on-location correspondent wrapped up, he took note of the fact that justice would seem to have eluded Baumann, an American who had made the UK his home for the past two years, and his loved ones.

As the network returned to its regularly scheduled programming, Fahey released the breath he did not realize he'd been holding. He pitched his empty cup into a trash bin and got up to leave.

He might go into work straight away, Lord knew there was always enough to do. But Fahey was reasonably sure Danshov's slaying and the now-vanished prospect of a lengthy trial would invite renewed conversations with top executives and producers about whether *Europulse* ought to do live remote feeds to promote viewership on the Continent, and he preferred to put those off for a bit. Now, he sensed, was not the time to resume his role as well-traveled journalist.

He might go back to the flat, but Fahey was certain another press phalanx would greet him there, seeking comment on the day's events.

He might go on to Aspect Ratio, but it was just after one o'clock and Chloe would have just arrived with the baby and a day's worth of duties ahead of her, in a full lather of her own about justice denied.

Fair Trade Hummus seemed as promising a destination as any, assuming the recent guests at Martine Gattus's townhouse had returned. He'd heard the New Court of Cruelty was back from two weeks in the Netherlands and Belgium, booked for another gig at the Little Goth Club. And he might have walked right up to the door, pressed the bell, and waited for someone to answer had he not seen what he'd seen as he approached: A wraith, dressed in a form-fitting aqua-and-black-striped dress that reached down to her ankles, black ballet flats, a black straw hat and dark glasses, kneeling on the walk, profile to him and nose to nose with a black Scottish terrier puppy, each with their teeth bared, the growls audible from where Fahey stood twenty feet away. Passersby were already beginning to stare.

"Chiara," he called, and she was quickly on her feet. The dog strained to reach him; she gave the leash more slack. Fahey patted the puppy's head, looked at its collar. "Mustafa."

"It means 'the chosen one.' He was not my choice, I assure you."

"Nor are you his, apparently."

"Senses a predator, rightfully so. Good thing for him I've never developed a taste for canines."

The puppy whimpered. She handed Fahey the leash and the dog began to bounce, hoping to be carried, or maybe comforted. Fahey picked him up, buried his nose in a soft furry head until Mustafa calmed enough to be set down on his feet again. "I'm guessing he demanded a walk."

"It was much earlier when he began to whine, hence my fashion choices. But once he did his business, he refused to move from this spot. He was most unhappy when he realized I was the only human available. He misses Martine, but he's far too young to travel just yet, or so I'm told. So the little beast is stuck with me for at least today, maybe tomorrow too, God help us both."

Fahey steered Mustafa in the direction of a park close to the river. They walked three blocks with the usual sniffing and stopping, and without snarling and snapping, though the puppy looked warily back at Chiara every few feet. When they arrived, Fahey let out the leash so the dog could wander.

He leaned against a tree; Chiara settled herself on a patch of moss, took off the hat and gloves.

"So, you're dog-sitting, not playing with the band?"

"House-sitting," she said, correcting him. "Ronnie insisted, said there were women wanting to audition who sounded perfect to replace Kat Nilsson but who'd never get a fair shot if I were there. No arguments, well not from me. I've read for a part in Stratford, as Miranda in *The Tempest*, which I'll very likely get; rehearsals start next week. Eric is unhappy, of course, but nothing I do will fix that. He's unhappy with me, unhappy without me; I've set his life off-axis again. If Ronnie could kill me, he would, his fingers itch just looking at me. Fortunately, he and I have an understanding after all these years."

Yes, well, Fahey mused, wasn't that what he wanted to talk about too?

Chiara stared at him; she'd heard his thoughts. "Living in

an ensemble, a collective with mutual goals, is essential to vampire survival. Hunting is time-wasting unless you're only in a city for a short time; even then, you either deal with other vampires and turf issues or chance it and get in, get what you need, and get out. A band, a theater company, a hospital, a factory, places where people join together daily in one pursuit, make the pursuit of food less predatory, more intimate for all concerned."

At Fahey's whistle, Mustafa scampered back, rolled on to his back for a belly rub. Fahey sank to the grass beside him. "What about vampire marriage?"

"And you're asking me why? Because I'm such a spectacular success at it?"

"*No playing coy, Jackson,*" her voice said inside his head. "*If you want to know, just ask.*"

"Fidelity is impossible, isn't it?"

"Only if you want to survive: One vampire cannot nourish another; the blood has to come from somewhere. And, as you know, pleasure—sexual pleasure—is all any vampire can reliably offer a human in return. Thus, infidelity is guaranteed in a union between vampires."

"So a mixed marriage, however limited its duration, has fidelity as an advantage? Theoretically, that is."

Chiara nodded. "Theoretically, if the terms of the relationship are clear at the outset. There has to be free will on both sides. Compulsion is difficult to sustain and can't, in such a situation, be particularly satisfying to either party. In my experience, vampires who hunt and kill are vampires without willing partners."

Suddenly, she was kneeling behind him, stroking and massaging his neck, kneading the knots that had formed there this morning after the email from Gippel. Flicking her tongue, tasting the skin beneath his collar, licking up the side of his throat and over his jaw. The tension ebbed, replaced by a different restiveness, a longing. She nipped his right lobe, licked away the blood, worked her way up the crest of his ear; her mouth might as well have been directly on his penis, which swelled in direct proportion to the pressure of her bite. He saw what she was doing: Who could argue in favor of fidelity when the persuasion was so pleasant and the desire so strong? She could take him back to Martine's house and have him within seconds of closing the door. Hell, even in this public park, even with the dog ready to attack her, she could take him in her hand now and milk him witless. Fahey twisted around and pulled her face toward his; he kissed her, plunging his tongue in, stroking, sucking Chiara's tongue in simulation of the act he needed but did not truly want. Not like this, not with her.

He broke away. "Point taken," he gasped.

Chiara licked her lips. "So delicious. Are you sure you want to stop?"

He wasn't and kissed her again, pulling her astride his lap, her breasts crushed against his chest. Fahey couldn't have said how long they kissed, how long he moved his hands across her dress, pressing the flesh below. He could tell there was no other fabric separating his skin from hers; he slipped his fingers under her hem, up along the inside of her thigh until he felt her wetness. His cock twitched beneath her, drawn to the warmth it sensed nearby, navigating toward the channel that would join him to this woman. All he had to do was free himself, sink into her, nothing but a zipper stopped him—until his brain engaged and reminded him who this woman was, and what she was to him.

He lifted her off his body. "I won't do this. I love Chloe, remember?" He willed himself to remember that he meant it.

Chiara smiled, amused or perplexed by his confusion, Fahey couldn't say.

"I love Christoph, I long to be with him, to be joined to him, and yet, well. . . ." She leaned in, a breast grazing Fahey's arm, its heat again torturing his focus. "This is not about sex. It's an exchange, an intercourse in the most basic sense of the word.

Sustenance for pleasure, between you and Chloe, between you and me, if you like. Achieving sustenance is pleasurable in many ways for a vampire. You understand that on one level, because you've felt it. You feel it now."

Fahey shifted uncomfortably on the grass, worked to slow his breathing, concentrated on bringing his throbbing friend under control, just the sound of Chiara's voice, in and out of his head, threatening to make him come. "It's the other level I worry about," he managed.

Chiara sat back on her heels, watched his struggle. Mustafa inched toward her. The dog knew who was in charge.

Fahey felt the caress of her voice in his groin, on his skin, against his lips, a soft, sweet mist floating around him, yet not touching him.

"We've been over this, Jackson. As a human, you have the reassurance that you and Chloe can be together as long as you both want each other. Fidelity will be possible, if that's also what each of you wants, as it would be in any relationship. You can grow old with her and your child."

"Growing old is not what I want." Fahey was sure of it, or as sure as anyone could be. "I want Chloe forever."

"Embrace your mortality and seize the time you have with her. Reconcile yourself to it, because you have very little choice. The baby changed everything."

It was true: Chloe would never try to transform him. Her one vampire life to give was most likely Avalon's, though it might be years before a blood hunger manifested, with its own set of complications. Chloe had miscarried Ava's twin, hadn't she? What more proof did they need?

"What if another vampire changed me?"

Chiara studied him. "You'd be bound by blood to that vampire forever, physically and emotionally. The bond would always draw you back to your creator, no matter who else you had pledged your loyalty to. Who would you give that much power?"

His eyes strayed to her wedding ring. Her eyes followed. "You can't be serious."

"You love the man, Chiara. You know him."

Her laugh was hollow, as though emptied of joy. "But I don't, do I?"

"So you don't trust him?"

"He had Will Baumann killed."

"You're avoiding the question," Fahey pressed. "Do you trust Zwilling?"

"What I think is irrelevant."

Yes, yes, it was his decision, Fahey knew that, and, yes, his every self-preservation instinct screamed, "Don't!" When it came to prospective vampire parentage, however, options were few.

"I don't think Christoph intended to kill anyone that day," Fahey said, wondering how much of that he believed and how much was him, rationalizing. "Do I think it was a dreadfully botched attempt at bravado, no question, but I don't blame Christoph for Baumann's death any more than I blame myself."

"That doesn't mean Christoph hasn't killed others, only that he hired better help."

"You haven't killed?"

Her eyes shimmered Emilie's brilliant green, just for a second, then turned a tear-filled hazel. "Not directly, but, yes, some died because of me. I've no desire to number you among them."

Well, then. Time to go; he had to get to the television studio. Fahey placed Mustafa's leash into her palm, felt Chiara's hand curve around his for just a moment.

"You haven't thought this through, Jackson. Christoph may have already sired a vampire. You don't know if this is possible."

It would never be possible unless Fahey asked. He yanked his hand away from hers.

"Play nice, you two. No biting."

The dog barked loudly, as if to say, "No promises."
As if there could be.

* * * *

Aspect Ratio was ablaze with light when Fahey arrived just after ten o'clock in the evening. Through the front window, he watched Benjamin, balanced on a ladder, hoisting a large textile piece into position on the main display wall. He was assisted by a twentysomething male Fahey was pretty sure he had not yet met, a new intern maybe, or just hired muscle.

Their backs to the window, Chloe and Daphne tilted their heads, assessing something. Fahey's former-videographer assessment: The piece washed out against the wall. They either needed something with more color or much diminished lighting, which wouldn't work in the primary gallery space. Heads shook; the young man dashed to the other corner and turned the lights down. Heads shook, and the lights went up again. Ben waited for his deputy, lowered the obviously heavy length of fabric down into his hands, and descended the ladder.

Fahey looked at the exhibit card propped up temporarily in the front window: "Textiles Reformed: Tapestry and Embroidered Works from Protestant Europe, 1460-1575."

More like works collected by Eugenie Verlaine Herz and Emilie de la Coeur and stored by the latter to display at her home outside Prague. These were the pieces Sebastian had mentioned in a letter Chloe found in her parents' safe-deposit box more than a year ago. She'd selected two dozen of the woven and stitched works, the ones in the best condition, some large and ready for hanging, others small and framed. Emilie had meticulously catalogued their provenance, including the details of her own purchases, complete with vendor and price, but Chloe still had spent weeks on independent verification, reaching out to every museum curator she knew from her past career. That accomplished, and climate control assured, and printing and catering arranged for, all that needed to be finished was the installation. The opening was day after tomorrow, Thursday night.

She would not be pleased. Couldn't be avoided.

"Need an extra set of hands with that one?" Fahey asked as he entered, shedding his jacket as Ben maneuvered another tapestry through the space. At Ben's nod, Fahey gathered fabric that was hanging down to the floor, swept it over his arm and took up a post at the far end of the dowel. The new guy held the ladder as Ben ascended again; Fahey pivoted to Ben's right, helping him lift the awkward rod higher into a support bracket and bracing the piece until the ladder could be moved underneath a second bracket farther along on the wall.

"You're a life-saver," Ben said when they were finished, shaking out a handkerchief and wiping perspiration from his face. "This monster was heavier than the last."

Chloe tugged Fahey's arm, pulled him toward the window, for the best view. "Jesus, yes, Jackson, you arrived just as Ben and Connor were running out of steam."

He offered his hand to the young man. "Jackson Fahey, provider of bulk."

"Connor Cleary, student of art," the young man said with an Irish lilt that reminded Fahey of his father's. "If I'd known what I'd be doing for this installation, I'd have spent some time at the gym."

Daphne fixed him with a look of sheer disbelief.

"OK, no, I wouldn't have, but it would have been a good idea."

Another arm tug restored Fahey to Chloe's side. "Better, don't you think? Doesn't wash out like the other did."

"Definitely more vibrant," he said and kissed her. She sniffed his hair, seemed to stiffen as his lips left hers. A cry from the other room gave him an excuse to walk away.

"Hello, pretty girl. How's Avalon tonight? How about a snack before we go home?" He lifted the baby from the small crib, walked to the refrigerator and found a bottle. Balancing her on his right hip, he flipped the nipple around, screwed it on tightly, and put the whole business into the bottle warmer for fifteen seconds. He settled into a chair, tested the breast milk's temperature against his wrist, and teased the baby's lips with the nipple. She was sucking at it happily and laughing, white bubbles dribbling from her mouth, when her mother appeared.

"Who's Mommy's favorite little slob?" Chloe turned to retrieve a cloth diaper from a stack on the file cabinet behind her and dabbed at Ava's chin. "She didn't get your shirt, I hope."

Fahey checked. "Maybe a little. I hope I have still enough laundered for a two- or three-day trip. We're doing a live remote from Zurich for Thursday's broadcast."

"Jackson, the opening-night reception . . ." She dropped into the other chair.

"Rotten timing, love, I know, but there was no talking them out of it; they've suddenly become sticklers about being true to the *Euro in Europulse*. They want me to do the program from the banking conference this week."

"Because now that there will be no Danshov trial, there's no reason you shouldn't leave London at the drop of a BBC producer's hat?"

Chloe seemed more eager to pick a fight than he'd expected. "Something like that, yes," he said. "It's the same conference I attended last year, just pushed back from November to September. You remember the one."

"When I dumped Will at your hotel room? Yes, I remember." She hated to be reminded of that night, just after her vampire coming out, when she'd left a nearly dead Baumann with Fahey, and then nearly died herself.

The baby hiccupped. Fahey set the bottle down, raised her onto his shoulder, stood and walked around the office, Chloe's annoyed stare blistering his back.

"It's fine; you have to go," she said. But it wasn't fine. "Fly out sometime tomorrow, back Friday night or Saturday morning?"

"One of those. My producer will text me the particulars." The baby burped, but he kept up the circuit around the desk, Avalon giggling each time he tickled under her ribs.

An uncomfortable silence settled between them. Fahey's right arm was falling asleep. He braced the baby against his chest, leaned in to hand her over, brushing his lips against Chloe's as he did.

"You smell of blood and lavender," she whispered icily, a mix of jealousy and vampire competitiveness in her tone. "I can't imagine why."

"Sniff more, there's also puppy and grass and moss and shaving cream and probably the tissue I used when I cut myself while trimming my sideburns," he countered, hoping that was all Chloe smelled.

"I didn't realize my mother was still in town."

"Back in town, I think. She said she had been in Stratford to read for a part, more Shakespeare. Oh, and Ronnie's auditioning new girl singers."

Chloe nodded, eyed him skeptically. "Don't stop now."

"We talked for a while, in the dog park near Martine Gattus's townhouse."

She sniffed again and plucked a long brown hair from his shoulder. "A dog, yes. And a bitch, in full arousal."

"They were nose to nose, teeth bared and growling, when I ran into them."

"Whereas you got a much warmer greeting." Chloe stood, laid Avalon into the crib. The baby fussed. "Too bad you're off for Zurich soon. Or is it? Maybe while you're reporting news of the European recession, you'll run into a fabulously wealthy Swiss businessman filled with special insights on one Chiara Nunnally."

She picked a strand of Chiara's hair off Fahey's collar and wound it around her index fingers until it snapped.

"Needless to say, I won't call to set up an appointment in advance."

She laughed. "He'll be aware of your presence the second you step off the plane; he'll know I'm not there with you."

"Counting on it, actually."

Her hands tensed around his shoulders, her fingernails dug into his flesh. "What's that supposed to mean? Are you negotiating on my mother's behalf now?"

On his own behalf, but Fahey dared not even think it lest she sense his motive. "I never said that."

"Shuttle diplomacy, you're Kissinger and they're North and South Vietnam? That is a historical reference you understand, isn't it, Jackson? You no longer seem to grasp the twisted history of the Herz family."

Christ, she could be a bitch, too. He let her hear that thought.

Confirming that she had, Chloe replied, "Stop trying to fix things."

Enough. He would not listen to that nonsense again. "No one else seems inclined to fix them. If I don't try, love, who will?"

Avalon cried louder. He scooped her out of the crib again, propped her up against his shoulder, facing away from Chloe. Ava twisted her head around to get a view of her mother; her little chest shuddered against his, a signal she was about to unleash a ferocious squall. The baby was as tired of this argument as he was.

Chloe patted her on the back, blew into her hair, tickled her ear, and the storm was averted. "Mommy's silly girl. Want to come?"

Ava buried her face into Fahey's shirt. "She doesn't know what she wants," Chloe said.

"An inherited trait," Fahey said in reply.

"Are you saying I'm ambivalent, or that you are?" Hands on her hips, Chloe looked as if she wanted to slap him.

"Pretty safe to say there's one thing I'm not ambivalent about. If you don't know that by now, I don't know what to think. I want you and only you. That's all I've wanted since the day we met, with or without enchanted pendants. Everything I've done, I've done so we can be together."

"Today's evidence suggests otherwise." Chloe took the baby from him, waving Avalon's little hand bye-bye.

It felt as if she *had* slapped him. Fahey rushed after Chloe through the hall, to the main gallery space, but she had already grabbed her things and walked out with the baby. He yelled his goodbyes to Ben, who was getting ready to lock up.

The street in front of the gallery was deserted. It was almost eleven o'clock, and the neighboring shops had closed for the night. She must have found a cab immediately, or else was running home under vampire power. Fahey sprinted to the Tube station, caught a train, and reached their building just as Chloe was disappearing into the elevator.

Once upstairs, he found her in the nursery, getting the things she needed for a diaper change. "Let me," he said, volunteering.

Chloe nodded and stepped away from the table.

"I went to see Chiara because I wanted to know where Christoph was, whether he'd be in Zurich. We started talking about vampire marriage."

She sighed, relieved, he hoped.

"Well, my mother would know all about that, wouldn't she?"

Fahey held up a finger to signal he wanted to finish with the baby. Chloe sank into the rocking chair behind him, its movement rhythmic as he cleaned their daughter and got her into her pajamas. He handed off a yawning Avalon, stepped away to wash up. He returned, finding them as he had left them, and sank to the floor at Chloe's feet. She looked at him expectantly.

"We talked about the third parties always involved in vampire romances. About how one vampire can't feed off another and has to find a bloodline, so to speak. The whole pleasure-for-pleasure thing."

"And she demonstrated."

"Yes," he admitted.

"And you responded."

"Yes, but I didn't want to; she's a vampire, for God's sake, she knows how to be irresistible. After today, I understand a whole lot more about your relationship with Will, and I'm sorry for giving you such a hard time about him. If I had that night with Danshov to do over, I'd figure out a way to save Will's life. I hope you believe me."

Fahey thought he saw tears brighten her gorgeous green eyes, but she quickly blinked them back. She seemed less angry, though sadder.

"Also, I had to determine whether Chiara thought Christoph could be trusted, given what we now know about him. What if he is your brother? Can you just turn away and pretend he doesn't exist?"

Chloe gave in to the tears, held the baby tighter to her chest. "I'm so tired of fighting this fight. I don't care if he and my mother never resolve their issues, I just want to know the truth, mine and his and my father's."

Fahey took her hand, kissed it. "I can make that happen for you, and I'm not just saying that so you'll forgive me for today. I don't want Chiara, the way I didn't want Kat, and I didn't want Emilie. I want only you."

She rested her cheek against his palm; she believed him. "What do you mean, you can make it happen?"

"The devil's in the DNA: Sebastian's, from the sample he gave Meredith before the phony suicide; Teppan's, from that morning with Meredith at the Castle; and Christoph's, from the swab the police took after Will was killed. It's all been cross-matched for paternity. Julian Gippel surely knows more now than is wise for us, but it was worth it. It's a story he can't repeat. No one would believe him."

Chloe's breathing grew ragged, as if she were about to hyperventilate the way she did when she was human only. "Tell me."

"I can't. If I learn the answer, Christoph will be able to pull it from my mind, and any leverage we might have will be lost."

"Leverage? What could you possibly want from him?"

Fahey put his arms around Chloe and their baby. He lowered his mouth to hers, kissed her as if he might never get the opportunity again. When he finally let her go, Chloe set Avalon down in her bed, then came back to him and flung her arms around his neck.

"Be careful in Zurich, Jackson. No tricks without a net, whatever you're planning."

One vampire had almost killed him. He hoped not to press his luck with a second.

Chapter Eleven

LONDON, MID-SEPTEMBER 2012

My challenge today: to make pestilence palatable. I am a designer for disease.

The grand tapestry that graces the main exhibition area at Aspect Ratio is a depiction of God's disfavor as revealed through an epidemic's destruction. Ironically, the piece is a vivid wheel of life's hues: the brilliant red of fresh blood; the bright blues of a sky heedless of the suffering experienced beneath it; the gaunt, yellow faces of those who stumble in the street; their violet bruises after they fall; the green grass turned to accommodate graves, and the brown-orange clay after they are dug.

What becomes a plague best? How to furnish, with but a few pieces, the space directly in front of this tapestry, simplistically titled *Demise*, to enhance the experience for the modern viewer, to replicate what contemporaries of the dying witnessed?

I have an idea, but it may be too Court of Cruelty, even for me. Ah, how my true colors show.

"A presence chamber. A dais, very low; a throne atop it, a queen's chair to minimize bulk. A rug that plays off the tapestry itself, with perhaps darker blues, to deepen the impact. A few tall potted palms or ferns, a brighter green to leaven the grim. Maybe a suit of armor, for a little medieval bling. What do you think?"

"Not terrible, if such items can be found on less than a day's notice. Or are they already in your vast inventory of stuff gleaned from Sebastian and Emilie's Prague collection?" Genevieve Hamilton, a textiles curator at the Victoria & Albert Museum, my longtime friend and mentor and, right now, my much-needed consultant, bounces a laughing Avalon on her hip. "Do you have something upholstered in purple, to pound home the royal imagery?"

I scroll through the photo files on my tablet, pull up a shot of the chair (purple, of course) I have in mind. "It's in storage, along with the rug and the armor, but I can probably have it here in under four hours. Also some standing candelabra, gilded, with thick, partially melted candles. We could build the dais from those shipping pallets in the storeroom—a carpenter could nail them together to stabilize them, if we could find a carpenter quickly enough."

Genevieve paces in front of the tapestry; Ava sucks on a pacifier, seeming fine with the monotony of the scenery. "Keep it intimidating and austere. No plants, no armor. No dais, either—superfluous, if the chair is tall enough."

I check the chair's specs on a list Daphne and I put together before crating most of the Prague furnishings. "Four and a half feet."

Gen approves.

"Let's get it in here then." I call the moving and storage company to set the delivery for this afternoon, probably no earlier than five o'clock, I am told. Benjamin and Daphne will be in at three to position tables and other necessaries for the reception area in the storefront next door, so all the caterer needs to do tomorrow is show up. Tonight will be a late one, but we'll get it done.

To keep the afternoon sun from bleaching the tapestry—a treasure I did not pay for, but that is priceless nonetheless—we've lowered and closed the blinds at the front of the gallery, yet the room feels as bright as the Sahara at noon, what with all the interior lighting. I punch up the app that controls the lights and dim the wattage just a bit. Ava notices the difference and looks up at the ceiling, a little drool dripping from the side of her mouth. Will she be such a happy baby in a week or so, once the teething starts in earnest?

The phone rings, a call on the gallery's main number. Ava twists in Gen's arms, toward the sound. The reflection of even the lowered light makes it difficult to distinguish numbers on the caller ID. We're closed, but it might be the movers, seeking some additional details.

"Aspect Ratio Gallery."

"I've a call for C.J. Hart from HMP Belmarsh. Will you accept the charges?"

The operator repeats the question, and finally I manage to say, "Yes, I will." An old-school collect call; I know only one person in prison.

"Hello?" A man's voice, familiar and not. A voice I've heard only a handful of times, but one that resonates through my thoughts often.

"This is C.J. Hart."

"I need to see you, Juliette!" he shouts.

My God, he remembers that. "This isn't a good time. I'm waiting for a delivery. I'm sorry."

He laughs, a throatier sound than I recall, likely redolent of too many cigarettes and talking over too many raised voices. "This can't wait. Come now." The line goes dead.

It's a quarter till two, just enough time to get there and back.

"Trouble, Chloe?" After all these years, Gen can read me pretty well.

"I have to run out. There's a bottle of breast milk in the mini-fridge; Ava will want to eat in about a half-hour. Give it to her and then put her down for a nap if she looks like she'll sleep. I'll be back before the furniture arrives. Thanks for baby-sitting, I owe you one."

More like six. Genevieve opens her mouth, but the objections

I expect go unspoken. Before she reconsiders, I grab my courier bag and dash.

Faster to run to the prison on vamp power than to venture out by more conventional means. I must not lose the moment. I cannot fathom why, after more than a year, he's contacted me. Adrenaline sweeps me along the miles, blurs me until, even if someone were sensitive enough to detect my motion, that person wouldn't be able to identify me as human. More like a swiftly flying bird—a hummingbird, maybe, darting amid the midday throng on London's sidewalks, hovering sometimes but never actually stopping. I've felt this way often since the night I ruined Anthony Kirkpatrick's life.

About a half-mile from the prison, I stop to pull myself together: run a comb through my wind-tossed hair, apply some lipstick (the same shade, Cinnamon Toast, I wore that night). I want to look beautiful for him, as if that will make him hate me less.

I slip into the short black boots I kicked off for my trip here and walk the rest of the way. At the entry gate, I step into the queue, allow the pat-down indignity and the bag frisk and the identification check, then flow into the waiting room with about two dozen afternoon visitors to Her Majesty's Prison Belmarsh. When my name is called, I jump, startled, this all seems so surreal.

"C.J. Hart," an officer shouts again.

I approach, and his eyes widen—he's recognized me, I think, maybe even made the connection. He hands me a visitor's badge, points to a door. "Carrel number five. No touching under the glass, nothing conjugal."

Conjugal? Under the glass? I can only imagine what prompted that warning. The security officer hands me a miniature bottle of hand sanitizer, as if he's read my mind. "That way, quickly, you've only got thirty minutes. Step inside."

As soon as I take my place behind the glass—my visit is being monitored on closed-circuit television—a wall panel slides to the left and my host enters. "Juliette," he begins. "I understand it's not your true name—women do that, give false names to men they've just picked up in hotel lounges."

"It is my true name, my middle name," I protest. "I never lied to you, Anton."

His blond hair is longer, shaggier than it was the night he was tending bar and I drank his blood, egged on by Esteban Gronlund into testing my vampire wings. Anton has bulked up a bit, his biceps strain the fabric of his shirt; his blue eyes are wary, where they had been friendly back then. He's handsome but guarded; wariness has to be a required life skill in this place.

I must be staring.

"Helps that everyone knows I cut a man's throat in cold blood. But this, you being here, that's gonna soften up my reputation. I wanted to talk to Fahey, but he's in Zurich; saw him on the news."

I nod.

"I'll have to listen to this sad lot talk about you for weeks, you know, they'll start on about my famous girlfriend, or is it ex-girlfriend? Like they don't know every word of the story already, we all know every word of every story. Just how it is in here, welcome to lovely Belmarsh."

"I'm sorry, Anton, for everything."

"Can't absolve you of a sin you didn't commit. I'm the one who was swept away by that beautiful, evil man. I still feel him touching me. I still hear his voice in my head."

That man, yes. "My father."

"Your father, Sebastian de la Coeur or Teppan Nilsson, whatever his name was. I call him the devil. I'm glad he's dead, Juliette, and don't tell me you're not a little glad, too. I won't believe it."

I won't, of course. I can't.

"Twenty minutes," a voice intones over a loudspeaker.

Anton gently taps his forehead on the glass, whispers, "Go

away, go away, go away, go away, go away," like an incantation that will shield him. When he stops, he raises his eyes to mine, studies me. "You look like him, you know."

I have his hair color, the shape of his nose and mouth. "I do, yes."

"So does Christoph Zwilling. Who is he to you, Juliette?"

Now *I'm* the wary one. "My cousin. It's been all over the news, how he hired someone to bully Jackson and my friend Will Baumann and how Will ended up dead, all because of some family squabble over jewelry."

Anton shakes his head slowly. "I'll ask again: What is Christoph Zwilling to you? I don't believe for one minute that he's your cousin or that this is about jewelry."

Can he see I have doubts of my own? "His father and my father were twins; except for their coloring, they were very similar. Zwilling looks exactly like his father."

"Too much like *your* bastard dad, in too many ways. I've seen him, he was here last night."

I know Zwilling was in Zurich yesterday morning, a news crew ambushed him outside his office with questions concerning Igor Danshov's death. Not inconceivable that he traveled to London afterward, but here?

"Belmarsh has no Tuesday visiting hours, and no nighttime visitation—the schedule's plastered all over the walls in reception, I just saw them. How could Zwilling have been here?"

"*Could you be any more naïve?*" Anton's expression suggests.

"I saw him poison a man in the dining hall last night, easy as you please, then disappear. Tell me he's not Sebastian de la Coeur's evil spawn so I can laugh myself the rest of way to madness. It'll be a short trip, trust me."

"Fifteen minutes," the disembodied voice announces.

"What difference does it make, Anton?"

"Stay away from him, that's what. You, and Fahey, and everybody else you love. Or is one dead friend not enough for you?" He reaches under the glass divider and pulls my left hand toward him. He feels the contours of my engagement ring, massages my finger. My mouth waters; I order myself to focus. Anton strokes the skin around my wrist, as I did back in that hotel bar before I sank my teeth into him and dragged him into my father's twisted plan for my future. He stares at me through the glass. *"Believe me,"* the expression in his eyes begs.

"I'm in the dinner line, getting a scoop of veggies and rice, a couple people ahead of a new arrival, Polish guy they'd just brought up from the detention center after he shanked another prisoner. Killed your mate Danshov, it seems, for almost killing his baby brother back in the old country, or that's what the chat was. Anyway, the guy at the steam table looks straight at me when he gives me my food. I swear on my mother's good name it was Zwilling, dressed just like I am now. Seen him on the news because of Danshov.

"Couple minutes go by, I'm tucking into supper when the Polish guy goes down, vomiting up his guts, then foaming at the mouth. Used to be an army medic, right, so I run over, stick my finger down his throat to clear his airway, roll him onto his side, but he starts to convulse. By the time they get a gurney to him, he's crashed, the medic has to climb on top to pound his chest, but it's over, they call time of death right there."

Anton tightens his grip on my hand. He jerks me closer to the glass, the chair moves under me, scraping the floor. "I look around for Zwilling but don't see him. I ask my mates about the new guy on the line, dishing out the peas and rice, and no one knows who I'm talking about, it's like he vaporized with the steam. This morning, I see one of the medics, sometimes we talk about the army, and ask what he knows about the Polish guy's death. Poison, he says, something quick. What more do you need to know, Juliette? He got in, did the kill, and got out. Sound familiar?"

The wall panel slides behind Anton, and a guard pushes his

way into the carrel. "What did we tell you, Kirkpatrick, look but don't touch. Time's up now. Sorry, miss."

Anton dips his head level with the bottom of the divider, brushes his lips against my fingertips before the guard hauls him back and away from me.

I wave goodbye, but Anton doesn't see.

Out in reception, I collect my bag and phone. I need to collect my thoughts as well, so instead of running back I join the flock of weary visitors taking the bus that Her Majesty's Prison Service provides to central London. My phone manages to connect to Wi-Fi; I check the national news feeds, find a four-line BBC item saying the man suspected of fatally stabbing Igor Danshov died himself at HMP Belmarsh just hours after being transported there, that authorities were continuing to investigate both deaths.

I call Jackson in Zurich, less than confident I'll reach him. But he picks up, and his voice is the most wonderful thing.

"Perfect timing, love. Need to head out soon to interview some bankers."

"I miss you. I can't tell you how much I wish you were here right now."

It's true, I can't, there are no words to articulate the apprehension I'm feeling. So I babble about our baby and the increasingly drooly signs that she's starting to teethe, and about Genevieve's consult on the exhibition. I envision him half-listening, multitasking with a script that needs completing or video that needs a voiceover—only in bed do we have time exclusively for each other. But then he says something that suggests he's been paying more attention than I thought.

"Are you on a bus? I hear voices and squealing brakes."

"Last-minute errand outside London," I lie, sort of. "Hey, did I hear that the guy who shanked Danshov is dead?"

"Yeah, weird one, that story. I called our friend, the prosecutor, for details; pending the toxicology report, he says the working theory is suicide, that the guy took something, maybe cyanide, either en route to or just after he got to Belmarsh."

How very plausible and convenient all around. "That's the end of it then?"

"Suspect so, love, not a lot of incentive to do a full-on investigation, is there? Sorry, my crew is waiting in the van for me. I'll call you later, Chloe mine. Kisses to the little one."

Which truth is truer, I wonder: Anton's or the official version? Was Zwilling at Belmarsh at all?

* * * *

Tapestries usually aren't buzz-worthy, but the brief mention Meredith, the PR goddess, has wangled for us on an influential London art blog—full of reminders about how these tapestries come from Emilie de la Coeur's remarkable collection, and how I, her daughter, am respected on the Continent as a conservator of textiles—brings most of the people who received invitations out to view the exhibit, probably just so they could say they'd been. Why ask why, when sales are unexpectedly robust? Little red dots mark the gallery cards of pieces large and small. Benjamin is taking checks and swiping credit cards with gratifying regularity.

We've positioned ourselves at our usual stations. I'm at the front, greeting our guests, answering overall questions about the exhibition, making chitchat about the more Calvinistic times these tapestries reflect. Textiles of the Renaissance/ Roman Catholic tradition are more my thing, but I've studied up on these pieces sufficiently that I can discourse my way through the Lutheran/Huguenot/Puritan era. Benjamin and Daphne circulate through the gallery's spaces, offering assistance where they can, explaining payment and delivery options. Meredith, who'll be in town for the whole two-month run of the exhibit, plays hostess over at the reception next door, networking on behalf of Aspect Ratio and making sure the champagne flows and the canapés keep coming.

About an hour in, Ben sidles over grinning from ear to ear, like me a capitalist-in-the-making. "Meredith's already landed us a corporate client. Big brokerage in the City, wants to lease a few pieces for its lobby through till the New Year."

"That's our girl," I tell her proud husband. "I'm sure there's something in the cache we still have in storage that's more festive than gruesome."

Actually, I'm not. I vaguely recall a scene of shepherds and herald angels that needs some small repairs and might be a possibility. Tackling a rehab project sounds invigorating right now, after weeks of cataloging and research. That is, after all, where my art love lies, born of the hours I spent at Emilie's feet as she stitched, staring up at the grand triptych of tapestries in my parents' bedroom at home at the Castle in New York.

As we roll into the last hour of three, I split my time between the gallery and the party, greeting return visitors to Aspect Ratio; accepting handshakes and air kisses and business cards from curators and collectors; answering questions about provenance as best I can and deferring to Genevieve about some of the younger pieces, whose era is closer to her specialty than mine.

After a while, I sense Daphne at my elbow, unwilling to interrupt anything important, but needing my attention. "Chiara Nunnally is here," she whispers. "She's not on the guest list, but I welcomed her and gave her the catalog. She asked whether you were free for a bit. I told her I'd fetch you if it was possible."

I excuse myself and cross back to the almost-empty gallery. I find my mother standing before *Demise*, the exhibit's centerpiece. I'm not surprised to see her, just surprised she has managed to stay away so long from the things she spent a lifetime or two accumulating.

Chiara paces and ponders the macabre tapestry. "I'd forgotten how arresting this piece was, how it embraces death rather than objectifies it. I bought this in Marseilles after

World War I; so many lovely artworks were on auction, so many once-noble families needed quick cash. I traveled there from New York to buy, and then had nowhere to store this great monstrosity and the others I acquired. I leased a space no bigger than a closet for years until we bought the Prague house and moved them there."

And when I sold the Prague house to Zwilling, she knew I'd move them again.

"I trusted you to love them as I did, though I guess I knew you couldn't afford to keep them all." I hear her words in my head. *"Your father guaranteed that with his messy suicide."*

So much still comes down to my father.

"Repairs to the Castle are only half-finished," I confirm, "and the craftsmen the work requires don't come cheap, as Ed Chestack reminds me weekly. Having to pay for it all just about makes him weep."

"Don't let it impoverish you, Chloe. It's only a house, and these tapestries, they're only things. Sometimes, it's good to walk away—you know that, you've done it twice."

She's trying for wisdom, but she looks so young, more like a sister than my mother. And she seems so, I don't know, adrift?

"Am I supposed to believe that?" I ask. "You miss your things. You miss your house. You were happy at the Castle, and that's not just some childhood delusion of mine, I remember Emilie happy. But you're stuck, aren't you? You wish you could go back, but you can't. You wish you could start over, but you can't. You killed off Kat Nilsson, but here you are, right back with the New Court of Cruelty, with not one but two new versions of Daddy, leaning on Eric because you can't have Zwilling and making yourself miserable."

Shining past Chiara's hazel is something of the green eyes I inherited from her, from Emilie.

"Mom," I whisper, and wrap my arms around her, but she stiffens.

"For a century and a half, I was part of a pair, and then

suddenly I was not. All those decades, most good but many not so good, your father was there to remind me who I was. Even when we lived apart, and we did for years at a stretch sometimes, we found our way back to each other."

I lead her to the queen's throne and make her sit. I sink down to the floor at her feet. "Tell me, please. For once, just tell me what your life has been, so I'll know, when mine becomes like it."

She runs her fingers through my hair. "*His hair,*" she says, though she is silent. "*So much of him lives on in you.*"

"After you left for Cambridge without a word of goodbye, ablaze with that teenage rage you spent a dozen years burning off, I was angry, too, Chloe, at myself and at Sebastian. I walked out of the Castle a week later and stayed away for six years. I threw a dart at a map, moved to Pakistan, and enrolled in medical school in Lahore. Crazy hours, plenty of available blood, a sense of purpose. Just what I needed."

Explains a lot: how she knew what to do with a newly transformed, pregnant vampire; how she knew I was about to give birth; and how she was able to tutor Will on delivering the baby.

"You were the doctor at the morgue in Dundee, weren't you?"
She nods.

I do the historical math. "Those years you were away, that's when the Cruel stopped recording and touring. That's when Daddy took up art photography seriously and started this gallery with Esteban."

Tears shimmer but do not fall; once again, she will swallow rather then shed them. "I pushed the Cruel out of the limelight; it would have happened eventually. But I couldn't stay away, I didn't feel like myself without Sebastian. I still don't: He was my husband *and* my vampire offspring; those bonds don't die with the man. Genevieve told Jackson I was a coward, all too willing to overlook my husband's flaws. Turns out I'm also quite good at overlooking my own."

Chiara slumps lower in the purple throne set before *Demise*, looking defeated yet regal. "My cowardice has trapped me here, in this half-life: with Eric and not wanting to be with him; married to Christoph and expecting him to be someone he's not."

"You love Christoph."

"I do," she says, "but I wanted to love him, didn't I? I wanted the promise of forever. Instead, my false start with him may bring a quick divorce."

Considering what I've learned about my cousin/possible half-brother, that might be a good idea, though fraught with its own peril. Who knows what lengths Zwilling might go to keep her?

"Anton Kirkpatrick says Zwilling murdered the man who killed Igor Danshov—walked into Belmarsh, poisoned him in the middle of the dinner crowd, then disappeared, all neat as you please. Sounds like something Daddy would have done, no? Like father, like son?"

She laughs at me, Emilie's laugh, too knowing to be merely playful; even when I was small, there was always a message in it somewhere.

"Do you believe Anton?"

"I believe he believes it. He asked what Christoph Zwilling was to me, and when I told him Zwilling was my cousin, Anton wouldn't accept it. He sees Daddy in Christoph. You do too. Yes, maybe you saw what you wanted to see at first, but you see the real man now, don't you?"

"The real man? I'm not certain he and I have met. But I doubt that knowing who his biological father is will do anything for Christoph but give him a convenient self-fulfilling prophecy to hang his misery on. If I were the most loving of wives, I couldn't conquer that."

Which would be the harder legacy for Zwilling to accept: Gregor Herz's depression, domestic violence, and suicide, or my father's depravity, manipulation and murder? Neither gives me any comfort, not with Jackson planning to serve as messenger.

"Jackson is in Zurich. He intends to tell Zwilling he has the DNA evidence that will set the record straight once and for all. He thinks it will give him some kind of leverage. I don't know what he thinks he's bargaining for."

She rises so swiftly, her regal chair tips over. "We need to stop him. Jackson mustn't confront Christoph with that, not alone."

"I have a child to worry about, and this gallery, this new exhibit. I can't run off to Zurich because you say so."

"Leave the gallery to your partner. Where is Avalon now?"

"Jackson's parents have taken her to stay with them. It's her first time at their place overnight."

"Make it two nights," my mother insists. "They'll all survive, unless you've seen signs of vampirism already."

I shake my head, I haven't. "Don't think Jackson will be grateful to have us rush to his rescue. He has too much manly pride for that."

Her fangs descend slightly, she's losing patience. "I'd prefer shattering his manly pride to having his manly blood spilled again, wouldn't you? Have you forgotten what your father did to him?"

Melodrama is not my mother's thing. She's always the cool head that prevails, but there's a panic here I've never sensed in her before, a lot like the dread I feel myself.

Go, we must, she says. So go, we shall.

We agree to meet in an hour at Martine Gattus's townhouse. A quick call and a little white lie to the Faheys, in which I plead a work emergency, an unexpected opportunity to meet in Prague with an artist I've been dying to have sign with Aspect Ratio. They understand, they say, no trouble at all since it gives them a chance to spend more time with their granddaughter. She's an angel, they say. I cross my fingers.

The last opening-night visitors to "Textiles Reformed" are

making their way out, and Benjamin stands at the bar with a couple dripping in couture. A pen is poised over a checkbook, about to inscribe an amount corresponding to one tapestry or another. No time to find out which; I snag Meredith to let her know I'm leaving.

"Jackson and Christoph the Terrible, enough said. What's the plan?" She asks because she loves me and knows anything having to do with my vampire relatives is an exercise in chaos.

"I'm not sure yet, I'm following my mother's lead here. If you don't hear from me by Saturday morning, call the media in and tell them Jackson is missing."

As I start for the door, I feel Ben's eyes on me and Meredith. He knows something's up. I wave and leave it to Meredith to fill him in. He'll worry and fret that he should be able to protect me, though he has no clue how bad things might get. I don't have a clue either.

Some instinct turns me back toward my office, toward the safe. I retrieve the two pendants, mine and Jackson's, and drape both around my neck. Warmth suffuses me, a gentle caress. I choose to take it as a good omen.

* * * *

When we walk into Jackson's Zurich hotel about four o'clock in the morning, the desk clerk stops us cold, shakes his head like a bobble-head doll and rattles off a string of no's, *neins,* and *nyets*. I am wearing a black leather jacket over a sleeveless black-and-white knit dress and black knee-high boots. Chiara is in a short red skirt with a black top, a red leather jacket and red heels.

"We are not prostitutes. Jackson Fahey is my fiancé," I explain in French, fixing the man with my vampire glare to compel his cooperation. "Call his room, I need to contact him immediately."

"He checked out about ten o'clock," the clerk says, and spins his computer screen around to show me; it reads, *BBC Fahey/*

O'Neill/Mincavage, 34E-36E-38E. "His colleagues remain. If you would like to talk to one of them, I will call."

Jackson worked with O'Neill and Mincavage in Brussels and insisted on bringing them to London for *Europulse.* "Did Mr. Fahey ask the concierge for help with any travel plans, or leave word for his colleagues where he was going?"

"No messages were left," the clerk says. "He did ask for a cab to be called, saying he wished to go to the Czech Airlines terminal. I had just started my shift, but I overheard."

I hand the man a twenty-pound note, with apologies that I have no Swiss francs. I give him a rueful smile and rush off with Chiara to regroup.

"Go on ahead to the Prague house," she says. "I'll check Christoph's home here. They know me, and if I show up in person, they won't dare turn me away or refuse to reveal his whereabouts. He won't have told anyone that we're estranged, he's too proud for that."

"I've tried Jackson's mobile twenty times. Even if he had to wait to get on a flight, he's probably in Prague by now. He should be picking up."

Why isn't he? If anything has happened . . .

"Tap into your blood bond, Chloe. It's strong, even more so since Avalon's birth. What does it tell you?"

I close my eyes and feel for it. I listen for the sound of his blood in my ears, in my head, through my body. "His heart is racing, he's worried or hurried, I'm not sure which. Agitated."

"Go," my mother orders, "I won't be far behind." As she opens the door to the street, she adds, "We need to find those DNA results. Christoph mustn't get them first."

A chill creeps through me as I imagine the consequences Chiara foresees. I call Jackson's phone again, but a recording says his voice mailbox is full. I try texting, but the message freezes on my screen. If he left no word for them at the desk, he must have told Mincavage and O'Neill in advance that he wouldn't be heading back to London with them. Is it possible he dropped off some of his gear, maybe his laptop, so he could travel lighter?

I circle back to the front desk, fix my eyes on the night clerk until he focuses completely on me. "I'll need the room keys for Mincavage and O'Neill." Without a word, he complies, collects key cards for 36E and 38E. I step into a waiting elevator and glide up three floors.

A sign in French and German points the way to the rooms I need. I take a chance that the order of names on the registration is the order of occupancy, as well—that I'll find O'Neill, the videographer, in 36E. He and Jackson have common interests; they are friends from back in Afghanistan, where Jackson shot video for the BBC until the ambush that took out the NATO unit he was embedded with and thrust him into the role of reporter in front of the camera. I cloak myself in shadow and hunt for a familiar black leather backpack. I locate it in a corner near the bathroom, nestled up against a camera case of rigid plastic and a tripod.

I slip Jackson's computer out of the backpack, slip quietly out to the hall. I sit on a square of teal and gray carpeting, greatly relieved to discover the laptop charged and Wi-Fi available. I've seen him log on a thousand times; I close my eyes, focus on the rhythm of his keystrokes, more right-hand motion than left, an eight-letter/four-number log-on that will get me into the server and then into his account. His password is always some number or punctuation variant of *Guinevere*, after the baby we lost. I guess at Gu!nevere5, for the five months he and I have been back together, and I'm in. Never again will I tease him for being sentimental.

He seems to have cleaned out his inbox recently; the email and attachments from Julian Gippel are at the top of the list. Because this account is synchronized to his phone, whatever mail I find now Jackson can also access. The same goes for his losing whatever I delete.

I open Gippel's email, view the attachments, memorize the

conclusions, and send the communiqué off into the trash bin, which I instantly empty. I check through four days' worth of email Jackson has sent; he hasn't forwarded this material to another account. My hands shake as I violate his trust. The dawn is coming, and I must hurry. My head pounds with the bass line from Court of Cruelty's classic "Heir Presumptive." I hear Sebastian's baritone impart a cynical lesson: "Take care whom you empower, lest you weaken your own grip."

I've empowered myself; it's the best I can do. I send Jackson an email he'll know could only have come from me:

"It's my DNA, too."

Chapter Twelve

OUTSIDE PRAGUE, MID-SEPTEMBER 2012

Sleep was not Fahey's friend, though he was back at a hotel he'd stayed in before, back in the village just up the road from Sebastian and Emilie's former estate. He passed the night fitfully, dreaming of Chloe, of feeding her, of making love to her, a dream that was on a continuous loop. As the thin light of the new morning stole behind his bed, he was hot and hard as stone. He kicked off the sheets and wrapped his right hand around that part of him in most urgent need of relief.

"You *are* the handsome specimen, aren't you? Little wonder my wife so enjoyed your interlude in the park the other day."

That voice, lacking warmth that might define it as even partly human, cut through Fahey's half-awareness. He shifted his hand, restored the covers to his midsection.

"No need for modesty, nothing I have not seen before. I try to choose wisely: amply proportioned young men eager to please. Someone like Anthony Kirkpatrick, willing to do just about anything in return for a fucking he'll never forget. If there was any doubt Kirkpatrick had forgotten his rendezvous with my late uncle, you should have seen his face during my necessarily brief visit to Her Majesty's Prison. Such a mix of bald desire and blatant horror—I found it quite stimulating."

The sheets snapped back, exposing what remained of

Fahey's erection. His eyes tracked the accompanying laughter to a shadowed corner near the door, as far away from the east-facing window as possible. Fresh late-summer sun fingered its way through half-parted sheer white curtains, casting Fahey's body in a striated glow that might, under different circumstances, be conducive to intimacy. This not being one of those circumstances, Fahey was instead grateful he had thought to reposition the bed closer to the window before retiring last night, just in case.

A throatier laugh, more feral, reacted to Fahey's recollected stratagem. "Clever *and* well-hung; a shame you have put yourself out of reach. Conversation rather than sexual congress it shall be then."

How, Fahey wondered, did he ever think to give this man the benefit of the doubt?

"If it was you Kirkpatrick saw at Belmarsh, it must also have been you who arranged Igor Danshov's death. Employee loyalty seems to count for nothing with you, Chris."

Zwilling dragged a chair into the still-dark corner. "One ties off loose ends before one is ensnared by them," he said, sounding the resigned, weary businessman.

"About loose ends, I believe there is one I can take care of for you." Fahey stood and slung the top sheet around his waist, careful to stay within the sunlight's protective field.

"Yes, you said something about a trade. If you want Chiara, Fahey, I shan't get in your way, however much I might wish to. I suspect dear little Clothilde would object though. Quite the woman, with her mama's fire and her papa's fury. Too bad she might be my sister."

"You're wasting precious time," Fahey reminded. He walked in the light's path to the bathroom, relieved himself, returned wearing yesterday's jeans, and sat as squarely in the sun as he could and still be able to look Zwilling in the eye. He grabbed his watch from the nightstand: It was already nearly seven o'clock. He estimated Zwilling had five minutes before leaving this room was no longer an easy option.

"You do want to know whether Sebastian de la Coeur was your father, correct? I have that information."

Zwilling dared to move closer, the better to intimidate. They stood toe to toe, almost face to face for several seconds before Zwilling retreated into the room's shrinking shadows. "How?" he asked with a rasp.

Fahey detected the smell of something singed and inched back toward the window, toward the wand that would allow him to sweep the curtains completely open and let the sunshine burst through. "Very simple: DNA—yours, and that of the man Stefan Herz became."

"The man who let the dawn set fire to him in his own home, by his own design, after almost killing you, Fahey. There was nothing left of him."

Oh, but there was.

"The Metropolitan Police in London obtained your DNA when they picked you up for questioning in connection with Will Baumann's death. A sample of Sebastian's DNA—or rather Teppan Nilsson's—came directly from his ejaculate via Meredith Grainger-Todd. They had sex the day before he died. I saw her before she'd had time to shower and, dear friend that she is, when I asked she collected a sample and gave it to me. I gave it to those investigating the deaths of the four sex workers found buried on the grounds of your new home, the former de la Coeur estate."

Zwilling clapped appreciatively. "Bravo, you are far more twisted than I gave you credit for. But more stupid, as well: I can easily compel you to reveal the information I require or scan your brain for it in a most unpleasant manner. "

Fahey gently tapped the curtain wand, widening the way for the incoming rays ever so slightly. "I said I had the results of the lab analysis, not that I knew which conclusion had been reached."

Zwilling bared his fangs, threw the chair at Fahey, and

swiftly opened the door to the hallway. As he vanished, his voice vibrated through Fahey's skull: *"Be at the house at noon, not a minute before."*

Any earlier, Fahey knew, and maybe both of them would end up dead.

A pot of overpriced room-service coffee, a couple of croissants, and a shower invigorated Fahey sufficiently to remember that he needed to charge his phone, which he'd shut off as he left the Prague airport so it retained the little juice it had. He plugged it in, watched text-message notifications march down his screen, all from Chloe, all asking him to call, or asking where he was, or asking why he wasn't calling. Nothing wrong with the baby, he hoped. Just Chloe wanting to talk about how the opening went at Aspect Ratio, he hoped.

As his pass code faded from the screen, the counter on his email app showed the usual several dozen on his BBC account. His personal account showed only one new message since he'd last cleared the inbox. He opened it to find an email he'd sent to himself.

Except he hadn't.

"It's my DNA too," it read.

An earlier email, the one with the attached lab analyses Gippel might have risked his career to get to Fahey, was gone.

* * * *

Autumn's promise stretched ahead of him, all red and orange and gold, a brilliant display of majestic trees and falling leaves, but Fahey found it difficult to concentrate on the scenery as he walked to Sebastian and Emilie's former home, now among the vintage architectural assets of Gregor Zwilling GmbH. Avoiding this appointment was not an option. Arriving without the goods, also not a wise idea.

He considered stopping at the coffee shop where he'd set up an impromptu office some months back, to visit with the owner/barista awhile, but that would just be postponing the inevitable. Fahey couldn't fathom what possessed Chloe to put him in this position. Whatever her reason, she apparently no longer wished to discuss it. She wasn't responding to texts or calls, and Fahey couldn't envision how she'd defend her actions anyway.

"Tell Christoph the truth," he imagined her saying. "Tell him I deleted the information before you looked at it. He'll know if you're lying, don't even think about it."

Except he could think of nothing else.

About two kilometers outside the village, there were fewer buildings and the road wound higher and tighter through the hills, affording a great view of the valley below but lousy sightlines of traffic ahead and behind. It wasn't until the long black limousine was upon him and failed to speed by that Fahey realized he was being followed. At the cutoff for a scenic overhang, the limo swerved across his path and the rear passenger-side door flew open. A muscled arm thrust out and hauled Fahey into the car, tossing him onto a seat as the driver burned rubber pulling back onto the thoroughfare.

Fahey's head hit the door handle on the far side of the car. He felt blood drip down the left side of his face, closed his eyes until the flashing lights behind his eyelids subsided. His stomach lurched, and he thought he might lose his breakfast. He righted himself slowly, leaned back against the soft leather, rested his head gingerly.

"Make yourself comfortable, we're going on an adventure. You've already seen my new home; I thought we would visit the town in which I was born. It's a lovely corner of Bohemia, especially this time of year, all crisp breezes and clear afternoon skies. A lovely place for a boy to grow up in the bosom of family. All of it stripped from me, when I was just seven years old."

Every bounce of the tires was like a hot poker to Fahey's head. The limousine had to be moving twice as fast as a vehicle its size should be, given the narrow road.

"It's a seven-hour trip, but that may be insufficient time for me to decide what to do about you. You don't have those DNA results, do you?"

Fahey opened his swelling left eye, saw Zwilling lounging on the bench opposite. "Chloe hacked into my laptop and deleted the email before I could read it on my phone. She knows whether your DNA plus Sebastian's equals paternity. I don't."

Brown eyes blackened then turned red with rage. "Such a stunning fool you are. She's compelled you to forget what you learned from the lab analysis because she doesn't want to give me what I want. She blames me for killing her precious Will Baumann, whom she loved so dearly."

Fahey sat forward, immediately regretted the dizziness it caused. It couldn't be true, she had never compelled him, would never compel him. "Chloe loves me, we have a child together, a future together. She stole the lab results before I saw them."

Zwilling's red orbs glinted white hot in the dimness. "An ill-conceived power play," he growled. "Clothilde doesn't realize what she's playing with, does she? Stupid girl doesn't comprehend just what it is you had hoped to trade the information for. Only a vampire's life everlasting. What else could I provide?"

"*You want to be sired.*" Zwilling hissed, his voice inside Fahey's head. "*I want to know what it's in it for me.*"

A forearm solid as a steel bar slammed him back against the seat, and Fahey felt his left shoulder separate. Incisors punctured the skin of his throat, bearing down until a vein opened. A large hand clawed at the collar of his jacket and shirt, and the humid warmth of a mouth descended on the wound to drink, the light stubble of a beard scratching Fahey's neck as a head moved over him.

Fingers tore at his fly and ripped open his zipper, pulled him from his trousers and grabbed the erection rising there. Pumped him in tempo with the drinking mouth until he climaxed and came into the grip that held him fast, until he was hard once more and aching to come again.

A tongue lapped at the clots on his neck, and the head lifted then lowered toward his hips. A mouth covered his cock and drained him until there was nothing left inside.

Gratification ebbed into humiliation and exhaustion into pain, as blood loss and dehydration dragged him from consciousness.

When Fahey came to, he could scarcely see. Shades had been drawn over the windows; the only light came from a lamp over the limo's bar. Zwilling cradled a snifter in one hand, his other arm thrown across the back of his seat. His eyes lowered to Fahey's crotch, and he smiled, knowingly.

Fahey was relieved to find himself still seated, his trousers still in place, though his zipper was open, his well-exercised prick peeking through. Blood and semen stained the fabric covering his thighs.

Zwilling leaned forward, tucked Fahey back into his pants, and tilted the snifter toward him, the brandy's potency inescapable.

"I thought your vampire code required you to give pleasure in return for sustenance?" Fahey barely managed to say.

"It's a more-or-less agreed-upon convention, hardly a universal decree. Oh, and don't delude yourself: You were quite pleased." Zwilling leered, slithered closer. "I could make a habit of you—it *would* be my prerogative as your sire."

Fahey willed himself not to recoil. Yes, sires had their privileges, the depraved consequences of a corrupt bargain; he'd known that going in. He knew what he wanted, and this man had just violated him because of it. He slipped past Zwilling to reach the limo's bar, poured some brandy for himself, and drank it down to wash the image away.

"Vomit in my car and I'll have to kill you, Jackson. Don't test me."

Fahey grabbed the bottle, raised it to his lips defiantly and drank, Zwilling's unwavering stare disturbing him less with every mouthful. Eventually, the alcohol, coupled with the motion of the car, lulled him to sleep. Chloe's voice whispered to him, as if she were there beside him, her head on his chest, her lips moving against his skin.

"Christoph won't believe anything you say about the identity of his father."

"I don't know who it was, I can't tell him anything."

"He prefers to believe that you know, and that I won't allow you to tell the truth. That gives you power."

Fahey kissed her hair, stroked the side of her face. *"Ignorance gives me power?"*

"Yes."

The limousine jerked to a stop, pitching Fahey onto the floor, onto a sticky patch of carpet; sticky from what, he didn't have to imagine.

"Disgusting."

Zwilling threw a container at him—baby wipes, the same brand sitting on Avalon's changing table in London right now. "Clean yourself, adjust your clothing. We're almost there."

"Where's there?" Fahey needed water, and aspirin, his throat felt like he'd swallowed ground glass.

"The house where I was born, where I lived with Marie Beatrisa and Gregor Herz, the man who may have been my father."

"Which man does he want to be his father?" Chloe's voice was clear, but Fahey wondered: Could he believe anything the voice said?

* * * *

At a dark turn in the road, the limousine pulled over and stopped. Zwilling prodded Fahey's injured shoulder. "Get out."

"What? Here?" Fahey felt for his phone. It was gone.

Zwilling kicked him out and exited behind him, carrying two electric lanterns. "We're walking into the town. The car will attract attention I'd prefer to avoid. The townspeople will overwhelm us if they are permitted."

No idea what that meant, Fahey struggled to his feet, took the lantern Zwilling held out. It was cold and black out there, and even with the lanterns they'd probably be mowed down by a truck. So much for immortality.

"How far, sire?" Provoking a vampire was never the best course, but this one had gotten on his last nerve.

"Two kilometers. You can see the dome of the Church of Saints Stephen and Gregory from here." Zwilling lifted his lantern.

"Quite the coincidence, that name. Not two saints one generally hears paired." Fahey was raised Anglican, but he thought he knew at least that much about saints.

"If one is Armenian Orthodox, one might. The church was built in the 1990s, after the USSR fell and an immigrant community formed here. An anonymous donor underwrote the design and construction."

"An ingenious way to honor his brother. I assume that's what Sebastian, or rather Stefan, had in mind."

Zwilling brought his lantern still higher, illuminating his own face, his anger obvious. "It was Emilie de la Coeur who donated the money. She signed the checks my company received as payment for locating icons of the two saints and installing them here. She's good, my wife, such a subtle quid pro quo. As the priest told the story, Emilie gave the congregation what it needed on two conditions: She would select the name, and she would decide the location—the scorched earth where Gregor Herz's forge once stood and where he made her precious pendants. I shall take you there for a tour shortly."

Fahey feared this fit of vengeful nostalgia did not augur well. "A church hardly seems the appropriate locale for me to sign my soul over to the devil, Zwilling. I'd envisioned someplace profane rather than sacred."

"Thus my mother's cottage will serve, since she conceived me there in either an act of rape or one of infidelity. It's just beyond that bend in the road, where the streetlights begin. Interesting, don't you think, that Gregor Herz thought to house his wife at the farthest edge of the village from his forge? God knows, I spent decades trying to escape her."

"Running away from home is a pattern for the Herz offspring: first you, then Chloe."

Zwilling's eyes glowed a wolf-like gold. "A trait shared by siblings, perhaps."

Country road turned to village lane, and the pair came upon a dwelling that seemed uninhabited but not derelict.

"The local citizens keep it up, restored it with my permission and my money. It's a landmark now. Tourists visit."

Fahey raised his lantern, noticed plantings along the path to the door, and flowers in boxes beneath each window. "Why is that?"

Gold eyes turned dark brown again. "A tunnel runs under the cottage back to the woods; many a Jew fled through the tunnel during the war. A family, eight members in all, hid in the root cellar under the house, under my protection for six years while I lived above as Gregor Herz's grandson, a man returned to the land of his ancestors. Nazi bastards had no idea."

"I wouldn't have pegged you as a humanitarian."

"No one takes what is mine. The Nazis seized this region too easily. Those people remembered family I lost or never knew. I would not allow the Germans to intimidate them," Zwilling said. "After the war, after I left, when the Communists tried to raze the cottage, the neighbors protested, for more or less the same reason: What was theirs, was theirs—their property, their legacy, not a government's to destroy."

Zwilling unlocked the door. For more light, he struck a match against the jamb and lit the wicks of a waiting candelabrum. Revealed was a room Fahey guessed was last decorated, minimally so, in the 1930s.

"An old woman gave me this furniture when I arrived with nothing but a bedroll. I recognized her immediately; she had been my playmate. It was as if she had been watching this house for years, expecting me. She remarked how much I looked like her friend Christoph, whom she presumed had been my grandfather and who had been taken to Switzerland when his mother remarried. She had missed him, she told me. I had not intended to stay more than the night, but I could not leave, that would have been too cruel, even for me."

The confession surprised Fahey. "You could not leave again with danger at hand. She was your friend, and she needed your protection."

Zwilling shrugged. "A stroke took her within the year. My protection was worthless." He pushed past Fahey, into the space beyond.

In the main room, the candles' light danced on glass fitted into nine frames hung on the wall facing Fahey. He moved closer and, squinting at each, recognized them as citations to those who had escaped certain death in this house. Czech words he deduced meant "honor" and "courage" were inscribed under each name, including the name Christoph Herz.

On a table in the center of the room lay a book, opened to a page with about twenty signatures. A guest book? Fahey examined the entries. The most recent was smudged, as if a tear had smeared fresh ink: *Chiara Nunnally*. He fingered the pen; it was moist to his touch.

A familiar fragrance of lavender floated up, as if rising from the page. Zwilling rushed back into the room, sniffing the air. "She was here."

"Yes, and recently." Fahey tapped the book and was jolted backward by an electric current coursing through his uninjured shoulder.

Zwilling seized the book and knocked the pen to the floor. Ink leaked and sparked up, igniting the paper. The pen levitated, wrapping fire around his left hand. He dropped the book, and it set the floor ablaze.

"Water, Fahey, outside!"

Fahey ran into the darkness. He banged his recently replaced knee into a pump, kicked around until he found a bucket. Backed away as the front wall of the cottage incandesced with the glow of the flames devouring it.

Zwilling struggled through the smoke, across the small square of lawn, shouting for the water, his voice leading Fahey and the bucket toward him and away from the wooden structure, now so much kindling.

Into the water Fahey carried, Zwilling plunged his left hand. Steam rose, blinding them both, the water simmering then boiling over the sides, scalding Fahey, poaching Zwilling's already burned skin. Fahey dropped the bucket, and tongues of fire leaped from the rubble of the cottage toward Zwilling, catching onto his ring, the one Chiara had given him. The rubies glowed red over his smallest finger.

"Pull the ring off!" Zwilling raged, the smell of his incinerated flesh inescapable.

Fahey gagged and covered his nose with his shirt.

"Get this fucking ring off my hand or I will kill you where you stand!"

He wouldn't have to: If Fahey dared step closer, the flames would jump to his clothing and set him alight as well.

"I can't, Chris. You have to pull it off yourself." He tested the handle of the bucket, hefted it again and doused the vampire's sleeve with the water that remained.

Using teeth that could flay a man's neck, Zwilling slit the sleeve open, and wet fabric slipped away. He shook it over his fingers. "Jesus, God, it's coming off! Everything's coming off!"

The ring skittered past Fahey's legs, landed in the grass, igniting the blades around it. Next to fly by was a blackened object, a small thing that smoldered on landing at Fahey's feet. Zwilling fell to his knees, keening in pain.

Fahey circled around the object, turned it over with a twig.

A charred, severed finger.

Zwilling's eyes gleamed white in anger and agony. Blood dripped onto the grass, extinguishing the fire that had just disintegrated a part of him, each wet hiss followed by the man's mournful shriek. Fahey reached for the finger, which pulverized on contact. The last of the now-cooling rubies sputtered, then shattered.

"She did this!" Zwilling screamed. He ran past Fahey into the night's blackness, leaving a luminescent trail of blood in his wake.

What choice did Fahey have but to follow? What the hell had just happened?

* * * *

A sliver of moon hung in the sky, the only light that remained as Zwilling's wound sealed and the hemorrhaging stopped. Would the finger grow back, Fahey wondered? Regenerate like a lizard's tail?

A hand slapped him, its heat strafing his skin, the stench of burned meat settling into his pores as surely as the imprint of its four fingers etched his face. Fahey snatched at his cheek, shielding his eye, flashing back to the death acid Teppan Nilsson's immolating body had splashed onto him.

The hand shimmered in the darkness, silhouetting Zwilling as he gulped air, seeking oxygen as if it had the power to extinguish his misery. "Go back," he ordered. "Find the finger; find the ring that witch cursed me with."

Brilliant and beautifully calculating she might be, but Chiara was no witch. Enchanting perhaps, but no sorceress.

"Why bother with ash and gravel? That's all that's left."

"Don't be a fool. Destroy them and she'll have no more power over me."

Fahey felt no compulsion to move, no pull to obey.

"Go!" Zwilling thundered, but the words were nothing but noise.

"I won't. The only power Chiara has over you is her love, and you're a fool if you believe otherwise."

Fahey strode in the direction of the church; he could just

make out its golden dome, outlined by the sparse moonlight.

"Just as your father's love still exerts its power over you," he said, glancing back over his shoulder. "You know whose son you are. Every bond you feel to this town brands you as the son of Gregor Herz. Admit it, Chris, and let the past be."

"Liar!"

Fahey knew it was the truth, no matter what the DNA revealed.

Chapter Thirteen

BOHEMIA, SEPTEMBER 2012

Each time flame touches wick, a new color sparks, cerulean, crimson, indigo, animating the saintly images in the stained glass before me. After years spent steeped in European iconography, I recognize them immediately: Saint Stephen, first martyr to the cause of Christ; Saint Gregory the Illuminator, who converted Armenia. The windows' symbolism here is obvious; my mother's proprietary behavior in this sanctuary, less so, but I've learned it is best not to question some things. She guards her secrets closely, reveals her motives when she is ready, if at all.

Damp envelops me. The scant candlelight only just relieves the darkness. The pew I slump into is hard and cold against my head, against my back and thighs. It may be sacrilege to sleep here, but my eyes struggle to stay open. We have run a thousand miles today, searching for my mother's husband and the man who wants to be mine. She has no blood bond to rely on in the search for Christoph but understands how his particular vampire mind works, she says. I *do* have a bond with Jackson, but it's one I'd prefer not to exploit, given the vampire in question.

Jackson's BBC London producer called me several hours ago, when the rest of the crew returned from Zurich without him, saying that Jackson hadn't checked in, and that his mobile last pinged in the Czech Republic west of Prague. Maybe somewhere between the village near my parents' former house and the hamlet my mother and I now find ourselves in? The Zwilling corporate offices, Christoph's homes in Zurich and Lake Como—we have looked for our men everywhere Chiara thought might be a possibility. She's been wrong so far, her insight proving less than reliable after all.

This church is a destination of last resort, she says. She paces the center aisle, then the space in front of the altar, possessed of—or perhaps by—an energy I cannot muster. I close my eyes.

A knee touches the marble floor, and she speaks softly, but not to me. *"Pardonne-nous nos offenses, comme nous pardonnons à ceux qui nous ont offensés."*

"For which trespasses do you want God the Father's forgiveness?" I ask.

"Any of them; all of them. Missteps, miscalculations, some minute, some monumental, several lifetimes' worth."

She pauses, as if assembling a list of her transgressions, picking among the small and large for the one she regrets most. Minutes tick by. My eyelids go heavy; I want only to rest, not to hear her confession. She's made mistakes. Haven't we all?

"I knew what Jackson intended," she whispers. "I should have warned you."

I rearrange myself on the pew; follow the sound of her voice over to the filigreed altar screen before which she prays. "Warn me now. What did Jackson intend?"

"To tell Christoph definitively who his biological father was. In exchange for the information, Jackson hoped to persuade Christoph to sire him. He wants to become a vampire, so he can be with you forever."

I sink my fingernails into the pew, slice through varnish and wood until I am bleeding. It's all I can do to keep myself from raging at her and squeezing her by the throat. My father, my vampire sire, was caught off guard by my strength. Surely

I am stronger than she is; surely I can punish her somehow for failing, yet again, to tell me an essential, urgent truth. The pendants, already heavy around my neck, grow weightier. I visualize strangling her with the longer chain Gregor Herz unwittingly fashioned for his brother. In this moment, I hate her, and I hate the thought of Jackson becoming like her, like me.

How much, I wonder, does Zwilling despise her for the lie he fell in love with? Did he think to grant Jackson's wish so he could exact some kind of revenge on my mother through me? What havoc have I wrought by foiling those plans?

"Jackson has nothing to trade, no DNA results. Unless he managed to retrieve them from an email backup, Jackson met Christoph empty-handed. I deleted the information from his phone before he could read it. He doesn't have the answer Christoph wants."

If Jackson were dead now, I'd know. I'd sense when the blood bond severed, wouldn't I?

"Chiara, why have we come here?"

"Because we eliminated all the obvious alternatives. The closer we came, the more my intuition screamed that whatever Christoph has decided, to kill Jackson or turn him, he will bring Jackson to this town, where Christoph breathed first, and ultimately to this church, where his father breathed last. Gregor's forge stood here, on this now-sacred ground. Whatever the circumstances of the fire, Gregor Herz died on this now-holy spot."

"So we wait for them to magically appear?"

"We reached the cottage before them, and it's been hours since Jackson's phone was heard from. They must be nearby."

The pendants, Jackson's and mine, start to radiate heat, warming the skin of my neck. I close my eyes and see him closing the distance, moving toward me, racing here. I feel rumbling, something vibrating to my right.

A ball of orange light crashes through the windows, slashing through the air, raining glass knives on top of me. Sharp, slicing shards. My blood flows everywhere the shards strike. Drops of it fall to the floor, catch fire, burn as they hover over the mosaic inlays. Flames lick at my legs as I dive into the space between the pews and shield my head with my arms. I will myself to remain conscious. Death by a thousand cuts takes on a whole new meaning. The odds of a fatal vampire hemorrhage, I don't want to calculate.

Moans rise from around the altar. I prop myself up on my elbows, inch my way along to the end of my pew, just enough so I can see up the aisle. My mother lies under a kaleidoscope of shattered glass, layer upon layer pressing on her chest, on her limbs.

Vampires, I am told, defy old age and live indefinitely because they can redirect energy and regenerate cells. But she's been crushed—if she can't get free, will her body fail her?

I haul myself to my feet and proceed cautiously through the debris. What remains of Saint Stephen's visage shudders with each labored step I take; the glass and lead strain, threaten to fall on me. Nothing survives of Saint Gregory's window save the sandals peeking out from under his bishop's robes; the pieces of his image have buried Chiara from chest to toes, compressing vital organs.

"Mom, can you hear me?" I stroke her cheek; her skin is icy cold. The contact ignites the smaller of the pendants around my neck. A length of its gold chain melts into the skin of my chest, taking my breath away. I gasp for air, wrap my sleeve around my fingers so I can pry the chain off. I manage to lift the nearly molten metal away and onto the leather collar of my jacket, insulated for the moment.

"Chloe . . ." A feeble moan and her eyes roll upward. "The ceiling . . ."

I follow her glance to the cracked skylight above us. The glass image of the ascendant Christ is pulling away, about to descend swiftly and destructively. I must move her, but with each step, new cuts and burns sap my strength. I have to replenish the blood I've lost, in addition to getting some into her. But we have no supply, and no time to spare. A slab of blue glass splinters and lands inches from my mother's head. I bite into my wrist and let my blood drip onto her lips. She licks at it feebly.

A pounding at the door sends more glass cascading from the faux heavens.

"Come out, witch! Come see what you've taken from me—it will be the last thing you ever see."

A more ferocious blow to the steel church door fractures the skylight instead, destroying the glass and the ceiling around it. For safety, I scramble behind the latest round of rubble that pins my mother to the floor. The impact of beams and bricks striking marble rattles the structure.

"You can't stop me with an earthquake, darling Chiara. I'll drag you into the rising sun and watch you fry. You destroyed my father's life. You destroyed what we might have been to each other."

"No," she gasps. "Christoph . . ."

Something batters the door a third time. The outline of a fist takes shape in the steel, not quite breaking through. A bellow of anguish follows from outside. The last of Saint Stephen crashes down and blocks my view of the entrance. The smaller pendant roasts another few inches of my skin, burning through the leather and the fabric of my clothing underneath it.

My rubble bunker shifts and knocks me over. Everything goes black.

* * * *

I am lying down, but the world around me sways, as if I'm in a sleeping car on a train. A gold chalice rolls away, ricochets off a mound of glass, then rolls back toward me.

Voices. Outside, I think. No, inside. More glass falls from the windows where the images of Saints Stephen and Gregory once presided. Another orange light streaks by and caroms off the opposite wall, knocking plaster down, revealing lath beneath. The pendants sear my throat. I lift myself onto my hands and knees, and the pendants swing down, away from me. Fire drips from them and races along to the edge of a carpet too close to where Chiara lies immobilized. I pull my arms from my jacket, maneuver the pendants into one of the sleeves and tie it off. The bundle sags from my neck, drags me down until my chin bounces. The sound of shouting pulses through the hard floor.

"Something is blocking this door! It won't let me push through."

"You said you worked on this church, Zwilling. Suddenly you need an invitation to enter?"

"It's her, Fahey, she's doing it. Chiara, you witch, let me in there so I can wring your neck! You've ruined my hand!"

The fury in his voice startles my mother awake. "I didn't," she says, so softly I can barely hear her. "Tell him I didn't . . ."

I crawl to her, kiss her forehead. "Don't waste your strength worrying about Christoph's accusations. All that matters is that Jackson is here. We'll get you out, I promise."

I have no idea how, or whether it's even possible. I rest my forehead against the marble, letting the floor take the weight of the jacket and the fiery pendants. Crying out might bring more of the building crashing down on us. Can't risk that.

"Jackson, the church is collapsing. My mother is mostly buried under fallen glass; she'll die if we can't free her. I'm too weak; I can't do it on my own. Get help, please."

Even these few unspoken sentences make me dizzy. I want to shut my eyes and sleep, but I feel my mother's breath, she has turned her head toward me.

"I'm so sorry. I love you, sweet Chloe. Tell him I love him. . . ."

"Shh, don't." I can't bear that she wants to spare the feelings of a man who stands cursing her just outside, laying more sins at her feet.

"Look at what she's done to me, my duplicitous vampire bride! I seek redress, nothing more than what I am due in recompense for what she has taken from me."

I spin quickly toward the voice, too quickly—the pendants slip from the jacket sleeve and brush my jaw, burning their way up to my ear. But a scream of agony dies in my throat as my eyes register a figure up in the space once occupied by the saints' windows: Zwilling, his left hand raised, light sparking gold off his wedding ring. A crust of black has formed where his smallest finger should be and wraps up his forearm to the elbow.

"Now do you see, Clothilde?" he bellows.

"What I see is your wife lying crushed under the weight of two stained-glass windows. Get in here and help her." I retie the pendants in my jacket sleeve and point to the space where she lies. "Chiara won't be your sacrifice, not tonight, not unless it's over my dead body."

I follow his glance, sense the twist in his gut, the one I also feel, as he recognizes how tenuous a hold on life she has. Zwilling punches at the air before him, recoiling as if he's struck a wall.

"The church won't let me enter. I couldn't help her if I wanted to."

"And you don't want to? Even if you don't love her now, you loved her once, even I could see that much. She loves you; she wanted me to tell you that. Will those be her last words: a pledge of her devotion to you, you undeserving shit?"

"She did this to me!" His condemnation echoes off the church's three still-standing walls.

"I don't know who did *that*, but I can assure you it wasn't her. I might have; she wouldn't."

He thrusts out his arms, falls back from the window. I hear him hit the ground below and run off.

That's it then. I edge as close to Chiara as I can and tear my jacket off, slashing the fiery metal hanging from my neck into the wrist I haven't already punctured. A vein empties onto my mother's lips. Despite a new collection of burns, a chill courses through me. She gave me my life. I'll give it back to her now, if I must.

"Take it, Mom. Drink, Emilie."

* * * *

Warmth seeps into me, past my lips, into my limbs, washes over me. My eyes flutter open. My mouth is locked onto a wrist, a beautiful masculine hand, its long fingers clenched in pain, but unmoving, unyielding.

"Take it, love. Chloe, drink."

When I can focus, Jackson's face appears before me, his features handsome and strong. But where at a moment such as this his body might melt into mine with desire, he leans away, favors one side. His left arm hangs limply as the other is welded to my face. With every gulp, I see him wince then smile weakly. His crotch bulges; his eyes cloud over. I swallow and gently push him away.

"That's all I need."

He stares at me. The blood coagulates on his wrist and the wound there closes. He regains his sense of who he is and where. He surveys the many lacerations the fallen glass has carved into my exposed skin, scans the bloodstains on my clothing. "You're sure? Saving Chiara won't be easy."

"Then you'll need your strength too, won't you?"

He nods and rolls away, wincing again. It's his left shoulder. I reach for him; he pulls back.

"It's badly sprained, I think, but not broken. Between us, we have three good arms; we can move her."

He scrambles to his feet, extends his good arm to help me up, raises his hand to the burn on my neck.

"I've had enough of these things to last a lifetime." Jackson tosses the pendants across the sanctuary. Sparks fly, but the rubies quickly cool down, their blazing red taming to a dull rust.

"They're demonic, I swear. Mustn't let anyone else be hurt

by them." Jackson retrieves the necklaces, stuffs them into his pocket. I'm not sure what he means by "anyone else," but I can't disagree with the sentiment, not with blisters forming on my throat and pus oozing out of them. Disgusting. I slip back into my jacket, gingerly settling back into the leather, the better to dig through jagged glass.

Gently removing pieces from the pile atop my mother's body, we stack them onto an altar cloth to be dragged as far away from her as possible, hoping nothing will shift and do further damage to her or the fragile structure that surrounds us. Jackson transfers the larger lethal pieces over to the far side of the church, away from the window wall. I see the pain in his face, but he soldiers on.

Progress is slow and exhausting. The glass bounces the little light we have back at us at odd angles, until a shadow falls over the sanctuary: Zwilling, back up where the windows once stood, a brighter sky behind him.

"Less than three hours remain until dawn. How is she?"

I press my fingers to my mother's neck, feel for a pulse. "Still alive, barely, no thanks to you."

He nods solemnly. "Not yet, no."

He beckons to Jackson. "The tunnel is open back at the forested end. We will be able to bring her through there."

"Is this end clear?" Jackson asks.

What are they talking about?

"I could pass only halfway through. Whatever bars me from this church also keeps me from entering the tunnel under it. But I was able to shine a light to the point where the tunnel divides into two paths. The way was clear." With a rope, Zwilling lowers a lantern; somehow, it makes it through space he cannot travel. "I also have acquired some road flares that will provide sustained light. Take a few now; I will place the rest at the midpoint, along with some food and bedding. We will have to spend the morning there, as far back from the portals as possible."

He lowers several large garbage bags down from the window ledge. "There's bottled water and some ibuprofen. Swallow a few, Fahey, it will ease your shoulder's inflammation."

Jackson drops the altar cloth between us, and with one arm collects the bags. "We just about have her free, but we still have to ascertain the extent of her injuries."

Zwilling points his charred stump at what remains of the altar. "There is a trap door. Look for a brass plate bearing my company's name. Press on it and turn counterclockwise and a portion of the floor will slide open. A ladder will take you down to the tunnel. Use one of the flares to discover whether debris is blocking any of the steps. I will go see to our accommodations."

"We'll need ninety minutes more here, at least."

"Work quickly, Fahey."

As Jackson gathers the supplies, I pull matches from his back pocket and light every candle I can find—we've just about depleted the sacristy's stockpile, but we mustn't waste battery power or the flares. When I return, I press my ear against Chiara's chest. Her breathing is more even, but still shallow. I can't tell whether she is asleep or unconscious, but she is, at least, still with us. I stand, numb, watching for a sign she knows I'm here, her face ethereally lovely, like that of an angel hovering between heaven and earth.

Jackson's good arm encircles my waist; his lips brush the top of my head. "She's made it this far. That has to be a good sign."

Who can say? I'm starting to believe less and less in vampire immortality. Still less do I want to believe that I am so insufficiently invincible I must rely on Zwilling to save her.

"I don't understand it. One minute Zwilling is shrieking that he wants to kill Chiara, and the next he's strategizing how to rescue her."

Jackson grips me closer to his chest. "He wants to kill her. Doesn't mean he wants her crushed to death by a supernatural storm of glass. Where's the fun if *he* doesn't get to actually punish her? After that email mischief of yours, you're lucky I'm not the nasty badass he is. I might just as easily want to kill you."

He bites down hard on my shoulder, hard enough to make his point: Jackson wishes he could hurt me, just a little. I deserve it; he deserved better from me. But now is not the time for that confrontation.

"You two have a plan. What is it?"

"*Christoph* has a plan." Jackson walks to the part of the sanctuary Zwilling indicated. "Here's the brass plate with the Gregor Zwilling company imprint. Can you give me a hand here?"

I put my weight into turning the brass plate, and as promised, a slab of marble flooring slides open, revealing a dark void.

"What's down there?"

"A Nazi-era tunnel that runs under this property out to some woods at the edge of the village. The Jewish family Christoph rescued, the one whose picture is at Marie Beatrisa's cottage, this tunnel is how he smuggled them into hiding." Jackson looks at me curiously. "You must have been at the cottage with Chiara, you know the rescue I'm talking about."

"And after we somehow get Chiara through the tunnel?"

"We'll stay there until after noon, of course, when it will be safe for the three of you to be outside. He'll arrange for a car to meet us. We'll get Chiara to a place where she can recover—a place where we all can recover." He pulls his arm away to rub his aching shoulder.

Why do still have my doubts?

"Zwilling despises me, behaves like a madman where my mother is concerned, and Lord knows how he thinks to manipulate you. We're supposed to trust him not to trap us in this tunnel, leaving Chiara to die and us to starve? No, wait, I guess I could postpone the inevitable by draining you dry."

"Would you die, trapped without blood?"

"I have no idea, I left my vampire handbook back in London."

He turns me around to face him, points to his right jacket pocket, where he's stashed the pendants. Smoke rises from a hole that wasn't there before. "Read up on these bloody things when we get back there, will you? I'd love to know what they're up to, all of a sudden."

He grabs a lit candle from the branch on the altar and strides to a side chapel, searching for something. Testing a door, he kicks it in when it doesn't budge. He glares at me, an unmistakable "get your ass over here and help" look.

I pick my way around the mountains of excavated glass and peer inside, where I see a trove of white linen cloths.

"Just what I was hoping for. Wet some of these and clean Chiara's wounds," he says, "then wrap whatever needs a tourniquet. We can't risk her losing more blood, right?"

Definitely not. I claim a stack of cloths, sort through to identify the strongest, and start ripping them into long strips. "Let's save the biggest ones to use as blankets. If her body is too weakened to vampire-heal, she might devolve back to human and go into shock. We need to keep her warm."

As Jackson drags load after load of Saints Stephen and Gregory's iridescent remains away from the trapdoor, I surround my mother with the water bottles and makeshift bandages. I wash the shallow cuts that have stopped bleeding, then bind them and tie off the ends of the strips. Several huge gashes on her scalp are still trickling blood. I cradle her head and wrap a long swath of linen around it repeatedly. Within seconds, she has bled through in some spots; I'm afraid to apply too much pressure. Lower down, ribs protrude from huge twin gashes in her chest. Her stomach is bruised; she must be bleeding internally. Her right leg is positioned at an unnatural angle.

Skating around on the blood-slickened marble, I sweep smaller pieces of glass aside and spread out the largest of the altar cloths, about seven feet of often-washed fabric. A shroud more than a blanket. I squat down, ease my forearms under Chiara, and, lifting with my knees, get her onto the linen, gently settling her and folding it around her, careful not to further damage her leg.

"I couldn't have moved her. Well done." Jackson flashes a thumbs up.

"My mother is strong, iron-willed, powerful. What's done this to her? What could cause a fireball like that, capable of bringing a church down around us?"

Rhetorical questions. He can't explain a supernatural maelstrom any more than I can.

"Love, while I scout the way ahead with the flares, you'll have to carry her to the trapdoor. I haven't quite worked out how we'll lower her down into the tunnel, though."

I haven't worked out how I'll maneuver her in any direction without making things worse, but he's right. I'm the one with two fully functioning arms.

"How did you hurt your shoulder?"

"Really, does it matter?"

"If it has something to do with Zwilling, it matters. Why should we trust him to do what he says he'll do?"

Jackson kicks still more glass out of the way. "We've got less than an hour until dawn brings a flood of sunshine through that hole in the wall. What else matters but getting out of here?"

He drops down through the trapdoor and disappears.

Chapter Fourteen

BOHEMIA, SEPTEMBER 2012

So fast was he plummeting into the black void, it felt as if he were flying—until his body slammed into something solid and sharp.

Impaling himself on the side rails of a makeshift ladder after dropping into an abyss was too simple a way to die, given his last brush with mortality. That dreadful morning at Castle de la Coeur with Chloe's father flashed before Fahey as he bounced repeatedly off the length of rough lumber. He knew he would not die this morning either, and was aware that, once again, it was not for any lack of stupidity on his part.

The splintered wood that tore through his leather jacket ripped the material cleanly before it finally snagged on a thickly rolled seam, slowing his momentum, preventing injury of an irrevocable nature. His right side was scraped raw, his ribs bruised, but the ladder had broken what might have been a crippling impact with the tunnel's floor. Fahey had grossly underestimated the distance he would fall, but his knees were still intact, both the one he was born with and the replaced one acquired after that December day at the Castle. He couldn't vouch for his left ankle. Fahey hoped the snap he heard upon landing was a rung breaking rather than a bone.

"Holy Mary and the saints, thank you." He took a deep

breath of the tunnel's musty air, and his ribs howled. "I think."

A road flare sailed down from the sanctuary above, landing maybe three feet away, followed by a green-eyed angel wearing torn black leather, just like him.

"Jackson, oh my God, I smell blood."

Chloe sank to her knees in the space just below the tunnel's entrance and sucked on the damp denim covering his right thigh, reaching up to open his zipper and tug his pants down. She licked at a small divot in his skin, tucked her tongue into it.

She patted down his right side, feeling for more wetness. She found the tear in his shirt and followed her hands with her mouth, cleaning him, feeding off the few small cuts. Fahey felt faint, though from pain, relief or arousal, he couldn't say and didn't much care. She kissed him hungrily then pulled him down to sit.

"Promise me you won't try that again."

"It was exhilarating."

"Idiot." Chloe kicked the ladder away from the hole above them. "That thing was ready for the junk heap even before you hit it."

Idiot, he was, indeed. "It was bad enough I failed to note just where the bloody ladder was before I jumped. How in hell do we get Chiara down here now?"

She picked up the flare she'd sent down to light her landing—oblivious to the heat it gave off—and walked several yards farther into the tunnel. "Chloe's Vampire Express. If I get a running start, jumping fifteen feet or so up into the church shouldn't be a problem. Then I'll jump down with my mother."

"Is that a good idea?"

"Do you have a better one?"

He didn't—but still objected. "You've been cut and concussed, burned and bleeding. And, sorry to put it this way, but Chiara is more than one hundred pounds of dead weight."

"I carried Will Baumann across France and much of Switzerland. He was seventy pounds heavier and almost a foot taller than me. Remember, Jackson?"

He remembered. That trip had nearly killed her and Baumann.

Fahey felt rather than saw her vault past him and seize the edge of the church floor. The fading light from the flare cast a halo about her perfect bottom as she hauled herself up inside the sanctuary.

* * * *

The tunnel veered off by several degrees every few feet, and the height of its roof varied with alarming frequency. Fahey held the electric lantern high and hunched low to protect his head as they moved through; his damaged shoulder protested loudly. Chloe gripped Chiara tightly against her chest, supporting her mother's head and back with one arm as she held her mother's legs around her waist with the other. So far, each flare Fahey lit had lasted about ten minutes. They had four flares left, roughly forty minutes to find their way through to the end of the passage. No way to know how far away that was. No way to know where, or whether, Zwilling would be waiting for them.

Chiara moaned; she was still alive. Fahey turned, waited for Chloe to catch up, leaned in toward her mother's face.

"Do you want us to stop for a bit? I think I see a straightaway up ahead."

"*Stone*," Chiara said wordlessly.

He looked at Chloe, uncertain if she had heard as well. "What does she mean, 'Stone'?"

"*Stone! Stone! Stone!*"

He dropped the lantern, tried to beat the echo of her cry out of his temples with his hands.

Chiara writhed, trying to free herself. Fahey saw despair in her eyes. Chloe set Chiara down then caught him as he sank to the tunnel floor. She grabbed a flare, lit it, and pitched it into the darkness.

"Rest here, I'll see what's up ahead."

He banged his head against the wall behind him. It was stone, of course, as were the disintegrating walls of the church above them. Pain jolted through his shoulder again, and a searing heat burned at his midsection. From his pocket, a ruby flame stole through the hole the pendants had made. He shoved his hand in, felt it blister as he pounded the wall behind him to smother the fire.

"*Stone!*" Chiara lifted her head, lifted her eyes to his. "*Blood!*"

"What are you talking about? I scarcely bled at all after I hit the ladder. I'm not bleeding now."

"*Stefan's, Chloe's!*" her panic tortured him. "*Christoph's, Gregor's, mine, all here! It will kill us all!*"

Her body jerked, her head bounced convulsively against the packed dirt. An opaque white liquid trickled from behind her left ear. Fahey scrambled to her side, forced his arms underneath, pulled her limp-again form onto his lap.

"Chloe, come back!" he screamed, as Chiara's words reverberated through his brain.

How many minutes passed, Fahey wondered, before Chloe hurtled through the black toward them? She swept the lantern across Fahey's face, startling him away from Chiara's prophecy. He saw Zwilling race toward them, saw Chloe pull her mother close, to shield her.

Zwilling stopped short, dropped to his knees, fell unconscious on top of them. Chloe kicked his suffocating weight aside, slapped him back to awareness. Fahey battled to slow his breathing, to force down the vomit climbing his throat, to ease his threatening-to-explode head. He rubbed at his temples, but he could not silence the sound.

"She's terrified," he said. "Screaming at me about stone, about how all our blood is here today, and your father's and Gregor's too, and how it will kill us all."

Fahey rose to his feet as if levitated. Chloe supported him with one arm as she hoisted Chiara onto her shoulder with the other. "Run like hell, Jackson! Don't look back!" They raced through the emptiness, as if fleeing Sodom. "The church can no longer protect us."

It hadn't protected them at all, though, had it? Was that what Chiara was trying to tell him? Fahey turned, shone the lantern back on Zwilling as he closed the distance between them.

Chiara suddenly levered herself upright, propelled herself out of Chloe's arms, and landed spread-eagled in the space separating her daughter from her husband.

Hemorrhaging from eye to elbow, Zwilling scooped Chiara up and cradled her against his chest. "Damn me, I still love you," Fahey heard him confess.

"Keep moving, wait for us up ahead!" Zwilling commanded, then he bit into his lips and fastened them, bleeding, to Chiara's open mouth.

Fahey felt his shoulder leave its socket as Chloe dragged him, in agony, into who knew what.

* * * *

They ran blindly, the lantern dangling from Fahey's ruined arm, banging against his thigh, its glow illuminating nothing that could tell them how far was far enough.

Tremors shook the earth beneath their feet. Small geysers of blood erupted from the dirt, spurting up and licking at their heels. Rocks fell around them. Fahey turned and saw the glimmer of a flare, its light dimming as the passage filled rapidly with debris.

Chloe stopped, to let him catch his breath. "It was all in vain, everything we've done. My mother will be entombed in there with Zwilling."

"You saw what she did, love, she vaulted out of your arms to be with him. It's what she wants."

"Stay here," Chloe ordered, "I'm going back."

Falling debris gouged his side, scoring the skin. Through the hole in his jacket, Fahey again saw a ruby burning bright.

Stone and blood, Chiara had shouted in her delirium: hers and Chloe's and Stefan's, Christoph's and Gregor's. Everyone's but his.

All were in danger of dying, she'd said, but Chloe's father and Gregor were gone already, and Chiara and Zwilling, as vampires, were technically dead. So was Chloe, Fahey supposed. She had transitioned from one type of life to another before his eyes during those terrible days at his Brussels flat last year. Only he remained as he had been born.

He blocked Chloe's way. "No, I'll go. It has to be me. That's what your mother was trying to tell me. Something about blood and death that does not include me."

She stared for a second then stepped aside, understanding, though Fahey wasn't totally certain he did. He folded her against his chest and kissed her. Chloe twisted out of his embrace, seized his arm and pulled, popping his separated shoulder back into position. The pain stopped his heart, and just as quickly was gone.

"Trust me to take your breath away again and again when this is all over," she said, pressing their last flare into his hand.

Fahey retraced their steps, picking his way through mounds of rock. A sulfurous smell assaulted him; a current of blood flowed toward him, splashing him, soaking into the cotton of his jeans. He trudged against the viscous red tide, until it pinned him where he stood.

"Don't come any closer!" Zwilling warned. "Go with Chloe to the camp I've set up at the end of the tunnel and wait there until you hear the village clock chime the noon hour. When the twelfth bell tolls, go out to the edge of the woods. My car will be waiting for you."

A pendant's clasp slashed into Fahey's flesh, urging his feet forward through the blood. "You expect Chloe to leave her mother behind, after all she's been through?"

The tunnel quaked with another tremor. "Stone!" Chiara

shrieked, her voice piercing through the roar of the collapsing walls.

"Jackson, get her out of there!" Chloe yelled, nearer than she should be, given where Fahey had left her.

"*I* will care for my wife. Escape is your priority, you have a child to consider. Must I compel you to obey?"

"Stone! Now!" Chiara entreated.

Zwilling swept Chiara up into his arms again. Fahey caught him off balance and yanked them closer to the tunnel's end. Zwilling bared his fangs, anger dripping like venom. Submission, Fahey knew, was what Zwilling demanded, comeuppance for his having dared to take charge. But to claw back the power, Zwilling would have to abandon Chiara, and that, Fahey wagered, he would not do.

"Chiara believes I'm our only hope—*your* only hope, Chris. Now get the hell out of here!"

Zwilling grudgingly obeyed and ran toward Chloe's voice.

Fahey waited until they were out of sight. Waited until he could no longer hear her screaming over the blood torrent raging toward him.

He ripped the smaller of the two pendants out through the hole in his jacket and lobbed it down the tunnel in the direction of the church. The angry rush of liquid fire turned and followed it.

The larger pendant, he smashed repeatedly against the tunnel floor, pounding it until the ruby ignited and the chain's heat forced him to let go. In seconds, the pendant pulverized, stone and metal both, and there was nothing left but iridescent dust. Fahey didn't wait to see what more might happen. He ran as fast as he could, flames singeing his behind, acrid smoke filling his lungs until he was sure it would eat its way through him, skin and sinew and bone.

* * * *

Chloe slept, heedless of the candy wrappers and water bottles and empty blood bags strewn about them at the tunnel's farthest edge, as far as possible from the fires that smoldered. As each hour chimed out in the village, Fahey startled awake, smoke and dust stinging his eyes. He counted the tolling bells— eight, then nine, then ten—listening for the one that would liberate them. Eventually, he gave up trying to rest. Instead, he watched the patch of ground opposite, where Chiara lay in her makeshift shroud. Watched Zwilling pace around her like the caged beast he was.

"Stop staring, Fahey," Zwilling growled when the eleventh hour tolled. "I'm not going to eat her."

"The gazelle is cornered. How simple to fire that one perfect shot that will finally rip her out of your heart?"

Zwilling's eyes turned a red-rimmed black, and his thoughts bit into Fahey's head: "*Better to devour you, perhaps, and make you my bitch for eternity. Take that sweet cock of yours as often as I liked. Remember how much you liked it, Fahey? Remember the bargain you hoped to make?*"

Fahey pressed Chloe to his side, revolted by the compulsion Zwilling threatened. His cock stirred anyway. Chloe felt it; in her sleep, she stretched and rubbed up against him, until he was as hard as the rock underneath them.

Zwilling's laughter woke her.

"Jackson and I have unfinished business, cousin. He is ready enough, as you have noticed. A well-placed bite, an expert coupling, and he is mine."

She reared up, shielding Fahey with her body. "I promise you epic hell, *cousin*, if you coerce Jackson into this. You will not sire him unless I hear him say the word."

"Forever with you is all I've ever wanted, love, however loathsome the price."

Zwilling applauded. "How sweet, quite the romantic hero, aren't you? Now, if Clothilde will lift her compulsion from you, we can finalize our exchange."

Not with her watching, Fahey didn't want Chloe to see him demean himself that way.

"*Don't worry*," her voice whispered inside him.

She knelt before him, placed his hands on her knees and covered his hands with her own. She gazed up at him, and her green eyes glistened with something Fahey had not seen there before. "You are free to give Christoph his answer, Jackson. Tell him who his father is."

Her eyes glowed white, then changed back; Fahey was sure he had imagined it. He yawned then stood, soothed somehow. From the box of supplies Zwilling had prepared, he took a bottle of water and a package of peanuts. He tore the small bag open and downed the nuts in a single gulp.

"My patience wears thin, Fahey."

He sipped at the water, capped the bottle, and handed it to Chloe, brushing her fingers with his. Electricity coursed through him, the way it always did when they touched. He broke the connection reluctantly.

"The answer? You've always known who your father was, Chris. You adored him; you look like him. How can you doubt Gregor Herz was your father?"

Would the pendants have reacted to his pronouncement, Fahey wondered, had he not destroyed them?

Zwilling sat quietly, long enough for Fahey to resume his place next to Chloe and finish the water. Long enough for Chloe to build a mental wall around his thoughts, he could feel her in his head, guarding him from compulsion. Long enough for Fahey to consider whether any part of the last twenty-four hours had been worth what Zwilling had to offer.

Zwilling closed his eyes. "It wasn't suicide, my father's death; my mother did not lie about that, at least. They found him at the forge. He had fallen and struck his head, dropping a mallet and scattering ashes that started the fire. He had been drinking, the fire brigade said, his breath smelled of alcohol. They pulled his body out of the burning building and carried him to our home. He must have been alive still, but barely. I remember a terrible scorched smell and his blood dripping onto the floor near the hearth. I remember my mother screaming that the blood would curse us for life. About that, she also did not lie.

"The day we were to leave for Switzerland, I ran off to the forge, to see it once last time. I had a small knife my father had given me; I sliced my hand open before I left our cottage, so my blood would mingle there, and here, with his." Zwilling covered his face and wept.

At the cottage where Gregor and Marie Beatrisa Herz had made their home and raised their son, that son's hand had just been sliced again, or rather partly burned off, and his blood shed anew.

Blood and stone, bond and sever—Fahey saw the pattern so clearly, as if it were etched into the walls around him: The pendants had the power to attract and repel, like magnets; the rubies burned hot, drew strangers together and made them lovers, he and Chloe were proof. Reverse that power, and the stones went cold and murderous: Tons of leaded glass had exploded out of stained-glass windows. A church had been destroyed. What else could be responsible?

Six years earlier, his own blood must have somehow doused one of the rubies at Sebastian de la Coeur's photo exhibition at Aspect Ratio, when the family chose Fahey to woo Chloe. But today, because Chloe fed off him as he bled at the bottom of the ladder, Fahey's blood did not soak into this earth, where the Herz forge once stood. Nor had he shed blood on the grounds of the Herz cottage.

Chloe had bled upstairs in the church, when the windows honoring Saint Stephen and Saint Gregory exploded, glass cutting into her like so many deftly aimed daggers.

Chiara's blood was everywhere: As Eugenie Verlaine, she had immersed the rubies in her blood before giving them to Gregor Herz to fashion the pendants that would draw his twin brother to her. As Emilie de la Coeur, she had passed those pendants on to her daughter and Fahey. She had carved pieces off the rubies to create Zwilling's ring, had bled nearly to death here when the church windows toppled onto her. And Gregor Herz's head had struck the ground at this place, a bloody blow that would claim his life and end it at the cottage.

Blood and stone, bond and sever, it fit together, like a puzzle. Except a piece was missing.

Zwilling rifled through the supplies he'd brought, searching for something. Fahey walked up behind him, and Christoph handed over two parcels, a knowing smirk crossing his hard, handsome features.

"Replacement passports. No doubt Clothilde traveled here by unconventional means; one might say you did as well, Fahey. A stroke of good fortune, in the end: An outlier proved to be what was needed, someone without the complicated history, the complex blood ties."

"I am the outlier, as you say, but hardly unconnected to your family. My daughter is the granddaughter of Sebastian and Emilie de la Coeur. Chiara's granddaughter, and the descendant of the man you knew as your uncle, Stefan Herz."

Zwilling pulled a blood bag from the supply box, bit into it and drank. When he raised his head, he flashed Fahey a fiendish red smile.

"My Uncle Stefan? I hardly knew the man. He swept in, rearranged my mother's life, and reordered my existence. He stole my childhood and my family from me and swept out again. Had I known him better, I might have recognized him much sooner as the famous Sebastian de la Coeur. I might, indeed, have succeeded in slaying the king. My biggest regret."

"He never came to the forge when you were a boy? Never visited at the cottage?"

"Never. He was the specter who haunted our lives, in them but untouchable."

The village clock began again to toll the hour. This was the one: eight chimes, nine . . .

"When the twelfth bell peals, we'll be free to go—or have you had a change of heart, cousin?" Chloe eyed Zwilling warily.

"You *must* go," he replied, and positioned himself near the tunnel's portal.

Chloe threaded her fingers through Fahey's and guided him to where her mother lay. She knelt and kissed her cheek. "You'll always be Emilie to me; I love you, Mom. I hope you'll be well again, but I can't bear to leave you with him."

Fahey crouched and tugged Chloe to his side. "We have to get back to Avalon. Come visit us in London, Chiara, as soon as you're able."

He and Chloe pushed the tunnel's portal open, and sunlight peeked in. A familiar black limousine coasted to a stop near a stand of trees. Chloe raced for the car and jumped inside. Fahey turned in time to see the portal close again. The noon hour tolled a brilliant autumn afternoon.

* * * *

The limo quickly covered the miles, pulling over after about an hour at a landing strip just off the road. A large private jet idled on the runway. The driver handed each of them a small suitcase. "Compliments of Herr Zwilling. You will find all you need."

Lord knew, Fahey stank dreadfully, was famished, and wanted to sleep for six or seven days. For a woman who'd been through what she had, Chloe looked and smelled remarkably fresh. A vampire thing, he supposed.

Once they were airborne, Fahey availed himself of the opportunity to shower. Hot water eased the ache of his injured shoulder and the sting of the nicks and bruises he suffered in his encounter with the ladder. When he returned in a clean sweater and slacks he recognized as Zwilling's, Chloe slid out of her seat, donated suitcase in hand.

"My turn to wash up. You should eat," she said, pointing to a covered plate of chicken and pasta a flight attendant had delivered in Fahey's absence. "I tasted it. It's good."

Food was far from his most urgent need, though. "Will you

marry me in London, tomorrow or the next day, however quickly we can?"

Chloe's eyes widened in surprise. "These last days have been unsettling, and there's still the matter of Zwilling becoming your sire. Don't you want to resolve that first?"

Fahey brought her right hand to his lips and kissed it reverently. "Marry me while we still have some time."

An enigmatic smile was her response. "It's not as if you'll look like a lecherous old stalker next week, you know. We have years. Are you sure you even want this?"

"You are the only thing I'm completely sure of."

"So you keep telling me. It's among the many reasons I adore you. But I would like to clean up a bit before resuming this conversation." She kissed him and left the jet's comfortable front cabin for its luxurious bathing area.

Chloe didn't have to say it, he knew she was afraid for him and relieved Zwilling hadn't defied her and sired him in the tunnel. Fahey was too.

When she returned, they sat silently, holding hands, their equilibrium re-established for the moment. In another few hours, they would pick Avalon up at his parents' house. They would listen to his mother's stories about him and his brothers and their accomplishments at Ava's age. His daughter had already worked miracles, if you asked him: She had survived Chloe's vampire transition and miscarriage. Ava was a fighter, a Fahey.

He tucked a finger under Chloe's chin and tipped her face up to his. "Families are so unpredictable. All that genetic material swirling about, creating unique individuals from the building blocks of centuries past. Some characteristics go unchanged; others recombine with random new traits. Look at you, love: You're your own woman, though you ultimately became what Sebastian and Emilie were. You're of them, but not."

"And?"

"Look at me: I look nothing like my father or my brothers. I'm taller, broader, darker. I favor my mother's side completely."

"You favor your Uncle John, the womanizing brawler who looked like *my* father."

"That's right. So very mysterious, this business of brothers and uncles and the like."

Chloe brushed her lips across his and shook her head. "Not so mysterious, really. Biology and genetics, secrets of the universe that Mendel and Darwin revealed centuries ago. Science, sweetheart."

Science didn't explain everything, though, did it? "Tell me," Fahey said, pulling her into his lap, "how many times have you compelled me to lie?"

Her green eyes gleamed like emeralds. God, he loved those eyes.

"Only once," she confessed.

"Thought so. Recently, was it?"

She squirmed invitingly and began nibbling her way up his neck. "Mmm, very recently."

"And that's it, is it? No re-compulsion necessary?"

She nipped at his jaw. "Christoph has what he wanted. He needed to feel in control of the situation."

"A lot like your father did."

"A lot like *his* father did."

In this family, what was one more secret?

Chapter Fifteen

UPSTATE NEW YORK, DECEMBER 2012

She flicks her pink, perfect tongue, in and out, in and out, until a fragile, frozen sliver glides onto it.

Wide baby eyes watch the snowflake vanish. Baby hands clap gleefully.

She spots the squat snowman, snatches at its broom. Crystals shimmer through the air.

Little purple boots thump joyfully.

She loses her balance and sits hard in the snow. Fingers sift the cold wetness. She giggles, a sweet, lyrical lilt. She is, it turns out, a champion giggler.

"She really needs to rest."

"Does she look tired?" I ask.

"She's already had a full day."

"Another minute or so won't hurt," I reason.

"She'll catch her death, or don't you care?"

How dare he even think it?

"My mother is pretty hard to kill. Haven't you realized that by now?"

Eric pushes me aside, flings the French doors open, startles the baby and starts her crying.

"Enough play!" he shouts. "Rehearsal now, Chiara."

She hands me my wailing daughter and slams her way

past the six-foot, two-inch blond god who adores her, as if he doesn't exist. Eric turns to follow. I halt him with a vampire grip he can't toss off. She needs a minute to settle down; he needs to take a breath.

"Don't push her. She came back to you, didn't she?"

"She always comes back but not to me, to the band. It's where she feels safe, she says, until she doesn't and runs away again."

He's right, of course, but I won't apologize for my mother or try to explain her, as if I could. The band, whatever its form, is both her refuge and the constant reminder that she can't find one. Without it, she feels unmoored; with it, much the same.

I lift my hand from his arm, and Eric rushes away. I watch him take the Castle's grand staircase two steps at a time. Above me, a chord bursts from Ronnie Hamilton's guitar, cranked up to its amp's highest. Lars's cymbals tremble above the chord, drawing Avalon's attention away from her tears to the source of the sound.

Rhythm and melody wash down from my late father's third-floor music studio, its repairs newly completed. Voices and instruments carry better than ever. Eric lays a bass line then retreats as the organ booms angrily and Anders fires off shots against a not-so-ancient enemy. Layered on top is Chiara, channeling her Emilie de la Coeur self, singing of lilies and loss and regret.

So familiar, those themes.

If you had asked me even six months ago whether there would be another Christmas at the Castle, I would have said no. Sorrow haunted this place, death's stench baked into every old plank and paver. Teppan Nilsson, my father's last earthly persona, left me a huge mess on his demise. Disturbing still to think how much worse his continued life might have proven to be.

Yet here we are again, about to celebrate anew the staying power of the Cruel, the band that just cannot be killed. It evolves, adapts as the vampires at its heart have. This year's benefit concert brings the band's new generation onto the big, bright US stage. In twenty-four hours, the masses and the media will swarm the house Sebastian and Emilie de la Coeur built, and this year it will truly be all about the music. No murder investigation into those women Sebastian/Teppan killed and their babies; no scandal of false suicides, Sebastian and Emilie's still-unaccounted-for cremated remains notwithstanding. Just a new appreciation, we hope, for the rock-and-roll institution my parents erected.

The Castle cacophony backs off suddenly, and the noises of carpenters and movers and roadies and techs at work echo off the walls of the Great Hall. Avalon kicks me with her purple boots, as if that will bring back the desired sound. I sink down onto a lower step of the staircase, unbundle her from her snowsuit and relieve her of her rubber weapons. A microphone squeals, the piano bench scrapes across the floor, and Chiara's soprano sweeps over us again.

"Still has it, your mama does." Ronnie descends the stairs. "If she weren't such a bloody pain in my arse, I might be hopelessly in love with her like Bohlander."

Avalon reaches out her arms, and Ronnie lifts her from my lap. "Instead, I'm saving myself for this little charmer. Who do you love, sweetheart?"

Ava loves everyone, as Ronnie well knows after a week of beguilement. The band, the Castle staff, the day workers, all have become my baby's family, just as they were mine.

A crash, followed by ear-splitting feedback, followed by arguing, interrupts the song. Chiara curses in French. Eric curses in Swedish, yells something about how she persists in idolizing a man who despises her. Unclear whether they're disagreeing about the lyrics or about my mother's husband.

"Christ, not again. They fuck up this song every time. They've got to get past this," Ronnie says. "We're recording the show live as the New Court of Cruelty's first full album. The EP has sold and sold and sold, but we miss this moment and there's no getting it back. You've got to help me talk some sense into them, girlie."

"Me? When have I ever been able to influence my mother? Anyway, if it's something to do with the song itself, she's probably right—she's feeling it, embodying it, that's what she does. Eric's just lashing out from nerves. Tell Lars and Anders to take him into town tonight and get him drunk."

Ava applauds, her hands cupped between Ronnie's weathered, calloused mitts. "Last thing Eric needs. He lost Katarina and got a second chance. Doesn't work out now, and we'll have a time of it, pulling him out of a deep hole. The new band members can pretend to ignore what's about to boil over between him and Chiara, but Lars and Anders can't. They knew Kat then, deep down they know it's her today. She's not even trying to compel them; she's daring them to acknowledge what's before their eyes. When they do, and they will, she'll own them—she won't want to, but she will. Seen it before."

Ronnie lowers Ava to her feet, lets her hang onto his fingers as her little toes flex to get a grip. She slides along the wood; he puts a hand under her diaper-padded bottom to steady her.

"That cousin of yours, Zwilling, he showed up at our gigs in Stockholm and Copenhagen. To his credit, Eric did not jump off the stage or throw instruments, thus no riots ensued. Don't know where I'd find another male singer. Replacements for your dad don't grow on trees, you know."

No, they are carefully groomed by my mother and Ronnie to be Sebastian's reincarnation. Can Christoph Zwilling sing, I wonder? He's got the look down, and a knack for tormenting others that would make my father proud.

"Promise me, Ronnie: no carnage tomorrow afternoon. I can't afford more repairs to this place." I crook a finger at Ava and she reaches out for me to take her—fickle little thing.

"Right. Too many people gone because of what happened last year: your dad, and Zeke, and this little one's baby sister. Miss them, of course, but the show's got to go on." He stands, knees creaking, and drops a kiss onto Ava's head. After a minute, he leans in and drops one onto mine as well.

"Talk to Chiara. You owe me, girlie, don't forget."

"You rescue me as I miscarry, and in return I spare you a prematurely terminated career opportunity?"

"Something like that, yeah. I'll talk to Eric. We'll be great tomorrow if we don't kill one another first."

That inspires confidence.

* * * *

I run along the back roads of exurban Ithaca, those rural New York routes near the Castle I've pounded since the summer I learned I was being packed off to boarding school, thrust out of the domain of the de la Coeurs and into the daunting world of cliques and mean girls. Once exiled in Massachusetts, I quickly learned the only things that made me at all remarkable in my classmates' eyes were my famous parents: a to-die-for hot dad and a mom whose outfits were so cool—their parents had dragged out Sebastian and Emilie's old LPs to show them. Oh, and what was my name again, the little darlings asked bitchily for weeks: Clothesline-dee?

That summer, before I could even anticipate the adolescent-female nonsense, I ran to burn off my hurt and anger. Later, during summer and holiday breaks, I ran to avoid the nonsense I came home to. Who knows how many layers of shoe rubber I've worn down here over the years?

I run with my eyes closed. I've memorized every turn. I can predict where the potholes will heave open each winter and where the black ice will freeze then thaw. There's something comforting about that: Sameness is an unappreciated virtue. Except that I am fleeing now the same thing my teenage self so often ran from: a confrontation with my mother.

Until yesterday, I had not seen her since Jackson and I walked out of that tunnel. I had only second- and third-hand knowledge that she had actually survived her Bohemian ordeal.

Calls, texts, and emails to Chiara Nunnally's phone went unanswered; all those, plus letters and telegrams to Zwilling's home and offices, also went unanswered. Sometime in late October, my phone began to buzz with alerts that Chiara had been brilliant as Lady Macbeth in Seattle and Portland. In late November came word that she had returned to the New Court of Cruelty. What she was doing, I knew. How she was doing, I had no idea.

Whether she enhances or aborts Ronnie's well-laid plans for the New Cruel's US debut doesn't concern me much. What I want to know is: How did she recover after being all but crushed to death in the Church of Saints Stephen and Gregory? What lessons can her recovery teach me about vampire survival?

What I *must* ask, however: Where do things stand between her and her husband? I don't like the idea of her with Zwilling, but stringing Eric along indefinitely seems wrong, too. I don't want him to be another Zeke Segal, her lover but never really her love.

I jog toward Zeke's old cottage on the Castle grounds, where I played as a child; his space apart from my parents, though never far enough apart—his suicide a year ago proved that. The door is ajar; I step inside. Shades are drawn at the windows; the space is dark, except for the glow of a dozen small white votives.

"Close the door, love, and take off your clothes."

In the center of the bed that overwhelms the tiny one-room house, clutching Axelrod, the aqua stuffed dog Zeke kept for me, sits Jackson. It's been seven days since I've seen him, seven days since I've fed, but it's not his blood I'm hungry for. I want to feel his skin on mine.

"You want my clothes off? You know what to do."

He rises from the bed and strides gorgeously naked toward me, takes my hand and twirls me as if we are dancing. He pulls me against him, my back to his chest, and reaches for the zipper at my breasts, tugging it down slowly, slipping his free hand into my leggings, massaging my bottom. His fingers inch forward between my thighs, to the wetness there, and pluck me until I sing. He pivots me so we are face-to-face, pulls my jacket down my arms, pulls me close and offers me his neck.

"Not yet," I whisper, and offer him my lips instead. He accepts, feels his way under my shirt until he reaches nipples strained to bursting. They weep milk; he tucks his head down and steals a breast. I squirm impatiently, needing more.

He carries me to the bed, sets me in front of him, strips my clothing away. He grips my ankles and enters me, sliding slowly, mimicking the motion with his mouth, sucking a toe on one foot, then the other.

I lever up to wrap my arms around his hips, my mouth roughly even with his navel, my tongue tasting the salt and sweat of him. I arch toward him until my breasts brush his belly and tease the soft trail of hair there. I fight back the urge to lengthen my teeth, to rake them over his sweet flesh and bite down. This moment is not about our blood bond, it's about our bond, period, the one that linked our lives inextricably. It's about the people we were then and will always be, Chloe Hart and Jackson Fahey, just us, with no one and nothing able to come between us. This is our forever, no matter how long it lasts.

He doesn't know what I'm thinking—or maybe he does. He picks up the pace, pounds harder, faster, head down, eyes closed, focus complete, skin to skin, pleasure for pleasure, until he quakes within me. I watch his climax, and I need to fly with him, wherever he has gone. I flex around him, to accept everything he is. I watch his surprise, his smile as I tighten around him, teasing another few strokes out until he stokes my fire into a blaze. He releases my ankles, lets my legs circle his waist, scoops under me and lifts me against his chest until we are face to face.

"Perfect," I say nuzzling his neck, expressing myself with lips and tongue rather than teeth.

"I'm jet-lagged, but give me a minute and I'll show you perfect again."

"A bit full of yourself, are you?"

"Perfectly so, though, don't you think?"

Jackson swings me off the mattress, spins and carries me up toward the head of the bed, knocking Axelrod onto the floor. Peripheral vampire vision catches the toy dog's descent. Catches the glint of a brown eye at the window.

Zwilling winks and walks away, laughing. Mocking me or this man who loves me?

"What is it?" that man asks.

"Nothing," I say and press my lips to his. *"Don't tell him what you know,"* I whisper in his head, a compulsion booster shot.

Once Jackson's desire for sleep overwhelms his desire for me, I slip out of his arms and into my clothes. I run back to the Castle, expecting to find my mother in the music studio with her band mates, but she isn't there.

"Chiara felt faint." Lars looks worried. "She was very pale. Eric wanted her to go to her room to lie down, but she insisted on looking for a dress to wear for the show. Look in Emilie and Sebastian's apartment maybe?"

Chiara is in the royal chambers, in her bathroom, alone, toweling her face dry, her porcelain complexion oddly white.

"Are you ill?"

"I'm not one hundred percent right now."

"Maybe Eric is right. Maybe you've been overdoing it?"

She sweeps past me into the dressing room, where the decades of her Court of Cruelty persona hang in numbered, catalogued array. She presses the button on the motorized rack that offers gown after gown for perusal.

"Getting your Emilie on for the concert?"

She picks at a garment bag. "The magenta, I think, from the 1978 tour. It draped beautifully, and I looked fabulous in this deep, warm silk."

She looks fabulous in everything, but she rarely acknowledges it. Being beautiful is what she is, what she's always been.

"Nineteen seventy-eight?"

She squats and studies a collection of numbered shoe boxes. "It was for the live album, *Peasants' Faire*, the shortened tour. When we discovered I was pregnant, Sebastian insisted on treating me like a fragile vessel for his heir."

How narcissistic he could be, and so unaware. My mother does not shatter easily.

"Your current husband is here. What does Zwilling want?"

She emerges with dress, shoes, and relevant accessories, hangs them from an ornate bronze hook, and manages to not look at me. "You'll have to ask him yourself. I haven't spoken to him since I left Zurich."

Why this surprises me, I really can't say. Did I imagine his willingness to assume the care for her broken body might translate into resolution of their situation, if not reconciliation? What was I thinking? Her vampire pragmatism will always trump actual affection, if my limited experience is any guide.

"You awoke recovered one day and just walked out of Maison Zwilling?"

"Yes," she replies, fussing over a bit of ribbon.

"And now Eric—or should I say, again Eric?"

She lifts her head finally, acknowledges the confrontational bent to my questions. "There will always be an Eric. He loves me. I am here for him because he is always here for me."

"Like Zeke was for how many decades?"

"Just like Zeke was." She sighs, looks at me as if I were still her stubborn little girl. "Or, in your case, just like Jackson. Really, Chloe, I think you'd understand by now how these things work, how vampires cannot nourish each other—and how this is really none of your concern."

She never ceases to amaze me: Just when I think some glimmer of human empathy remains in her, she extinguishes it. Hardly like Jackson, how dare she?

Wardrobe elements slung across her arm, she exits the dressing room, heads into Emilie and Sebastian's grand bedroom. She flings the dress and accessory bags onto the bed, unzips them and begins to inspect for stains, insect damage; I've seen this drill before. The dress is lovely, her artistry as a seamstress is superb—it is as well-preserved as she. She will look stunning in it; the color will enhance her current pallor.

She works around me, but I won't be ignored.

"Not my concern? *Au contraire, maman*, it is all my concern: This house; the fifty people employed in it and at Vineyard de la Coeur; those clothes, the chairs, the sound equipment and the instruments your band will play in the Great Hall tomorrow; the recording and video that will be made; the security for the concert that benefits your charitable foundation; and the care and feeding of your fans, people who come back to this place year after year because they love your music. You dumped it all on me when you and dear Daddy decided to fake your deaths. Your legacy occupies so much of my life I scarcely have time to live it. Don't you dare tell me it's none of my concern, and don't you dare insult my relationship with Jackson by equating it with yours and Eric's."

She sits on the bed, looks past me toward the door. I know without turning that Eric is there, that he has heard. He rushes to kneel at her feet, brushes his lips across the knuckles of her right hand.

"Are you feeling better?" he asks.

Chiara nods, caresses his cheek. "I think Chloe and I are just a little nervous about the concert tomorrow." She raises her eyes to mine, challenges me to disagree.

I defer. "Even the great Chiara Nunnally is entitled to a little stage fright, Eric. I'm sure she'll rally." As if she isn't performing even now.

Eric stands and helps Chiara to her feet. "Ronnie wants us to run through 'Queen and Country' again. Says he's not getting the right vibe, not enough passion." He leans in and takes

Chiara's face into his hands. "I assured him we'll get there. Passion, we can give him."

"You work on that," I say, turning to leave. "Make it perfect. Ronnie is depending on you to sell your slavish devotion to each other."

She moves so quickly, I don't see her, and her slap shocks me, the sting of my mother's hand hot against my face. *"You're good at leaving, Chloe. You stayed away for thirteen years,"* she snarls inside my head. *"You know where the exit is."*

"Have it your way." I rush into the corridor that leads from the apartment back to the Castle's public areas, past the sitting room that was my parents' inner sanctum, the place where my mother's tapestries told their vampire-origin stories and then mine. Catching my eye is a new tapestry, swimming in the space the large triptych once dominated.

The switch is just by the door; I reach in, flip it, and soft light bathes the wall. Without stepping into the room, I can see this piece is delicately wrought, modern-looking yet unmistakably her work; I know textiles and my mother too well to think otherwise. If she's exhausted herself creating some new mirror of hell, I'm not sure I'm ready to witness it, but I can't resist. I am drawn in.

A small hanging, maybe two feet by three feet, it would have been dwarfed by the bloodthirsty tapestry trio Emilie de la Coeur crafted. Its subject also smaller: just a dark-haired woman, her face mostly obscured by the head of a baby, which she nuzzles as it rests against her shoulder.

Avalon and me.

A step closer and I can see one of the woman's eyes. Not green.

Not me after all. With a simple choice of thread color, I am the thirteen-year-old she banished to boarding school once again.

* * * *

Jackson and Benjamin scan the intermission crowd, the

buyers of souvenir T-shirts and vintage vinyl, bottles of Blood of the Bards wine, and early Court of Cruelty memorabilia. Avalon's head swivels, following the thrum of voices, the swirl of color that comes at her from all sides. I give my blue velvet mini-dress a smooth-down to keep the sheen even. The baby reaches out to touch the fabric. Please let her fingers not be sticky; I can't bear to venture back upstairs to change. I want this concert over. I want to go home.

Jackson doesn't understand this new impatience of mine, and what I've told him amounts to this: I am done with my mother—whatever she chooses to call herself—and with this house. I have spent the last year of my life trying to resurrect them both. No more.

My restlessness registers with Benjamin, who can read my moods better than Jackson most days but who is just as bewildered now. "The show has been fabulous," Ben says, gushing, "and this house, it's just as you and Meredith described it. I thought I knew what to expect, but I couldn't have—it's magnificent. The album art alone is priceless. The music studio's restoration is remarkable. If I had one, I'd raise a glass to C.J. Hart, miracle worker."

"I did what I had to do," I grumble, refusing to take the compliment.

Ben is always on the job, or rather, jobs. Today, he is not only business partner/cheerleader and art curator, but also security expert. Cameras now monitor the Castle's public spaces outdoors and in; there are no alcoves left on the ground level for the secret trysts and blood-lust liaisons of Sebastian and Emilie's era. Ben insisted on eyes, subtle yet all-seeing, in every location but the bedrooms and baths. Last year's tour-bus bombing was one tragedy too many, and this year we must anticipate the possibility that someone might take violent exception to the New Cruel's liberties with the Classic Cruel's music.

Then, too, there is Christoph Zwilling, provocateur. Once

noticed, he has been intent on being seen. Disrupting, just by being here, Chiara and Eric's focus during the first set, throwing them off their harmonies. He stands now at one of the interior doors to the Great Hall, watching me, watching Jackson, watching Ben. Watching concertgoers come and go, watching event staff mill among the masses. I have been watching him all day long, too, watching him stare at his wife as she strokes Eric's arm during their duets, watching Zwilling do a slow, dangerous burn.

Heralds' trumpets signal the intermission is about to end. Zwilling approaches. Jackson tightens his hold on Avalon. Ben grips my shoulder as I take a step forward.

"Gentlemen, Clothilde, why so tense? Have I not minded my manners in my uncle's home? I have come to hear the New Court of Cruelty, to see my wife perform. Where is the harm in that?"

Ava's little fingers stretch toward him, and Zwilling tucks his right thumb into her tiny grasp. "Hello, my lamb, you're so much bigger now than when you visited my house." Zwilling looks from the baby, to me, to Jackson. "So beautiful, like you both, though she favors you, cousin. Her eyes will likely change, of course, from blue. Perhaps they will be brilliant green, like her mother's—and her grandmother's."

Except her grandmother's current persona has hazel eyes. Just like the woman holding an infant in the new tapestry upstairs.

The trumpets sound again, summoning us back to the Great Hall, and the tide of fans flows forward to the seats. The music will not resume until I have greeted my guests, as a good host should, but my heart is in my throat, and not because I fear facing the audience. I disengage Avalon's fingers from Zwilling's, step into the space between him and Jackson.

"Describe Zurich," I whisper, so low only a vampire can hear.

Zwilling smiles a wistful, longing smile. "A bounty of pleasure, weeks of wonder. One day, we could not untangle our bodies. The next, she was gone."

I sense his yearning, the pain within him. *Wretched man, don't make me feel sorry for you.*

"Gentlewomen and gentlemen, knights and vassals," Meredith's voice announces from backstage. "Bow to the princess of the realm, Sebastian and Emilie de la Coeur's daughter, C.J. Hart."

A spotlight tracks to a small platform in the center aisle. Heads turn. Silence falls. A sound tech hands me a wireless microphone, and I proceed to my mark.

"Thank you for joining us again for Christmas at the Castle, for visiting with us once more and offering your kindness to the medical-research charity my parents founded. Because of you, the hard work of fighting blood and bone marrow cancers continues, unceasing and unstoppable.

"Equally unstoppable is the band you're hearing today, undeterred by tragedy, undaunted by history, worthy of your allegiance because it is both the embodiment of my parents' musical legacy and the evolution of their musical genius through the guidance of veteran guitarist Ronnie Hamilton and former drummer Eddie Check. From the loss of not only my parents, but also guitarist Zeke Segal and Matins and Vespers vocalists Teppan and Katarina Nilsson, grows a new determination and a new generation of monarchs. Please give a welcome worthy of royalty to Eric Bohlander, Chiara Nunnally, and their company in the New Court of Cruelty."

Lars strikes the cymbals, a cue to kill the house lights, and all heads turn toward the sound. A blue spotlight bathes Chiara at center stage, and the crowd gasps. She is wearing a diaphanous silver mini-dress that is molded to her curves and concealing little—the silver bra and thong underneath visible and carefully chosen to enhance more than cover. She parts her lips and the Latin lyrics to "O Come All Ye Faithful" rise a capella, filling the room. Eric steps up behind her, places his hands over her stomach protectively.

The story of the new tapestry reveals itself, because of what it says about my mother rather than about me. I hear a faint heartbeat, small, weak, and I understand.

I rush to the back of the Great Hall, to Zwilling, and when I see his face, I know he has read my thoughts. Benjamin grips his arm, though if Zwilling wanted he could split Ben in half. I fix Ben with a stare and compel him to stand aside.

"She is pregnant." Zwilling's voice could freeze fire. "My child will not be raised by Eric Bohlander."

"There will always be an Eric," I hear myself echo my mother's words. "You know you can't nourish her. If that is your child, you need Eric as much as Chiara does."

"If? Do you think I will stand for this?"

Not for a minute. But who will reason with him if I don't? "You don't know this baby is yours. The odds in Eric's favor are quite good."

Zwilling glares toward the stage, flashes fang ever so briefly. "I'll kill him."

"You won't," I command, steel in my voice, in the fingernails I jam into his clenched fist. "You will bide your time, or you will lose her. You're a patient man, given to careful strategy. This is not the time for rash action."

He growls at me, like the wounded beast he is. I don't fear him, but I know I should keep my distance. I retract my claws. I walk away, as my mother so recently urged I should, to the grand staircase and up the stairs. I approach Sebastian and Emilie's apartment, where Jackson walks the hall outside, Avalon asleep on his shoulder.

"Did I miss anything exciting?"

I press a kiss to his smiling lips. "Do you have to ask?"

He shakes his head, aware that any given day holds potential for a vast spectrum of odd experience, human and vampire.

The New Cruel rocks beneath our feet. Eric's bass reverberates, Lars's drums vibrate through hardwood imported from my father's Bohemian homeland. Chiara's soprano blends with

Eric's baritone, and I recognize "Divine Insurrection," the title song of the band's now-oft-downloaded EP.

No one knows what God intends
Only fools have certainty
And in his name, virtue pretend
Evil is all I see
Rise up against the hypocrite
Rise up against the throng
Rise up and let the just prevail
We must not go along
We won't just go along

The lock on my parents' chambers has not yet been replaced; the door jamb is still splintered where I shattered it a year ago. I cross the threshold, and the two people I love most follow. Candles burn in the sitting room, but I flick on the museum lights.

There are two tapestries now. I stumble toward them, astonished.

Jackson sees what I see: Chiara, her lips lowered to the head of a newborn nursing at her breast. I sink cross-legged to the floor.

"She's not?"

"She is."

"The father?"

"Maybe Eric, maybe Zwilling. Each had opportunity, it seems."

Jackson sits beside me. Avalon fusses and wakes. She holds out her arms, and I gather her up. He folds us into a hug. "Still want to leave tomorrow?"

He knows the answer: I can't leave now, not until they all do, despite my every instinct to run. The Castle is the family fortress, mine to defend without a single effective weapon. No simple paternity test is possible; no simple rules apply here.

Zwilling still had a vampire life to create, so if this baby is his, my mother faces the same risks she faced with me and my father, a sire's sexual obsession with his offspring. If I hadn't interfered with Jackson's wish to be sired, could I have prevented this?

A kiss on my cheek. A voice beside my ear. "It never ends, love, does it?"

No, it doesn't. We're vampires in this family. With us, trouble lives forever.

COURT OF CRUELTY
DISCOGRAPHY (LPS/CDS)

Born to Slay the King (acoustic, 1975)
Miserere Nobis (1976)
Children's Crusade (two-disc, 1977)
Peasants' Faire (live, 1978)
For My Liege, My Life (greatest hits, 1979)
As Albion Mourns (1980)
Heir Presumptive (1981)
Fiefdom of the Feral (1982)
Corpus Incorruptus (1983)
Gifts of the Holy Ghost (1984)
Auto Da Fe (live, 1985)
Heir Apparent (1986)
Circles of Hell (1987)
Maiden's Madrigal (1988)
Blood Sacrifice (1990)
The Rack (1992)
Monarch's Kiss (live, 1994)
Plague of Fools (1995)
Knights Errant (1996)
Communion of Saints,
Commingling of Sinners (last studio album, 1997)

Matins and Vespers
In Service to the Court of Cruelty (tribute album, 2011)

New Court of Cruelty
Divine Insurrection, (six-song EP, 2012)

Noteworthy Songs

Court of Cruelty

"Feudal/Futile"
"Inquisition"
"Lady Anna's Disgrace"
"Sanctifying Grace"
"Faithless Servant"
"Wisdom"
"Fortitude"
"Piety"
"Fear of the Lord"
"Plague of Fools"
"Bride Price"
"Slaughter of the Infants"
"Wifely Duties"
"Croix de Guerre/Cri de Coeur"

Matins and Vespers
"Weapons of Class Destruction"

New Court of Cruelty
"Queen and Country"

ABOUT THE AUTHOR

Joanne McLaughlin has worked in public radio and at newspapers in Philadelphia, upstate New York and northeastern Ohio, involved in coverage of everything from politics and murder, to sports and interior design, to fashion and financial markets, to Pulitzer Prize-finalist architecture criticism. As vice president of a musicians-management firm and record company, she publicized blues artists and produced and promoted their work. She lives in Philadelphia. Learn more at joannemclaughlin.net.

Twitter: @joannemclaugh
Facebook: Joanne McLaughlin Writes

Also By Author:
"Never Before Noon" and "Never Until Now," Books 1 and 2 of the Vampires of the Court of Cruelty trilogy; and the short stories "Peppina's Sweetheart" and "Grass and Granite" (both available for Kindle).

www.ingramcontent.com/pod-product-compliance
Lightning Source LLC
Chambersburg PA
CBHW060316260626
47160CB00007B/2633